OCCULT DETECTIVE
MAGAZINE

MYTHOS SPECIAL #1

edited by

John Linwood Grant and Dave Brzeski

CATHAVEN
PRESS

OCCULT DETECTIVE MAGAZINE
MYTHOS SPECIAL #1

ISBN: 978-1-9160212-7-3

http://greydogtales.com/blog/occult-detective-magazine/
occultdetectivemagazine@gmail.com

Publishers: Jilly Paddock & Dave Brzeski

Editors: John Linwood Grant & Dave Brzeski

Logos & Headers: Bob Freeman

Cover by: Sebastián Cabrol (https://cabrol-art.blogspot.com/)

Interior design by Dave Brzeski and Jilly Paddock

Published by
Cathaven Press,
Peterborough,
United Kingdom
cathaven.press@cathaven.co.uk

CONTENTS

INTRODUCTION

This is a somewhat unusual event for Occult Detective Magazine. Over the years we have, on the whole, avoided the Mythosian and Lovecraftian zones. There are, after all, plenty of other outlets for such stories, even though there are undoubted crossovers with investigators of the unusual and abnatural. However, we finally decided on an indulgence – two 'specials' (alongside our regular issues) which would focus unashamedly on such areas. Being ODM, we also chose to blur the lines by including tales related to Robert W. Chambers' *'King in Yellow'* sequence, a brooding sandpit in which a number of Mythos writers have also played.

What the above terms mean in practice is, well, open to debate. H.P. Lovecraft never chose to lay down a clearly mapped-out or cohesive 'Cthulhu' Mythos, and despite August Derleth's somewhat questionable later attempts to impose order, so many other creators have visited the area since that it can be hard to work out whose footprints are whose. HPL himself wrote both Mythosian stories which contained what people often call 'cosmic horror', and cosmic or speculative horror stories which weren't Mythosian.

Later writers have added everything from straight Lovecraft pastiches, new Mythos monstrosities, and playful re-interpretations of his ideas, to serious examinations of Lovecraft's concepts, shorn of their original fictional baggage. In addition, more recent times have seen many stories which directly (and rightly) challenge some of HPL's attitudes, or which rework the tropes in his fiction.

We have tried to reflect such variations within, and so are pleased to present a brand new unpublished novelette by James Bennett, a twisting and twisted tale which is totally Mythosian but which involves protagonists you would certainly not find in HPL. Alongside this, we have a wide selection of reprints from recent years. Paula Ashe provides a dark, epistolary-style glimpse into cadaverous horror, whilst Will Murray gives us something closer to a Lovecraftian version of The Men in Black; Nick Mamatas has a very different and highly inventive take on the Mythos's Mi-go, and Pete Rawlik offers smart, futuristic noir in his story of shoggoths and much more.

Denise Dumars explores moving, contemporary echoes of Lost Carcosa, and supernatural horror dwells in Michael Keyton's story of a mirror with a dreadful secret. Added to this we have an unusual tale by DJ Tyrer set in the era of early post-war atomic tests in the Australian desert. For those who appreciate classic period settings, we have William Meikle's recounting of a brush with cosmic horror for William Hope Hodgson's archetypal occult detective, Thomas Carnacki, plus I.A. Watson's story of another Miskatonic expedition which did not go well – accompanied by wry derring-do and Shub-Niggurath from Tim Mendees, and an appearance of that old 'devil' Aleister Crowley dealing with the result of dubious pacts, by Bob Freeman.

We hope that such a range intrigues, shivers, or amuses you, and that we will see you again in our second Mythos special, due in a few months. Oh, and at the time of writing, Occult Detective Magazine #10, with our usual eclectic mix of damn fine stories and four longer novelettes, is also on its way...

John Linwood Grant

THE FACTS CONCERNING THE FIRST ANNUAL ARKHAM PARADE

JAMES BENNETT

Boston, July 1951

Dear Quentin,

Forgive me for leaving without any warning. An urgent phone call took place this morning and I feel obliged to respond in person, a question of decency, I guess. My trip north couldn't have come at a worse time, what with the backlog of accounts in our Pearl Street office, and it hardly amounts to a vacation when one considers my destination. Arkham! That ancient, mouldering Massachusetts town that legend tells us was cursed by a witch.

You'd have thought that the Essex County Tourist Board would've made more of an effort to paper over such bull! It seems that little has changed since the '30s when, according to my old man, the back pages of the *Herald* often featured articles like the torpedoing at nearby Innsmouth in the winter of '27 and the disastrous Pabodie Expedition, which was funded by the town's own university. Lord knows there's little to recommend the place unless one likes sagging gambrels, overgrown graveyards and the salt marshes north of the city. My only saving grace is that the distance is short – forty-five minutes from Downtown Crossing – so I hope to head home in a day or two. With any luck, you'll find this note where I leave it, and skip thinking me a jerk.

As to the why of it, the call came from one Wanda Olmstead, who looked me up in the blasted Gardener-Athol directory. Mrs Olmstead is the mother of one Walter Olmstead, my old roommate at the aforementioned Miskatonic University. We're talking a good nine years ago now. Walter was a student of archaeology and dead languages whereas I studied law, as you're aware. It won't shock you to hear that Walter was a bit of an oddball on campus, with his head often buried in books, and yet we became 'study buddies'. I suppose he found security in my practical nature, which might sound familiar to you. Walter was never one to join in on the hockey pitch, but he was reliable when it came to helping with homework! In time, I came to learn that I was in fact Walter's only friend. I guess this is why his mother has reached out to me following his strange disappearance.

For reasons unknown to me, Mrs Olmstead appears to place no faith in the Arkham Police Department, and has begged me to help her locate her son, AWOL these past two weeks following some incident in the town. I hesitate to say a violent one – I don't want to rattle your cage! Mrs Olmstead mentioned a summer parade that escalated into some 'ruckus' or other. Since the incident, Walter has been nowhere to be found.

Forgive me, Quentin. I know what you'd say were you here beside me and not catching zeds in the king-size upstairs. I'm sure you'd remind me I'm no detective, but a humble tax collector, and that I should leave the matter to the cops. I'm afraid that my conscience won't allow it. If nothing else, I'd like to honor my friendship to my alumnus and comfort his mother in any way I can. Please don't fret. I'll return to you with the job done and my mind at rest.

Until then, think of me with affection.

Jack

Letter #1. *From the evidence file of the Boston Police Department, 154 Berkeley Street, Boston. Submitted by Mr Quentin G. Fields. August 23rd, 1951.*

I. *In the Rattling House*

Jack Elwood was shaken and damp as he stepped off the train and into the squat stone building that passed for the Arkham railway station. The train that had brought him hence was in need of repair, rattling along tracks that had only been fitted for a slow commute, with so little traffic seeming to travel along the coast road. Most with business in the city lived in the suburbs these days. Looking out the window, already missing Quentin and homesick, it wasn't hard to see why. Low bleak hills rolled into the rural corners of the county, the odd leafless tree on the rise. The landscape was draped in a greenish fog that rendered everything skeletal and dull, suggesting that he didn't even have the country air to look forward to.

Nevertheless, Elwood found himself mourning that wasteland the moment he stepped into myth-haunted Arkham, strutting with valise in hand under Georgian eaves that dripped with gloom as much as with the clammy atmosphere. The fog wreathed around lampposts that had been quietly rusting since the turn of the century, and there were potholes in the road that made progress irksome for trucks and cars, which filled the air with a clamor that was somehow louder than Boston, setting his teeth on edge.

Blank windows and half-empty drugstores regarded him, and he had the sense of being watched, the hairs prickling on the nape of his neck within minutes of him stepping off the train. In his immediate vicinity, all he saw was some joe in a gabardine, smoke curling from behind his crumpled copy of the *Herald*, and an old lady feeding shabby pigeons on a bench. When he looked over his shoulder, however, he caught sight of his observer. She was standing by a pillar in the station foyer, her eyes aglitter in a powdered face. She was wearing a lime green suit-and-dress combo, and she was tall for a broad, he thought, kind of willowy, if not Amazonian. The purse under her arm, an equally vivid yellow, was so stuffed that it looked like a Canary melon ready to burst. Atop her head, a pillbox hat rested on a pinned updo of wild ginger curls. He frowned, puzzled by the woman's glare, the pinch of her red-rouged lips. Noticing him, she turned away at once, her high heels clopping as she fled.

What's your tale, nightingale? he thought.

He was a stranger in these parts and for all that, unremarkable, just a young man in a flannel suit and overcoat from Boston. Unable to find a reason for her attention, he tutted, shaking off the zorros. Deciding that the trolley looked too medieval and complicated, he hailed a cab for nearby Water Street.

* * *

Elwood believed he'd made a mistake the second that Mrs Olmstead opened the door. Or rather *half* opened it. The portal in question only offered a crack and a face peering out at him in the mid-morning gloom. The woman's head seemed perfectly shaped to navigate such a fissure, and her eyes, each one bulging and round, appeared to have evolved as a result of the casa behind her, abyssal thanks to the weather. Elwood had all but decided to light out for the station again when Mrs Olmstead flushed, becoming animated. His name hissed off her lips, although there wasn't so much as a twitch of the curtains in the houses on either side of them and no reason for discretion that he could see. Silently, he realized he'd missed his chance to skip this business, but he doffed his hat all the same. It was him alright, he told her, Jack Elwood, former roommate of Walter, her son.

Soon came the matter of Walter's disappearance, which left Elwood far more uncomfortable than the overstuffed armchair the woman ushered him into, while she sat opposite him on the couch. The living room curtains remained drawn, which he didn't blame her for, considering her concerns and the miserable day. A floor lamp lit the space in an unwholesome glow, the color of faded tax chits. In the weak radiance, Mrs Olmstead appeared to him a forlorn creature, with flaking skin in the folds of her neck and an oddly flat nose. Discomforted, he found he preferred to look around the room.

There were pictures of Olmstead Junior on the wall, the man as scruffy and pale as Elwood remembered, his eyes haunted by a surplus of forgotten dialects and old stones. Walter was never going to be a dreamboat, but it might've done him some good to pay more attention to exercise, and choose sunlight instead of a study. He wasn't smiling in any of the shots. Elwood found he had no memory of him ever having done so, not even after he'd woken one night in the dorm from a bad dream — some nonsense about benthic realms and golden ingots, if he recalled correctly — and Elwood had done his best to soothe him, the beginning of their brief fling, teenaged and boneheaded as it was...

The pang in his chest surprised him. Before he had time to examine it, Mrs Olmstead was handing him a cup of tea, and at first he thought that the saucer was rattling so much due to the poor woman's nerves. Then he realized the entire room was shaking. The pictures clapped against the clapboard walls. The lamp trembled, guttering. Cheeks flushed, Mrs Olmsted informed him that it was the eleven o'clock train to Portland, the city thirty odd kilometers north. She went on to say, without any prompting from him, that she'd had to move to a smaller place after her husband passed six years ago. The only house that Arkham made affordable to her was this one down by the railway track.

"It was long before Walter had his trinkets, of course," she said, and shivered.

6

"Trinkets, ma'am?"

"Oh, he must've read about them in his books," she said. "Awful tomes. Ancient, moldering and damned. He told me he was reading up on some pagan cult over in Innsmouth. You now, the old seaport. Something about golden idols and human sacrifice. Ingots dredged up from the bay. A nasty business by all accounts. I wish he'd never bought them home!"

"Books or ingots, Mrs Olmstead?"

"He traded the books in Innsmouth, or so he said," the woman went on as if she hadn't heard him, her large eyes glazed. "This was a month or so before he… you know. Got his big idea." She smiled, apologetic. "Though who pays gold for old library books is beyond me. Nothing in them but squiggles and symbols, as far as I could tell."

She told him there were six trains a day, passing either way, and that he'd get used to the noise. Before he could reply that he'd booked a room at the Excelsior, Mrs Olmstead – she insisted he call her Wanda, although manners forbade him – launched into the facts concerning the First Annual Arkham Parade. The Widow Olmstead spoke of her son with weary affection, but she never seemed to blink, no emotion lighting her bulging eyes.

As if she noticed him staring, she lowered her head and said, "You know how he is," to which Elwood gave a nod, remembering the stack of books that used to litter Walter's side of the room on the Miskatonic campus. Were they similar to the ones he'd sold? He sipped his tea and hid a wince, the brew lukewarm and brackish, with an aftertaste that brought to mind the salt marshes north of the town.

It happened that the runaway (heaven forbid that Elwood should think him an 'abductee') had been frequenting some of the… less salubrious establishments in town, most notably 'Pink Jenkins', a dive bar at the lower end of Peabody Avenue. "Over the river," the widow said, and pursed her lips, which was all one needed to say about the area in general. Elwood was familiar with the joint, of course, and had reason to stare at the carpet to hide the color in his cheeks.

A haunt of rivermen, farmhands and factory workers, 'PJs', as it was locally known, was the only establishment in the city for men of a certain nature – and an illegal nature at that – to go, hence the requisite mercantile frontage. Passing PJs by day, one would've taken it for a hardware or a tackle store and never have imagined the bar in the back where local men gathered after dark, smoking and watchful in the shadows. Elwood knew better, having frequented the place on more than one occasion, and on the arm of Walter to boot. He'd even attempted a foxtrot to Ella, the recollection the source of his blushes.

"Why," Mrs Olmstead told him, "Walt claimed there was a 'shadow over Arkham'. He had him a mind to bring the fellas at PJs out of it, if you take my meaning. 'It ain't right,' he said one night, 'that we should live in shame when all we're doing is lovin' each other.' " Mrs Olmstead looked away at that, concealing her feelings on the matter. After stealing a sip of tea, she continued. "Walt planned to hold a parade, you see. Fifty men or so, marching bold as brass down Church Street on a Saturday morning, past the university and up to Hangman's Hill for a grand old cookout in the cemetery. And he wouldn't heed my warnings, no sir!"

Elwood sat back at this, with a sudden hankering for something stronger than tea. Such exhibitionism shocked him, and not merely because it sat at odds with the withdrawn and muttering Walter he'd known. Typically, the practical tax collector of Pearl Street came at once to the fore. "You'd need the mayor's say-so for such an event," he wondered aloud. "Not to mention dough from the county council."

Mrs Olmstead was shaking her head like an echo of the eleven o'clock to Portland. In a low voice, she informed him that Mayor Armitage hadn't only rejected Walter's proposal, but threatened to alert the local police. Most might prefer to overlook the small, seedy bar in the Merchant District, she said, and spare themselves the paperwork. A brazen display of libidinous behavior would only shatter the veneer of tolerance that Arkham had deigned to muster in the first place.

"That wasn't going to stop my Walter," she said. The house creaked, settling. Elwood barely heard her when she leant forward, her eyes wide, and admitted that her son had sworn to go ahead with the First Annual Arkham Parade regardless. "A friend in need is a friend indeed, Jack. Will you help me find him?"

II. *The Statement of Samuel Wentworth*

In the name of thoroughness, Elwood spent the rest of the day getting a slant in the local stores. Had anyone seen or heard of Walter? It took him only an hour or so to confirm what Mrs Olmstead had told him (there was an outside chance that Walter was simply avoiding *her,* he'd thought), and to confirm that his search was going to take him longer than he'd foreseen. He considered getting on the horn to Quentin, to feel some reassurance by hearing his voice, if nothing else.

Arkham was weirdsville and no mistake. The Federal style buildings and the ceaseless fog were one thing; the taciturn disposition of its residents was quite another. In the cigar shop, he learnt of a 'strange violet twinkling' that was said to occur on occasion in the windows of houses on Parsonage Street, but the shopkeeper clammed up on sight of the photograph that Elwood showed him, borrowed from the wall of Walter's jittery mother. In the kiosk of the Sarnath Theater, a broad muttered to him about the 'large, deformed fish' that her husband had seen while out fishing on Gravelly Pond, yet she was much less talkative when it came to his quarry, informing him that she had business to get on with and that "fish weren't the only unnatural things in these parts", which he ignored for the sake of politeness. When he stepped up to a pedestrian with his picture held out, he found a wad of tobacco spat at his feet, a passage from Leviticus squawked up at him, and his company abandoned on the sidewalk. Some, it seemed, knew Olmstead well enough. Knocking on doors wasn't going to help him.

Feeling much further than forty-five minutes away from Downtown Crossing, Elwood had decided to give up for the day when once again he sensed eyes upon him. He spun in the direction of the pharmacy and the bank, the gloom at the end of the street. There, he caught a flash of eyes, bright and glaring, and a blur of a lime green skirt as it vanished around a corner. Who was she, his stalker? What on earth did she want?

High heels echoed into the fog like the death knell of his inquiries.

* * *

Queer goings-on in Arkham were far from unheard of, Samuel Wentworth, the general clerk of the Deputy Mayor's Department informed Elwood in his small and caliginous office the following morning. Despite some garbled chitchat down the wire, Elwood had been unable to secure an appointment with the mayor himself and the secretary's tone had made it clear that Boston city tax collectors didn't merit special treatment. Elwood soon found himself squirming in the presence of the bug-eyed old clerk instead, who insisted on keeping the blinds drawn throughout the interview that he'd so reluctantly granted.

The wood-paneled office was dampish, and allowed not the slightest draught. In minutes, Wentworth's pipe shrouded the file-cluttered space, making Elwood cough and wonder why the fog outside was considered so noxious when tobacco smoke was not. Curiously, the clerk had the same broad-lipped and oleaginous look of Mrs Olmstead, the narrowness of his skull some hereditary quirk of these parts. Degeneration, perhaps.

Querulously, Wentworth confirmed that the First Annual Arkham Parade had gone ahead one morning in June two weeks prior. And despite a rejected proposal for funding and repeated objections – both legal and moral! "The youth of today," he said, and mumbled on about the war and liberty and those who took them. Pipe dancing in the corner of his mouth, Wentworth told the happenstance investigator that Walter O. had informed the mayor's office he'd keep his 'protest' limited, for the most part, to the Merchant District where, 'it wasn't likely to upset anyone sensible'. Walter planned to lead the march up Church Street and past the gates of the Miskatonic University, nevertheless. Then on to Hangman's Hill where he'd organized caterers, a band, fireworks and a grand old cookout as advised.

Here Elwood raised his eyebrows. The unemployed Olmstead had hired no less than eight farm trucks to serve as floats and adorned them all with gaily colored ribbons, streamers and balloons. Men and women, Wentworth said, squeezing the arms of his chair, had hired all manner of couture and painted themselves from head to toe. "Glitter. Lipstick. You name it," the elder spluttered through a particularly explosive cloud of smoke. "Men in ballgowns!" Some sported feathers and tassels, he went on, that weren't politely viewed outside of speakeasys. Reportedly, some men wore undershorts and loafers ("and nothing else!"), leaving naught to the imagination and flaunting themselves before the good Christian people of Arkham that morning in a kind of 'immoral assault'. There had been music and dancing, radios on each float playing a 'barrage of rhythm and blues'. Astonished onlookers had to cover the eyes of children. Members of the local clergy gasped as men and women 'made unseemly and ungodly displays of affection', Wentworth concluded with a shiver of contempt. He explained that he quoted from the letter of complaint that Pastor Gideon Hawley had sent to the mayor's office the day following the uproar.

Propriety aside, it was the uproar that Elwood was interested in, having been the last time that Walter was seen. He squeezed the old man for further details, perspiring under his shirt at the description of the incident, a fracas so unusual in a backwater like Arkham – though he'd have found it startling even in Boston. The rags were buzzing with the so-called 'Lavender scare', which had seen some dismissed from governmental positions and was set to filter down into every industry and every office, instilling in Elwood the utmost discretion, along with an undercurrent of panic. In these times, when men like him were deemed 'perverts' and 'criminals', he couldn't help but admire Olmstead's bravery, even as he shrank from its consequences. As Wentworth continued, Elwood put on an award-winning performance to conceal his growing discomfort.

The trouble, he learned, had blown up on the junction of East Church Street and Peabody Avenue where the warehouses sat closest to the river. A rumble had ensued between the fifty odd members of the parade and a mob of presumed 'factory workers' who'd crept out of the surrounding slums to mount an attack on the floats.

"Poured out the warehouses, they did," he said, and again he shuddered. "All of them wearing these... masks. Strange, froglike masks, I heard. Must've been near double the amount of the folks in the parade. Guns were fired off from the floats. The mob wasn't dissuaded. By the time the police got there, most of the revelers had fled. Some folk were lying in the street unconscious. The tires of the trucks had been slashed. Blood was on the sidewalk. And the mob had retreated, slipping back into the gloom of the warehouses. The police weren't going to chase them in there."

Elwood, who'd walked through the district on his way to PJs, and never beyond the safety of the streetlights, could well imagine why. The area known as Oldport was a maze of warehouses by day, and dive bars, can houses and clip joints by night. If one happened to get lost in the backstreets, they'd risk a mugging or worse. On top of this, he suspected that the local heat weren't too put out by the fact of 'factory workers' doing their job for them. The parade had disbanded. No one had been seriously hurt, as far as Elwood could tell, and only one rube of a resident was missing, likely on the lam. It was hardly a top priority for the Arkham PD. He was beginning to see why Mrs Olmstead had got him on the horn yesterday morning.

To that end, Elwood pressed on with his inquiries, drawing the clerk's attention to the matter that had puzzled him the most during their smoke-bound exchange. If the town hall had refused Walter dough for the parade, he asked, then how on earth had he managed to hire trucks, caterers, fireworks, musicians and all the decorations?

"Oh, there's gossip," Wentworth told him, sitting back with a wheeze. "All I'm saying is that there was no parade along Pickman Street, which lies two streets over from Church. Nonetheless, someone broke into Levensky's jewelers at around the same time as the brouhaha. Turns out Olmstead had sold some trinkets to Henry the week before. Gold, as I heard it, though where a bum like him got it is anyone's guess. If you're fixed on poking your nose in, maybe start there."

Elwood tipped his hat and assured the clerk he would. To which Wentworth shook his head, vented smoke and concluded the interview by advising him against it.

III. *Watchers in the Mist*

Elwood's mind was glittering with trinkets (the word *ingot* was niggling at his mind) as he made his way to Levensky's jewelers, trudging under his hat through the mist. He didn't have to think too hard about where the gold had come from; Mrs Olmstead had told him that Walter had traded some old books over in Innsmouth, a queer kind of town beyond the salt marshes on the New England coast. As far as he recalled, there'd once been a refinery in the ancient seaport, and whispers of treasures salvaged from the reef out in the bay. Whatever the truth of it, the US Military had cordoned the place off in 1927 to test torpedoes or somesuch, a matter that had contributed to the harbor's depopulation and decline.

These days, most knew Innsmouth as a godforsaken place, near derelict after the crash of '29 and never close to recovered, the local industry sliding from boom to bust. Fish still came from Innsmouth – not as much as rumors, however, swimming even to Bostonian ears. Most said that the seaport was cursed, bedeviled by ill luck and a haunt of hoods, vagrants and strays, those who society couldn't find a place for. "They ain't like us, the Innsmouth folk," a drunk informed him on the steps of the Arkham Municipal Library in return for a buck to spend on hooch. "What yer askin' after 'em for, anyways?"

That was the best result from the inquiries that Elwood made on his way downtown. No one liked to talk much in Arkham, but he learnt that no trains travelled direct to the coast, preferring to rattle north for Newburyport and Portland beyond. "Demand don't warrant it," a shopkeeper said before turning her attention to another customer. "Nor sense." Whatever Walter had been up to, it seemed a straight up black market trade, enough to raise funds for his parade certainly, and courtesy of some shady Innsmouth source.

None of which explained the boarded up window of the jewelry store before him. The trays behind the patch-up job were empty, he saw, and the space beyond them dark. Most of the glass had been removed, the frame bearing witness to its shattering in splinters and fangs, dull under the weather. Shards crunched under his shoes on the sidewalk, and coupled with the stench of the Miskatonic, his nerves were doing the rhumba again. An unpleasant thought was forming – about theft, about revenge – but Levensky's wasn't offering any answers and the jeweler in question had refused all his calls. No wonder if the guy had been up to no good. Last time he checked, receiving stolen goods was a criminal offense. The smash and grab had taken place during Olmstead's parade, someone (or *someones*) getting the bulge from the uproar over on East Church Street. He didn't kid himself about it being a coincidence; Walter had fenced his gold at this particular store and none of the others had been ransacked. Whatever business had gone down here, ingots for easy greens, it had clearly gone bad.

The idea was an omen. Hearing footsteps to the right of him, Elwood swung in that direction, half expecting to see the same lime green dress, the same powdered face that had dogged him since the train station. Instead, he made out figures in the fog — two or three silhouettes that made him wish the hour were later and the streetlights on. Scrawny, they were, and moving in a peculiar fashion, lurching towards him as if they weren't quite comfortable in their shoes or with the blacktop, a thought that slipped hands around his throat. There were no other pedestrians around and he had no reason to think the strangers an immediate threat. Menace emanated off them all the same, causing him to take a step backwards.

"Hey, what's the grift, fellas?" Elwood managed before a growl cut him off, the nearest member of the gang hastening his steps, heels scraping. He made out a cap, a narrow face under it, the features masked by a scarf. Did they intend to mug him right here on Pickman Street and in the middle of the day? They'd make off with his Bulova watch, a gift from Quentin for his thirtieth birthday (an ache in his chest made him wish he'd got his partner on the horn now), and a handful of dimes. But he didn't think so. He wasn't too far from French Hill, the wealthy suburb of Arkham, with its rows of impressive yet decaying houses surmounted by the spire of a church. Oldport was streets away and even if these were factory workers on the warpath (his next breathless thought), what business did they have with him? He noticed more of them now, shapes further back in the fog, approaching.

"Gentlemen—"

It appeared he'd been wrong about being attacked, for the nearest gang member made a grab for him. In a blur, Elwood glimpsed a ragged sleeve, clawed fingers on the end of it. The sight tore a cry from his throat, along with the water that speckled the ground, informing him that his assailant was soaked to the bone, and the stench of the river, which made also him gag. Arm raised to fend off a blow, Elwood shot a look around him, seeking escape. One heavy he might tussle with. Six or seven would see him counting bluebirds in seconds. He was no more a brawler than a detective. It was time to make like a tree, he thought, as his attacker lunged for him again, a knuckle sandwich darting past his shoulder.

The next moment, a squealing sound was filling his ears, a wash of radiance lighting the place up like the Olympia Theater. Hissing, the figures fell back from the headlights blazing through the fog, the harbinger of the car that came tearing around the corner. It was a Cadillac, he saw, an old, beat up coupe with bullet shape fenders and a chrome grille. In a blink, the bucket was screeching to a halt beside him, rubber greasing the tarmac, exhaust fumes blending with the brume. Wide eyed, he could only gawp as the driver shouted out of the rolled down window, her pillbox hat and lime green dress a beacon of salvation in the gloom.

"Get in," the woman told him, wheeling a glove at the passenger door. "Unless you fancy a trip to the bottom of the river."

Elwood needed no further encouragement. Wrenching the door open, he hoisted himself into the wagon, the vehicle roaring off down Pickman Street a second after his soles left the sidewalk. Illuminated by the headlights, he drew some satisfaction from the factory workers – or whoever they were – leaping out of the way of the Cadillac. It snuffed out the moment he took in their faces, no more than flashes in the fog, each one a strange and unearthly green, their eyes bulging from their narrow heads, their skin squamous, covered in scales.

IV. *The Plight of Miss Lillian Crow*

For a while, they drove in silence, Elwood gathering his wits. Soon enough he realized, from the same bare hills and cadaverous trees rolling by the window, that the woman was driving him out of Arkham and into the open countryside. Traffic was light and telephone poles waltzed off across the flats of sedge-grass and stunted shrubbery. It was late afternoon and darkness wasn't far off – if it ever truly left this hellish corner of Essex County. Embarrassed, but grateful for rescue, Elwood asked his most pressing question first. Who the devil had attacked him?

"Cultists," the woman replied, her voice husky and low, perhaps due to lack of sleep or too many cigarettes. Suit rumpled, Elwood pulled himself upright, glaring at her as she sat with her gloves on the steering wheel, her eyes set on the road. "Second generation hybrids. Guess they're hoping to score brownie points from the Order by getting their idol back. Guess they reckoned you'd lead them to it. To *me*. You can hardly blame them, sweetheart. You've been shooting your mouth off all over town."

This admission, bizarre as it was, washed over Elwood like drizzle. He leant in a little closer, peering at the woman's profile, her powdered cheeks, sharp nose and the wild ginger curls under her hat. Spying a trace of the familiar under her make-up, he sat back in his seat and shook his head.

"Olmstead. Walter Olmstead. I'll be—"

"Hey, now!" He – she – shot him a glance. "That cat is dead. Or as good as dead. It's Lillian Crow to you. To anyone. Capice?"

Elwood snorted. With her wig and paint job, his rescuer looked a world away from the scruffy student he'd roomed with at the university. Gosh, but he'd been wasting his time flapping his old photograph around, and he was in no mood for theatrics.

"Look, *sister*, your mama got me sniffing after you and it hasn't exactly been a boat ride. Seems you've caused quite the ruckus in town and I don't blame you for the disguise, but..." he shrugged without a shred of nonchalance, "you and me need to have a little chat."

"Firstly, Jack, that isn't my mother." His alumnus shot him another glance, a knowing one. As he digested this, remembering the Widow Olmstead's narrow head and bulging eyes, and the brackish cup of tea, his driver hit the brakes and swung the Cadillac over to the side of the road, parking in the shadow of an old, blasted tree. Birds took flight, squawking. She turned to him, the engine rumbling. "Secondly, you need to listen up. *Walter* was the disguise. I wore him for thirty odd years until the morning of the First Annual Arkham Parade." She held up a hand to check interruption. "Honey, just nod once for yes. Otherwise, keep your trap shut, OK?"

Reluctantly, Elwood gave a nod. Such things weren't unheard of, of course. He'd been to PJs enough times (along with some well-appointed basements in Boston) to know that guys and dolls could play 'musical chairs' if they wanted to. What was it to him? No one would think him a model citizen if they happened to find out about Quentin, an African American clerk employed by his Pearl Street office... It was shock talking, he realized, and thought of his partner helped him to master it, straightening him in his seat. Christ, he needed a drink.

"I got no beef with that," he said. "Like I said, I came up here to find you. And though I ought to bust your chops, I'm glad to find you alive." She smiled at that, but he plunged on, his lip curling. "Look, unless you want me to hitch a ride back to Arkham pronto, you better start spilling the beans."

In response, Lillian reached for the purse in her lap, a leather melon ready to burst, and flung it over at him. Elwood caught it, heavily, and found himself staring down at bulbous golden eyes and fat, drooping lips. The hideous visage – what one might rightly call *batrachian* – leered up at him, the idol sculpted to resemble fins and gills, the aspect of some long forgotten, thalassic god.

"Dagon," she explained. "Say howdy-do."

"What the heck is this?"

"The Father of the Deep Ones," she said. The object gleamed even without much light, some strange alloy in its making rendering it chromatic, alive. "The folks worship him over in Innsmouth. They reckon a city lies under the reef, you know. 'Cyclopean and many-columned Y'ha-nthlei'," her tongue tripped over the quoted name, which surely had no place on human lips, rouged or otherwise. "I don't know about that. I do know those freaks have a truckload of gold. I read about it at the university, some discovery back in the '20s. Never thought I'd catch the fever myself."

Elwood pushed back his hat and scratched his head. Archaeology and dead languages had never been his forte. Piece by piece, he was putting the puzzle together.

"Books. Old books. You traded—"

"So I got greedy," Lillian said, as if he'd accused her of something. "I should've stuck to ingots, sure. But why stop at a parade? I had me a mind to open a coffee-shop in downtown Arkham. You know, somewhere for folks... for folks like us to go. And that costs dough. So..."

"Where...?" Elwood's mouth was dry. The idol stared up at him, making him squirm at the blind condemnation in its blank, glittering gaze. "Where did you get this... Lillian?"

"I took it from the Innsmouth Masonic Hall."

"You... took it?"

Lillian flapped a hand. "Jesus. Are you a cop now? It was left out on the altar. It was night and no one was around. I'd come from the Old Marsh Refinery — Bobby Williamson keeps a pawnshop there, not that it's advertised — and the hall doors were open, the congregation down at the shore. Before I drove back to Arkham, I thought 'Why the hell not?' No one was gonna miss an old statue."

"You were wrong."

Lillian looked at him. Her eyes betrayed her honest sentiments, as did her trembling voice. "Jack, they're not gonna stop." She bit her lip and didn't need to say who. He'd seen them for himself. "I only took a down payment on that thing. How was I to know they'd come looking, attack the parade and smash up the shop? I'll have to settle with Levensky later... Oh God. Jack. My mother..." She sobbed, panic climbing into her voice. "You have to help me."

Elwood swallowed. "Help you do what, Lillian?"

"Why, we have to go to Innsmouth. We have to give the damn thing back."

Elwood let this sink in for a moment. Then he offered her a humorless grin.

"Oh, I don't think so, lady," he said. "My job was to find you. If you want my advice, you should high-tail it out of here why you still can."

"They're not gonna stop, Jack," Lillian repeated, reaching over to squeeze his arm. A little too hard, he thought, making him chew on the damsel-in-distress act. "Don't you see? If they don't get what they want, well, they've *seen* you. They know who you are. The Miskatonic isn't the only river in Massachusetts. There's the Charles River too. The Mystic and the Neponset, all flowing through Boston. Let's just say that the Order prefers to keep its secrets... secret."

As she spoke, Elwood stared at her with growing horror. Quentin! His mind went skating over thin ice. What about Quentin? His dread only mounted as Lillian reached over and flicked a switch, the glove compartment dropping open, mirroring his jaw. Inside, he saw a small, pearl handled revolver – loaded, at a guess.

Before he could say another word, Lillian tutted and put her foot to the metal. Lurching back in his seat, Elwood began to object. The squeal of tires cut him off as the car pulled out and ripped along the road, no doubt heading for the coast.

"Terrific," he said.

"We all make mistakes," she said. "Buckle up, hon. Time to kiss it better."

V. *Frog Soup*

Considering the attack on the parade and the way that the 'cultists' had come for him, Elwood proposed that a joyride into Innsmouth probably wasn't the smart course of action. Lillian hushed him. "I told you I had a contact, didn't I?" To that effect, she pulled up at a rundown gas station that emerged from what seemed like an ocean of marshes, flat, grassy and reeking of brine, stretching to the town and the physical ocean beyond. After tapping him for quarters, Lillian's high heels clopped across the forecourt to a rusted payphone where, she told him upon returning, she'd fixed up a meeting at the Old Marsh Refinery for midnight. "Williamson will get the idol back to the Order," she told him, checking her hair in the rear-view mirror with a calmness he found hard to believe. "No harm. No foul. Then we can get on with the business of living, such as it is in these parts."

Elwood didn't share her confidence. There was something about her breeziness that niggled him, but he was too shaken to put his finger on it.

And he was in too deep to turn back now, knowing if he did he'd never sleep again, starting at the drum of rain on the window of his North End apartment, every gurgle of the drain. The muddy stretch of the Charles River would never look so innocent again. And it sure as hell wouldn't be fair of him to put Quentin at risk, or to even tell his partner about this unhappy jaunt, what with his nervous disposition. Pouting at his ashen face, Lillian reminded him that he knew what to do if things went south, nodding at the glove compartment. Then she fired up the bucket for the last mile or so to the seaport. High above, the moon rode with them, gibbous and laughing in the sky.

Innsmouth wasn't much to look at. On the outskirts of town, stately old mansions rose from overgrown lawns, the weed-choked statues and boarded up windows blurring like ghosts as they passed. The faded opulence soon gave way to strangled streets and cramped, unremarkable houses, most of their windows dark, the odd one emitting the light of a feverish lamp. Heeding his advice, Lillian refrained from taking the main road into town, turning off at the Ipswich Junction instead and heading north along what a rusted sign told him was Adams Street. Where it met Bank, which appeared to be the port's chief thoroughfare, Elwood noticed a rumbling in his ears, faint yet drawing his gaze to the bridges they passed. It seemed that the Manuxet River went plunging through the town, carving a series of waterfalls through the terraces of dark and rickety streets to the equally shadowy harbor. Subsequent bridges spun a web across the sea, a vista of ink and bronze at this hour. Out there lay the bay, and the rocks which Lillian informed him were called 'Devil's Reef', her voice a murmur over the engine. According to her, it was the fount of all myths, mad sailors and ancient gold, lost where the bay gave way to the sunless, saliferous depths of the Atlantic.

The last of the light was bleeding from the sky as Lillian pulled up on the corner of Federal and Paine, selecting the lone bar and grille in town for supper, a joint known as Gilman's. The hotel, a Georgian monstrosity, lurched over the square like a penitent. A tug on his sleeve drew Elwood's attention to the Masonic Hall, the building set on the sparse, triangular green at the southern end of the confluence of streets. Its belfry and pillars looked ordinary enough for a hall of its kind, he thought, though he saw no cross, or for that matter, any recognizable religious symbol on its spire or architrave. Instead, he made out the lines of graven waves and an almost Grecian pair of eyes set above them, watching him with a portentousness that he could only attribute to the building's role as the source of all his troubles. In this godforsaken place, it didn't seem so strange that some might cling to the beliefs of old, forgotten sea gods and pagan idols, but the realization didn't make him happy to be here.

Along with Lillian's manner, her impious looting bugged him too, the casual way in which she'd confessed, rebellious parade or no. He could understand her reasons and her resentment well enough. Men like him were considered roaches to the privileged classes and few had qualms about stepping on them, let alone what they made of those who dared to step across genders. The notion must rattle their safe and tidy world in the same way that Lillian's boldness rattled his; he'd grown too accustomed to life in the shadows. The truth was her defiance made him feel ashamed. Whatever her motives, the doors to the hall were shut now, locked against the weather and the darkening sky. Against thieves in lime green dresses. Could they truly undo her mistake? Make amends for her crime?

The dusk made no difference to the atmosphere, which dripped with abandonment and penury. Half of the stores looked empty and the few pedestrians along the sidewalk darted from streetlight to streetlight, collars up as if fleeing the glare of the Cadillac. When Lillian killed the engine, a tightness crawled into Elwood's chest and he spared a glance for the eaves above him, perhaps elegant at the turn of the century before last, now cracked and sagging with the weight of the sea fog. He'd come here out of altruism, he reminded himself, to honor his alumnus, the friendship they'd once shared. The glow of the restaurant window, a cancerous yellow, did little to assure him he'd been right.

* * *

Inside Gilman's, Elwood ordered soup of the day – in reality, a clam chowder – and he wasn't at all surprised to find it lukewarm and brackish, with flakes of unidentifiable herbs floating on the surface. Still, he was hungry from his wrangle in Arkham and the interminable drive, and he slurped it down in the hope of reviving himself for whatever was coming next. To this end, he wiped his lips and subjected Lillian to another round of mild interrogation.

"What happened to Mrs... to your mother, Lillian? Were you suggesting—?"

"If only I knew," she said, putting down her fork. She'd only been playing with her salad anyway. "All I know is when I went back to the house after the parade, my mother wasn't there. Or rather, whoever *was* there, it wasn't her." She grimaced, recalling some unpleasant memory. "They're in the town, which won't come as news to you. They've been creeping in for months now, I guess."

They, Elwood thought, and loosened his tie. He was feeling queasy, out of sorts. The room was cramped and empty of diners, the windows shut against the weather. All the same, he experienced a chill. He recalled the widow in the rattling house, her glassy, bulging eyes, the way she'd spoken about golden idols and human sacrifice. "A nasty business by all accounts", she'd said. And he remembered how she'd pointed him to Mayor Armitage and the wrinkled clerk he'd been presented with, who'd sat in his gloomy office and coughed, his lozenge of a head wreathed in smoke, his eyes large and watchful. The whole thing had been a set-up, sure, a way to find the missing thief. But—

"The cult." Somehow, he wasn't certain that's what Lillian meant. Or not *entirely* what she meant. He suppressed his dread with practicality. "What do they want? Sounds like more than a stolen statue."

"Who knows, mister?" Lillian said, and her shoulders sank. "Expansion of the Esoteric Order of Dagon? That's what they like to call themselves. To establish churches from Portland to Boston, no doubt..." Lillian fumbled for a cigarette in her overstuffed purse, lit it and went on through a swirl of smoke. "As to what they *believe*, well, that's a little more complicated. According to the books from the Miskatonic library, there's some unholy union between Innsmouth and the folks of Essex County. They say that ambassadors came, rising from the drowned yet ever living city of Y'ha-nthlei, fathoms under the waves. There's more than gold down there, Jack, or so I read. There's old things. *Old Ones*. With the proper incantations, the right sacrifice, the Cult of Dagon longs to establish the Deep Ones on land, and make way for the oldest of them all. Great Cthulhu, who in his house at R'lyeh waits dead and dreaming. *Fhtagn!*"

"Come again?"

"Just something they say. The cultists. In the old tongue."

"Boy, you've done your homework." Elwood steepled his hands under his chin, impressed. The woman before him was frowning, an echo of the student he'd once known. It dawned on him that Lillian's dress and make-up wouldn't have changed an iota of that, and he found he couldn't dismiss her claims as easily as he'd have liked. Rattled, he took another spoonful of soup to hide his expression, wincing at the taste. The revolver, pearl handled and cold, dug into the small of his back like a comforting hand. "You sure did wander into a snake pit when you got all cranked up about your parade." He held up a hand at her protest, offering what he hoped was a placatory smile. "I'm not saying I blame you. What those bastards think, all scripture up front and cruelty behind closed doors, well... it ain't right. But you know there are people out there who'll hurt you. You gotta be careful. Use the shadows like a friend." He sighed, wearied by his own words. "Let sleeping dogs lie, isn't that what they say?"

"Sleeping *gods* in this case, Jack," she replied, and pursed her lips. "You know, there are worse things a girl could do. We're all of us equal in God's eyes. We all cry, laugh, love, hate, shit, bleed and die. Judge not, isn't that what He said? Well, all I see is a whole lot of judging. Why do some folks think it's fine for them to live with the sun on their faces while it isn't for us? You're damned straight it ain't right. That kind of selfishness goes beyond any words you'll find in a book, Jack. That kind of shit is... *inhuman*. We have to show them that. They have to learn. That's why I wanted my parade. What else do you suggest? Hiding forever?"

"Spare me the sermon. We're not the only ones living in the shadows in these parts, babe. You'd have thought the Arkham PD would've noticed something. The townsfolk. Anyone!"

He said this and recalled the lack of response from the department in question, the morning of the Church Street parade. How deep did the conspiracy go? How far had the cult infiltrated? Just what in blazes was going on here?

"Like frog soup," Lillian told him.

"Huh?"

"Frog soup," she said, looking at him like he was some chump. "You know, from science class. Put a frog in boiling water and it'll jump right out of the pan. Put a frog in cool water and slowly turn up the heat..."

"Yeah, I get it. The frog won't notice. So that's how—"

He belched, cutting himself off. The chowder churned in his guts, a sudden tide of queasiness. Regretting his appetite, he looked across the table at Lillian, tasting brine and alarm. It wasn't her cigarette that had her swimming in his vision. Blearily, he watched as she stood, one glove climbing to her breast, her eyes wide. But she wasn't looking at him. Following her gaze, Elwood turned in his seat, mute with horror at the figure who'd entered the dining room. At once, he fumbled at the revolver in his belt, but it fell to the floor. He attempted to stand, his chair skittering out from under him. Leaden, he dropped to one knee, the gun sliding away on the carpet. The room seemed full of fog, the walls rippling around him.

"Thank you, Jack," the Widow Olmstead said from the doorway. "A friend in need, yes?"

Spluttering, Elwood stared up at Lillian. In his mind, all the pieces snapped together in a terrible kind of sense. Her lack of grief for her mother, for starters, glaring now that he placed his unease. Her strange knowledge of the cult and its aims. The idol in her possession, simply 'taken' from the hall. The way she'd known where to find him on Pickman Street – a wolf in sheep's clothing, all right. Or in this case, in a lime green suit-and-dress combo.

"You... you brought me here on purpose..."

Croaking, he tried to say more, to question or rebuke her for her double-cross. All he caught was a blur of curls and red-rouged lips before the waves closed over his head.

VI. *Upon the Black-Sailed Altar of Dagon*

"The right sacrifice," Lillian had said. Elwood sneered at the memory as the world swam back into focus. A senseless span of time had passed where he'd been lying on a floor somewhere, drifting in and out of consciousness. A door had opened, closed. Footsteps had come and gone, echoing on stone. When he came to, his hands were still bound, but he was upright, tethered to a pole behind him. A groan escaped him, more of a curse. Though anger simmered in his breast, he had no time to vent it, rankling at the trick for which he'd fallen. Yeah, fallen hook, line and sinker. Someone must've doped his soup, Lillian or the waiter. How could she do this to him? He'd come all the way from Boston to find her (he knew it was only forty-five minutes from Downtown Crossing, but he might as well have crossed an ocean). It seemed his former friend had only plucked him from the clutches of the cult for her own nefarious purposes, offering him up, he suspected, in place of stolen gold...

There was something skewed in this thinking, but the roaring in his ears, a cacophony that he took for the sea at first, made it hard to pin down. The air was full of wind and salt, the spray on his cheeks rousing him to full awareness. Even a humble tax collector could recognize music, the deep drums and the cheering all around him, the wail of some flute-like instrument assailing the starless sky. It was far removed from Ella, the song speaking of anything but love.

"Iä! Iä! Cthulhu fhtagn!"

Hardly daring to open his eyes, Elwood drank in his surroundings, his breath going out of him. The first thing he noticed was that he was elevated, placed several feet above the street. Night had fallen, the moon wreathed in scraps of cloud, and it was impossible to orientate himself in such an unfamiliar place as Innsmouth. The crowds didn't help. Shadowed faces lined every inch of the sidewalk or hung out of the windows of houses, arms waving in time with their cries. There must've been a hundred or more spectators, their godless chanting thrumming in his head. It was the sight of them that reeled his gaze inward again, his mind threatening to snap. Was he hallucinating? The dope was still in his blood... Chowder rose in his throat, his flesh cooling to match the fog, and he knew that what he was seeing was real. Every eye on him was a sallow, amphibian orb in a narrow, fish-shaped skull. Every face was a pale and pelagic green, the color of rotting limes. Yesterday, he'd taken these features as some hereditary quirk of backwater New England. Now he suspected a different source, some untold ancestry rising from Neptunian depths, the unholy union that Lillian had spoken of. The dwellers of Innsmouth weren't human at all...

"Iä! Iä!"

Like a bird tossed on waves of the queer cry, Elwood's gaze was drawn to the heavens. Whatever god reigned here, he feared it lurked in the darkness of the bay and wouldn't deign to help him. The black sail that billowed above, coupled with the lurch of the ground under him, brought home the fact that he was mobile. From starboard to port, the boom and the rigging overhead, he was in no doubt what vehicle carried him. Shivering, dazed, he flashed that he was in a boat of some kind, a small schooner or ketch on the back of a truck. The sight of the seaweed and shells above, weaving and clacking like banners, spread a ball of cold through his guts. In some grim, benthic distortion – perhaps a mockery of the violent incident that had drawn him to Arkham in the first place – it dawned on Elwood that he was in a parade. *A parade of all things!* The boat was bedecked like a float, navigating the surging streets. He was bound to the mast, he realized, the blasphemous procession winding down to the harbor and the lightless waves beyond.

It was then that he noticed Mrs Olmstead – or whatever aped her plain and lanky guise for this (he suppressed the thought 'ritual')... nightmare. The woman stood at the prow and Elwood saw that it was she who was whipping the crowds into frenzy, her popish hat resembling a tiara, tall in front, with a freakish and irregular periphery. Gold glimmered in the murk, suggesting the tiara was of a set with the ingots and the statuette, containing the same strange and lustrous alloy. Her vestments, long and flowing, belonged to no orthodox prelate. Even in the gloom, her aquatic aspect was unmistakable and she swayed like an ancient reborn, some latter day priestess of the sea. What little hair she had left was a sketch on her lengthened skull. The last of her skin had peeled away from a broad, supra-terminal mouth and the same round and unblinking eyes that had become so familiar to him in such a horribly short space of time. Closer up, he noticed the gills that flapped on her neck and her webbed hands, a wedge of solid gold clutched between them.

"The Children of the Deep shall never die!" the imposter shrieked, the reclaimed idol held high. "The faithful will return to Dagon who birthed us, who gave us breath. Hearken to us now, father! Open the gate to sunken Y'ha-nthlei. Accept our earthly sacrifice!"

The crowd roared – '*Iä! Iä! Cthulhu fhtagn!*' – incomprehensible words in a language that Elwood guessed had bitten the big one long before history as he knew it had begun. It didn't take a genius to realize who the priestess meant by 'sacrifice' either, any more than it did to realize where the float was heading. Looking beyond the creature's rapturous form, Elwood took in the view, the truck turning a corner and heading along the harbor wall, the black waves rolling beyond it. The knowledge wrenched a groan from his throat, lost in the hubbub. He was a catch and had never been more, lured by the bait of his conscience, hooked by secrets and lies. The cult meant to give him to the sea, to the seething waves around Devil's Reef and whatever foulness lay beneath it.

He heard another groan, closer than the celebrant horrors and their raving, foam-lipped doyenne. The mast shook and creaked, mirroring his efforts as he struggled for release, rope burning his wrists. Craning his neck, he saw Lillian tethered behind him, her pillbox hat lost to the chaos, her wild curls streaming as she looked up and around her, her falsies blinking. She took in the scene with mascara-streaked eyes – though her shock seemed dwarfed by his own. She'd seen these abominations before, he knew. Hell, she'd done business with them.

Frowning, her lips a smear, Lillian caught him staring.

"Jack! You're alive. Damn it, the newts did a number on us..."

In that moment, he knew it was all true. This bright and rebellious creature had seen a way to lift herself and her friends – men such as himself, women and whoever – out of the shadows, to confront Arkham with its bigotry. And refuse to accept it. In a surge of relief, Elwood forgave her her thievery, her madness, grinning despite himself in the gusting air.

"Lillian!" He had to shout over the crowd. "I thought that you... the idol... the soup—"

He shrugged, a schoolboy, and she caught his meaning.

"Yeah, well, thanks for nothing." Then she shook her head. Neither of them had time for it. "Can you reach my leg? I'm wearing a garter. There's a nail file..."

Relieved as he was, Elwood didn't think such a weapon would save them. Nevertheless, he strained against his bonds, his wrists smarting, fumbling for her thigh. As luck would have it, his captors had appeared to rely on the drugs, his constraints giving enough for him to reach the object in question. As if he were handling bone china, he tweaked out the thin metal tool, gripping it between his trembling fingers. Like he'd seen Lex Barker do once in a *Tarzan* movie, with Quentin sat beside him at the drive-in, Elwood maneuvered the blade upward and began to saw through the rope.

"Open the gate, Father! Accept our meager offering!"

With her cry skimming over the waves, the Widow Olmstead spread her arms and spun to face her captives. The truck had reached the wharf now and come to the top of a slipway, a slope of cracked brick leading into the water. The crowds thronged the harbor wall, chanting, and they were too far away to notice that something was up on the boat. The priestess, however, was not, her round eyes flashing as the rope snapped and Elwood wrested free of the mast. Behind him, Lillian sagged, released from her bonds. Like an amateur matador faced with a bull, Elwood slashed at the air with the nail file, silver under the moon. He might as well have wielded a paper-clip. With a snarl, the priestess curled back her lips, revealing a row of tiny teeth, each one yellow and piranha-sharp. Dropping the idol, she came lurching towards him.

"Jack, the crate! The crate!"

It took him a second to grasp what Lillian meant. Then he was darting forward, reaching for the mess of equipment in the middle of the deck. Perhaps he could find a mallet or a pike pole, a more suitable weapon to fend off his fiendish assailant. He'd managed to fling the lid open when the priestess descended upon him, her fingers – in truth, claws – sinking into his shoulders. Crying out, he sprawled on his back on the deck, arms raised to keep her at bay. She snapped at him, drool and brine peppering his face. Her gills seethed with her efforts, her back a hunch of spines, designed for the fathoms and not for dry land. He could only hope it gave him an advantage. The woman, or whatever she was, had some strength to her, and Elwood knew he couldn't hold her off for long. In his ears, her vile croaking, which was doubtless summoning the cult to her aid. Faint splashes confirmed his fears, the creatures diving off the harbor wall in their haste to reach the slipway. If they managed to do so, he and Lillian were fish food.

Then Lillian was there, a lime green blur over the creature's hump. Lips a fierce moue of red, she raised the oar she was holding and brought it down hard on the priestess. With a crack of splintering wood, the priestess wailed and slumped to one side, giving Elwood enough time to leap for the object he'd seen in the crate. Grabbing it, he climbed to his feet, dizzy and swaying along with the deck – the truck was driving straight into the water, the driver giving no thought to drowning, and the bowsprit of the boat, which overhung the roof of the cab, was following. Despite the sails above, it was plain to him that the vessel served only a ceremonial purpose, some foul oblation to the heathen god these creatures venerated. The truck was meant to see them into the bay, sinking into the depths of Devil's Reef. Lillian and him were the cherry on top, grub for the blasted deep.

Worse, the inhabitants of Innsmouth, hideous to a one, were swarming through the water and clambering up the sides of the boat. '*Iä! Iä!*' In seconds, they'd reach him, his flesh torn apart by a hundred claws, his lungs bursting as he spluttered his last. He'd never see poor Quentin again, never bask in his furtive smiles in the Pearl Street office or feel his warmth next to him... It was this that spurred him to action, shouting at Lillian to stay back. Recalling how the denizens of the half-abandoned seaport had hissed at the Cadillac's headlights in Arkham, shirking the light, Elwood raised the flare gun over his head. With a nonsensical cry, he pulled the trigger and light blossomed over the bay.

In the crimson radiance, the priestess shrieked, shielding her face. As one, the creatures hissed, the would-be boarders falling back, some of them crashing into the water. Half-blinded himself, Elwood grabbed Lillian's arm and pulled her to portside. He had no idea what he was doing – he was still just a tax collector from Boston, dammit – but it was clear to him that they had to get off the boat. There were other, smaller, vessels bobbing in the gloom. One of them must have an engine...

The light from the flare was fading, an arc of smoke and phosphorescence over the bay. Before Elwood could take the plunge, the deck was shuddering under him, the seaweed and shells rattling overhead. It reminded him of the way that the eleven o'clock to Portland had shaken the house on Water Street, an event that seemed an age ago. The tide was sucking at the slipway, drawing back over shingle and sand. Here was the approach of something else, he realized, something much larger than a train, rising from the place where the shallows met the Atlantean depths.

As soon as he thought it, a tremendous bubbling sound filled his ears and he looked beyond the prow to see the waves chopping and churning, a whirlpool troubling the surface. In moments, the reflections scattered and dimmed, the flare winking out overhead. The fog closed back in, the waves doused in darkness. Waves sloughed across the bay, some crashing over the harbor wall, carrying the odd creature with them. And with the disturbance, the sprawled priestess and every terraqueous eye on the boat turned to face it, gazing with palpable adoration out into the bay.

Elwood looked at Lillian, finding an answer in her pale, streaked face.

"Dagon," she whispered.

The sky shook, some terrible, submerged bellow thundering through the water. Rigid as stone, Elwood saw the great fan of spines break the surface of the bay. Scads of seaweed and fish poured from the membranes between them, escaping where Elwood could not, his feet refusing his will. The muck slopped from the anemic flesh of the jagged titan that bore it, tons of silt sliding off its bulk. Its shoulders, each the size of the Masonic Hall, rose, thrusting a colossal skull from the sea, scaled and horned, its snout a grille of encrusted fangs. Caught in the glare of one gargantuan eye, Elwood gagged, his brain hurting, fit to burst. Humans weren't meant to see such things, the understanding spearing through him. How long had such a beast waited, he wondered, its name remembered by only the damned? Had it lurked for a thousand aeons, patient and hungry under the sea? What chaos did it bring now, summoned as it was from slumber by the arcane and insidious Order? Beneath the leviathan's imagined claws, the buildings, roads and bridges of New England would crumble like matchbox toys.

As if to echo Elwood's dread, the priestess and all the creatures on the boat prostrated themselves, their heads to the deck, their claws clasped in prayer.

"*Nog!*" they murmured in the same dead tongue, hushed now and reverent. "*Nog ng vugtlagln vulgtmm!*"

Looking out at the harbor, Elwood saw a similar scene, the crowds falling silent, their toadish faces to the ground. His heart, beating like an echo of their drums, cringed to see them. Some deep, unplumbed part of him longed to follow suit and he suppressed the urge to sink to his knees before the rising giant, to beg Dagon for mercy, for his pathetic, land-bound life...

Lillian didn't share his awe. Taking advantage of the lull, she grabbed Elwood's tie, wrenching him towards her.

"I don't regret it, you know," she said. "Any of it."

Elwood met her defiance. "I know. If this is the last time we speak, I want you to know that I'm proud of—"

"You should be."

In her eyes, he could see she'd lost her lust for gold, and had probably heard enough dead languages to last a lifetime. There was pride, sure, and then there was survival. Before he could stop her, Lillian was grabbing his shoulder and pushing him backwards, the two of them tumbling over the side and crashing into the water.

* * *

Portland, July 1951

Dear Quentin,

I know you'll never forgive me. I'm sorry for leaving the way I did and it pains me double to send you another farewell. Hopefully by now you'll have read the facts concerning the First Annual Arkham Parade and found this letter enclosed as a postscript, which should make a little more sense of things. You'll be pleased to hear I'm as well as can be expected, currently heading west with Lillian Crow to a 'safehouse' in an undisclosed location.

How did we escape from Innsmouth, you might ask? Well, it wasn't easy. While the inhabitants were distracted by the horror in the bay, Lillian and I managed to swim to an empty speed boat and fire up the engine. Navigating the reef was a horror in itself, and I'm afraid to say that we were pursued. Some in the crowd noticed we were taking off and came after us. Needless to say they swam pretty fast and we rounded the headland narrowly, barely missing the rocks. Once we'd navigated into Plum Island Sound, and with dawn on the horizon, we found ourselves alone, left to drift or to drown when the gas ran out, I guess. Instead, we made it all the way to Newburyport and there I was faced with my godawful choice – and the writing of this letter.

Please believe me. The Esoteric Order of Dagon is real, as real as anything I've put in my account. You may think me a walk-out or a cheat – I ask you to remember my practical nature and ask yourself whether I'd lie to you. If only my trip to Arkham had concerned a missing friend and an ill-advised parade! To my regret, I've come to learn that an inhuman cult, the spawn of some ungodly race that dwells deep in the waters of Essex Bay, has infiltrated New England with an eye to greater expansion. Arkham has already fallen under its sway, presumably with Boston to follow. As sole witnesses to the truth, Lillian and I find ourselves hunted. Though it weighs on us daily, for now the shadows are our friend.

In light of this, you must understand that to return to the city would lead our enemies straight to you. The reason for my continuing absence is only for your protection, my dear, and I beg you to respect that. DO NOT CONTACT

THE AUTHORITIES. Don't show anyone this letter. Throw it on the fire and mention the matter to no one. Take what you can from the safe in the Pearl Street office and head west as soon as possible. Under no circumstances come looking for me. Steer clear of Innsmouth! You'll only discover the truth of what I've told you. I'm afraid that you won't survive it.

This isn't over. Somehow, some day, I'll make my way back to you. We'll dance in our own parade or just stand hand in hand with the sun on our faces. One day, Quentin, all the shadows over us will be gone.

Until then, think of me with affection.

Jack

Letter #2. *From the evidence file of the Boston Police Department, 154 Berkeley Street, Boston. Submitted by Mr Quentin G. Fields. August 23rd, 1951.*

Graphologist note: *After initial analysis, the signature on letter #1 makes an inconclusive match with letter #2. Details to follow. September 17th, 1951.*

DEAD MEDIA

NICK MAMATAS

At Miskatonic, like most liberal arts colleges, nothing is ever thrown away, but almost everything is misfiled. Lenore Reichl was a junior and knew her way around, but she needed help for what she wanted this time – an actual Dictaphone. For that, she had to appeal to Walt McDonald, the ever-present work-study student in the A/V office. The trick was to figure out whether Walt was simply unwilling to leave his seat, or actually really too stupid to know what a Dictaphone was. Lenore tried bending over the desk, just showing a little bit of cleavage and most of her teeth. Her piercings glinted. She tapped the toe of her stompy boot. That got Walt away from Facebook for two seconds.

"Look, I don't know," he said. "I did all the tagging here last year. Everything has a barcode now and there's no code for a Dictaphone."

"Just because there's no code for something doesn't mean it doesn't exist," Lenore said. She and Walt had shared a class last semester – Semiology, which involved watching lots of television commercials. They weren't friends. The mildest of acquaintances, really. They didn't even nod to one another when they passed on the quad, but Lenore did feel comfortable using Walt's name. "Walt," she continued, "just because there's no signifier doesn't mean there's no referent." Walt had been in charge of the video projection unit and had saved the day more than once in Semiology. "C'mon," Lenore said. She licked her lips. Not too flirty, just, more like anxious.

Walt glanced back at the screen, looking at his reflection rather than the status updates of his online friends. He didn't have too many friends here in Arkham. Not a lot of black kids made it to Miskatonic, and those who did were often subtly abused and suspected of such crimes as petty theft, Affirmative Action status, and facility with a basketball. Walt was too fat for basketball, too fat for Lenore. Not so fat that he had to go around doing pretty girls with purple hair special favors for no reason, though. "What do you even need a Dictaphone for?" he asked, more to himself than to Lenore.

"I'm glad you asked," she said and reached into her shoulder bag. It was an Emily the Strange thing, and what came from it was pretty strange itself. A small cylinder wrapped in yellowing paper.

"Is that what I think it is?" Walt asked.

"Yes!" Lenore said. "It's a cylinder, the Wilmarth cylinder. Brattleboro. The mysterious recording of the so-called 'Bostonian' and the Mi-Go. And I need a Dictaphone to play it, to hear the voices. This is primary source material."

"Oh," Walt said. He glanced at his monitor again. "I thought it was something else. Anyway, yeah, that's cool, but we have mp3s of everything, so why bother?"

"We have mp3s of DAT tapes of a cassette of reel-to-reel tapes of a 78 record of this cylinder. Luckily, I'm into vinyl, so I managed to work my way back through the dead media – stuff is definitely dropping out with every generation. It's like oral folklore, what's on here. It's been, you know, changed."

Now Walt was interested. He shifted in the chair, held out his hand for the tube, then carefully undid some of the paper and uncapped it to peer at the wax cylinder within. "All right, but you're coming with me. Four eyes are better than two."

The A/V archive was in a dusty Quonset hut off the library, and it was stuffed with dead and dying machines: VHS players and overhead projectors – the old analog kind with Cyclopean lenses atop craning necks – shelves of slide projectors, and that just on either side of the large entrance. Walt clicked on the light and Lenore saw the problem. Floor to ceiling desks and blown-out televisions and snake-coils of coaxial cables spilling from ruined cardboard boxes. The dust was oppressive. If there was any rhyme or reason to the storage at all it was simple – oldest stuff in the back. "The Dictaphones, if we even have any, are on the other side of this. So, let's start moving stuff out of the way. There's a dolly in that corner and we can use a few of the TV carts that still have four wheels to move shit outside."

Lenore wasn't much help. She had on the sort of long lace dress Walt would call 'kooky', and needed to hold up the hem with one hand at all times. But boy, did she talk. "I know; it's all basic term paper stuff. Is the so-called 'black goat of the woods' a separate figure from Shub-Niggurath or not?"

Walt shoved some old monochrome computer monitors out of the aisle he was making, and leaned in close to Lenore just so that she could see his eyes roll. "C'mon," he said. "Nobody knows. That's why it's a term paper topic – you can argue pro or con, and everyone knows the arguments and rejoinders and whatnot. It's a religious argument, not a real research question at this point. Not for undergrads, anyway. Wilmarth couldn't comprehend what he got on wax, so I can't imagine what sort of research you have planned to find out... eighty years later."

"Field..." Lenore said, the word rolling off her tongue tentatively, "... research."

Walt didn't know what to say. But he found the machine a moment later.

* * *

It took some time to get the Dictaphone working. Walt appropriated some copper wiring from a dead filmstrip projector and put Lenore to work wrapping it in insulating tape. She frowned when Walt cracked the still-sleek black case to get at the innards of the Dictaphone.

"This is totally steampunk," Lenore said. "They don't make equipment like this, anymore. Everything's so sleek and sterile, these days."

"If you like vintage, you came to the right friggin' college, that's for sure," Walt said. It was true. Miskatonic felt lived-in. Every stone on the quad was worn. The lights flickered during the frequent winter storms. Monocles, sideburns and grandfather's moth-bitten and frayed frock coat were perennial student affectations. Corned beef hash and liver had regular rotation in the cafeterias. There wasn't even a single vending machine on campus.

"Why does anyone come here?"

"Pfft, you know," Walt said. "You have the rich idiots who couldn't get into any of the *real* Ivy League schools; ninth-generation inbred legacy College Republicans; locals from across the river the College Fathers give full rides to just so nobody swims across and burns the whole place down; Californians who want to be close to skiing, and..."

"And?" Lenore asked, her voice lilting as she stretched the word. She liked this.

"People like us. You know, people with *reasons* to come here."

"So, you'll do it." Lenore didn't have a car. Walt did.

"I'll plug this thing in now and give it a whirl." Walt tried putting it in backward first, by mistake. Lenore had her notes with Akeley's transcript of the recording – or, at least, the transcript Wilmarth claimed to have received from Akeley – spread out under her palms. Walt touched the sapphire point to the cylinder. The recording was tinny and distant, more crackle than voice. Was that a Boston Brahman chanting, "... abundance to the Black Goat of the Woods. *Ia!* Shub-Niggurath! The Goat with a Thousand Young!" or a toothless old Vermonter putting on airs?

"Akeley himself, running a scam of some sort?" Walt said, but Lenore shushed him harshly. Then that inhuman buzz of a voice, near-chanting, "And He shall put on the semblance of men, the waxen mask and the robe that hides..." What a voice! Like auto-tune, or a nail across a chalkboard. Walt didn't hear it so much as feel it. But then, Lenore was skeptical. "What if he recorded this on another Dictaphone, then played it back... wouldn't it sound all hissy and strange?" They played the cylinder again, then a third time. Lenore had a pocket watch, yet another Miskatonic fad, with a second hand and took notes with each pass.

"This is some wild shit," Walt said after the fourth round. "But is it telling us anything? Are we debunkers now? Skeptics, all of a sudden?"

"Get one of the blanks. Let's try it," Lenore said. She recorded herself – "the waxen mask and the robe that hides" – then played it back, recording that on her cell phone's voicemail, then re-recorded the playback of her voicemail onto the wax cylinder. "You're a freakin' genius, Walt," she said, "getting this thing working." Walt found himself thinking that Lenore wasn't too shabby, herself. He wanted the experiment to fail, so they could do that field research, so that he could spend more time with her. And it did fail. A tiny little Lenore voice, with a trace of a microchip accent, spilled out of the Dictaphone's old speaker. No vibrato, no buzz of the sort that made Walt's molars cringe in his mouth. "Ah, well," Lenore said.

"Maybe... the cave's acoustics made it easier to fake such a voice?" Walt said.

"Why would Akeley bother telling the truth about the cave if he was running a hoax?"

"You said that there were things on the cylinder not on the mp3s, that you heard them on the old records and tapes."

"There are." She slid the transcript over to Walt and reloaded the Wilmarth cylinder. "Listen closely. Listen *past* the words." Walt and Lenore shared a look – Walt confused, Lenore confused by his confusion. "At the recording artifacts, you know," she said. "With the copies, they've either been digitally erased or just degenerated beyond hearing from the process of copying."

Walt got up and turned off the lights in the little office. "The fluorescents, you know," he explained. "Buzzing." He even turned off his computer and threw his wristwatch – yes, he still wore one as a Miskatonic affectation of his own – into a desk drawer. Lenore had a keychain flashlight with which to illuminate the transcript and a purple-painted fingernail to follow along. And there was something there, in the opening sounds of the recording. *Ii eh lu uh uh wu*. Then, after the hysterical and uncanny buzz of 'a thousand young!' *Ah ih ah ca t'pa*. Just a little hint of *And it has come to pass* but not in that Boston accent.

"The 'Bostonian' is being fed his lines?" Walt asked.

"Sounds like it."

"By Akeley."

"Or by whoever actually made the recording. Or by someone standing next to him."

"Or maybe it's just an echo of some sort. In the cave."

"Again with the cave!" Lenore said, but she laughed. She was a pale girl, nearly aglow in the darkened room. "... but maybe," she conceded.

"So, the original recording has a third speaker. That's great, Lenore. Senior thesis stuff, maybe, if you feed it into the right program and manage to extract it, but it's not literature. It's not a determination about Shubby and the black goat." Lenore snorted at *Shubby*.

"One more time," she said and reset the point on the cylinder. This time, just thanks to expectations, Walt heard the other human speaker and he heard something else. Some of the hisses and crackles themselves seemed to be phonemes now – stage-whispered prompts or at least preliminary throat-clearings from beings beyond the stars. "Ahem, ahem," Walt said. "Did these things, if there were any, even have throats?"

"Here is my proposal!" Lenore said. She shot up from her seat and reached for the light switch herself. "There were other speakers! Let's assume that, just for now. At least one other human speaker, be it Akeley himself or a confederate, or who knows. Many people have tried to determine who 'the Bostonian' was, but maybe he's not important. Maybe he was just an actor who was fed lines by someone else? I say we head to Vermont and find that person, or traces of the same. Field research," she said.

"And then just ask him if Shub-Niggurath *is* the Black Goat of the Woods with its thousand young?" Walt asked.

"Of course not. But we have already expanded the number of people who knew what was going on from two to three. That means that there may have been more; there still may be more. So, come on."

"You know I'll say yes," Walt said. He was always being tapped for favors by non-drivers, but mostly just to the local liquor store for party supplies. "But what were you going to do if I said no?"

Lenore shrugged. "Like you said, I knew you'd say yes. And if you didn't, Peter Pan to Boston, then Amtrak to Vermont, I guess..." She glanced away from him.

Walt spun in his chair and typed something on his keyboard. "I'll take tomorrow off... thank *you*, EZLabor; now check Google Calendar... okay, I'm free. We can go—"

"Now," Lenore said.

Walt laughed. "The stars are right?"

"You know it, kiddo," she said.

* * *

It was a tedious two-hour trip across the top of Massachusetts to southern Vermont. At night, the trees are black and the highway stuffed with tractor-trailers. Walt idly wondered if Lenore planned on killing him in Brattleboro, but decided against. She wanted a ride, after all. How would she get rid of the car, get back to campus? And the huge mess they'd left from burrowing through the supply hut of old A/V equipment would be a great clue in itself. Fingerprints everywhere in the dust, the friggin' Dictaphone, half-gutted and left on the workbench. He had nothing to worry about, he decided, this time. In general, though, for students like Walt and Lenore, those few who came to Miskatonic for *reasons*, a bit of curricular violence was never far from their minds.

"Do you have to pee?"

"I'll pee in Vermont," Lenore said. "I've never peed in Vermont."

"It's good to have dreams and to accomplish them," Walt said. "We're going to run out of shitty mill towns to turn off onto in a few minutes, though, so if you wanted to pee—"

"Do *you* want to pee?" Lenore asked. "Or did you just want to visualize my vagina, somehow, and let me know you were doing so?"

Walt laughed. "You have a mouth, woman!"

Lenore arranged her Emily the Strange purse on her lap for the millionth time.

Right outside Brattleboro, they stopped at a motel and spent the night tip-toeing around one another, in their separate beds, around the door of the tiny bathroom. Neither had brought a change of clothes, but Brattleboro was full of used bookstores and people who shopped at the food co-op and places like Save The Corporations from Themselves – "hemp clothing for ugly girls," Lenore declared as they walked up Main Street the next morning – so they weren't out of place, not Lenore in her lace nor Walt in his oversized sweatshirt and low-riding jeans.

"Think the town's changed much?" Lenore asked. Then she nodded at a news rack. "The *Reformer* is still publishing."

"I saw a building dedicated to milk cows and there was that truck full of lumber rattling down High Street," Walt said. "But yeah, this place is fucked up. One-third hick, one-third yuppie, one-third dirty hippie. So, anyway, what's the deal, Missus Peel?"

"Huh?"

"Your plan. *Field* research, remember? We didn't drive two hours to have smoothies for lunch and go back home." Walt pulled out his phone and tried to call up a map of the environs, but didn't get any service. "What the—? No bars."

"Verizon only 'round here!" some too-helpful old timer in coveralls called out as he passed by. "Happens all the time to the casual trade."

Lenore turned on her heel and walked after him. "Excuse me," she called out. "Where might someone new to town find... goats?"

"For what?" the man said, his vowels flat. Now he was suspicious. He looked past the purple porcupine spikes of Lenore's haircut to take in Walt. "Not a good idea to go around upsetting livestock, especially other people's."

"It's for an art project," Lenore said. She made a little gesture at her own clothing.

"Just pictures," Walt said. To Lenore he added, "We'll have to find a drugstore and get a map. And a disposable film camera, too."

The old-timer recommended the Price Chopper – *Choppah!* – he said, and then beyond that there was indeed a goat farm. Then he nodded and continued his walk.

"Weird," Walt said.

"Why's that weird?"

"It's weird because it's not weird, if you know what I mean," Walt said.

"Well," Lenore said, "remember, the whole thing with Wilmarth could have been a hoax. There's almost too much evidence – the cylinder, the newspaper articles, letters. If all the stuff happened here, why isn't it mainstream science or literature? So, maybe this isn't weird because there's nothing to be weird about."

Walt just gawked openly now as they walked back to the car, looking, looking for something. And he found it in the public parking lot behind the shops of Main Street, on the side of a Dumpster: Goodenough Rubbish Removal.

* * *

The Price Chopper was easy enough to find and maps were plentiful there. There was even a phone book available at the customer service desk, but it wasn't necessary because the answer was right there – Goodenough Road. "As in, Akeley's son, George Goodenough Akeley," Lenore said.

"Well, they've been breeding, I suppose," Walt said. It was a sunny day and Goodenough was sufficiently winding to be interesting, lined with tangles of trees. "Where are we going, for real?"

"Yeah," Lenore said. "Maybe we should stop and buy a gun. There are no gun control laws in Vermont. We can go in *strapped*!"

Walt glanced over sidelong. "Ever fire a gun?"

"I've never been motivated to even touch one before. It's just... you know." Again with the lip, her teeth clicking. She was eager for something.

"Right. It's a road, on a map, mentioned in the documents. We could end up at a goat farm at the end of a long line of Japanese tourists and gamer nerds looking for something real."

"Exactly. Where we're headed there's either nothing important at all, or something so horrific that...," she gulped. "Nobody! Has! Ever! Returned!" Lenore rolled her eyes at herself.

"Does this look like a farm?" Walt nodded out the window. "Hey, a cow."

Lenore glanced over. "City boy. That's a friggin' horse."

"In the city, garbage hauling firms are all Mafia. Maybe that's why anyone else who ever had the idea to check out Goodenough never came back."

"Hey, a goat," Lenore said.

* * *

The fence stretched on endlessly, somehow, and the mud of spring was thick under Walt's feet. Tired of looking for a gate or door, he made a brace with his hands and boosted Lenore over, then popped up atop the gate and, with some struggling, managed to swing his heavy legs over.

"Now we're breaking and entering for the sake of scholarship and hijinks," she said. "It's so sunny today; I just feel like nothing can go wrong. The air isn't like this by the Miskatonic River."

"Yeah, I guess no cotton mill spent eighty years dumping poison into the local water table," Walt said. "Anyway, about the cylinder..."

"Mm-hmm?" She was already striding toward the far-off end of the field, kicking up those knees.

"How did you get it? Where did you find it?"

Lenore turned to look over her shoulder. "Jealous? Or suspicious?"

"Incredulous," Walt said. "It's weird."

"I was looking for something else, and came across it in the library," Lenore said. "Let's play pretend. You're Wilmarth."

"Okay, I'm Wilmarth."

"Akeley... goes missing, but you've just talked to him. You rush home and write up a monograph. You even make a note of having retained your flashlight and revolver and suitcase."

"And so, how come I didn't snatch up a little canister with the word *Akeley* written on the side too? You know, have something to show later, to prove my claims?"

"Right. And the talking machine. Clearly, on a literary level, it was just Wilmarth taking a look at a Dictaphone and a wax cylinder and thinking, *What if this office equipment were crazy alien technology? What would that look like? How would it end up on Earth and what would it do?* So, assume that. What are Shub-Niggurath and the black goat of the woods? One thing, or maybe two things. Maybe he gets some students from the theater department together, feeds them lines as he's recording, just for kicks or for some kind of literary immersion – to create a faux 'document' that gives his story more authenticity, more verisimilitude."

"Like an ARG?" Walt said.

"Aaargh," Lenore repeated. She was only half-joking; one of her boots had sunk into the sod.

"An alternate reality game. Internet games that bleed over into real life, with phone numbers that really work, things you can find in real life, actual people to talk to who give you clues as to the next step. They're huge," Walt said. "They usually just tie into some movie or TV show, but really, people are playing ARGs all around us."

"Sure, maybe it's just like an ARG. Or maybe we'll just go into that farmhouse and some kind old lady will offer us lemonade and tell us about the pet black goat her mother had as a little girl." Lenore shook the mud from her boot and trotted, bored of Walt now. Trotting up to the farmhouse and its adjacent greenery, she even muttered *Shrub nigge...* – could that be the secret within the old Akeley farmhouse?

No, it was a man with a shotgun leveled at her on the other side of the screen and when the fat kid pounded up the three steps of the porch to give Lenore a piece of his mind, the old man covered Walt with the gun, too.

* * *

So, here's what happened. I found the same Dictaphone cylinder Lenore did, back in 1977. It was really something. Like I said before, some kids attend Miskatonic for *reasons* and I was one of them. I wanted to know what was going on behind the veil, as it were – I was just a mass of pimples and stringy hair named Marie Anne, and not into anything girls were supposed to be into, and even Women's Liberation couldn't change that. The boys in my classes were all so competitive and as sexist as anything. So, when I found the cylinder, I listened to it till I'd memorized every audio element, every exhalation and smack of the Bostonian's lips. I even figured out how to do the Mi-Go voice. It's easy enough: just a paper and comb kazoo. Practice enough with it and you can 'sing' dialogue that sounds uncannily like some sort of vaguely insectoid alien. But I didn't want anyone else to find the cylinder, and I couldn't bring myself to destroy such an artifact, so when I returned it to the campus library, I did so unofficially by placing it on a random shelf in the stacks.

It's easy enough to find the Akeley farm. Wilmarth, who was still alive and teaching a course every semester when I was a student, practically appended directions to his syllabus at the beginning of each semester. He'd made an agreement, you see, with the Mi-Go. They're from Tyche, a great gas giant in the Oort Cloud. A cold and slushy minor planet like Pluto could never support intelligent life, but in the lower depths of a Jupiter-like planet, atmospheric conditions are right for life. Think of jellyfish hundreds of times the size of blue whales, floating in the hot clouds for thousands of years, riding storms older than human civilization. And inside those huge gasbag beings is another kind of ecosystem, one in which smaller, *harder* creatures evolved. They were born, and died, in the hundreds of generations in the bellies of these city-sized jellyfish, and when they finally pierced the membrane of their host organism and were exposed to the elements of Tyche ... they were torn to shreds by the winds.

Gas giants are mostly hydrogen, of course. But life will out and so will intelligence. The harder creatures, the fungal-crustacean Mi-Go, learned to communicate with one another across long distances, over the roar of the endless storms of Tyche, with a form of hypersonic communication that bordered on telepathy. The mind was elevated to the center of Mi-Go civilization. But they were a lonely race. The only other form of life on the planet was the gasbag jellyfish in which they lived, like *Escherichia coli* in the hot guts of an Earth mammal. People used to think the Earth was alive and called her Gaia, worshiped her in mud-soaked and blood-drenched pagan rites. But imagine *knowing* that the thing in which you lived was alive and without any form of intelligence. How lonely would you be, if you couldn't even pretend that you were anything other than a speck in a blob floating along on the chaotic and deadly winds of a planet hidden a quarter of a light year from its sun? Lonely enough, indeed. So, the Mi-Go reached out to find new life, new minds. And they've been collecting us for quite a while. Such a long while.

Lenore and Walt found out what they wanted to know, just as I did back in '77. Of course, there's no such thing as a 'brain canister' – someone was probably eating too much expired pork brains from rusty cans when he came up with such a ludicrous idea. The mind is nothing but a system of electrochemical responses embedded in a network of cells and gaps. Easy to copy, to record onto a new medium. Like the medium of a gasbag membrane. And that's where we are now. I'm here. Lenore is here and so is Walt. In our new 'body', we're immortal and the constant focus of the attentions of the Mi-Go. It took me such a long time to learn to communicate with them, but they're patient. Long-lived, anyway, though I've had a dozen generations die within my gasbag body. They spirited me away from my human body; it's only fair that I gain my sustenance from breaking down their corpses, from eating them. The Mi-Go have even picked up the idea of religion from the human minds they study – death is a quaint ritual now. They tear their dead apart and smear their innards against my inner membrane to encourage decomposition and ingestion. And they sing when they do it. The Mi-Go also go to war. Gasbag against gasbag.

In fact, I killed Walt and Lenore just now. Now is a relative term, I admit. Time's very different out here, with our 6000-year solar revolutions and endless, changeless lives. Of course we go to war. We're human and we have nothing else to do but fight over the only commodity we have – our lives, our selves, our memories. And the Mi-Go live to please. I liked Walt and Lenore. They were like me. *Homo sapiens sapiens*, Anglophones, Americans. They drove cars and drank tonic, like I did. Walked across the Miskatonic

University quad on crisp winter nights, the snow like mounds of sparkling diamonds on either side of the cobblestone paths. It's been such a long time since I'd 'met' someone so much like me. I barely recognize most of the 'humans' encoded upon the medium of a gasbag's membrane I come across these days. It's been three million years. The Green Mountains of Vermont have long since fallen to dust, but there's still a little something on the spot of the Akeley Farm, a few feet above sea level, that attracts the tiny, hairless and half-witted daughter species as different from my human life as *Australopithecus afarensis* is. It was so good to encounter the gasbags encoded with Walt and Lenore, to have *my* Mi-Go tear into them, to drink their memories and, for a moment, remember what it was like to have limbs, to breathe air, to say words I know with a human jaw.

I hope I find some more like them soon. Soon is a relative term. But I'm patient, and old.

LOOKING FOR JOEY SHOGGOTH

PETE RAWLIK

Suddenly she's just standing there; I didn't even hear the office door open or close. I don't even remember unlocking it. I'm still in my nightshirt waiting for my morning dose to finish dissolving. She's made a mistake I think, but nobody comes to my office by mistake, not in Delta, not on Third Avenue, and not up three flights of stairs. The ceiling fan spreads her perfume through the office, she's wearing Valentine '43 and the scent digs deep into my memories. She's not a local. Her hair is blonde and done up in a tight bun that reminds me of a flower. Her features are small and tight, her skin fair. Her long neck tapers down and vanishes into the grey coat that she has cinched tight in all the right places. When she walks her legs flash way too much thigh, but she seems oblivious to the fact that she oozes sex with every step.

I grab a shirt as she opens her tiny cherry mouth, "Are you Mister Noone?" Her voice is thin, the accent mid-Atlantic American, and it wavers as she speaks, there are tears buried somewhere down in her throat.

As I button the shirt and tuck the tail into my pants I turn to face her. "Just Noone, how can I help you?"

"My name is Lora, Lora Melisande, I need help, you come… well… recommended." She sits down, uninvited.

I let the comment roll off and drain my medication in a single shot. "I don't handle divorces Mrs Melisande."

She looks down at her left hand and her eyes linger over the ring. "My

43

husband died in the war."

I pull up a chair and sit down in front of her; I make sure I'm close, well within her personal space, forcing a connection. It's a cheap trick, but as long as I play it proper it'll have the desired effect. "My apologies, occupational hazard, what can I help you with?"

"I'm looking for my brother Joey... Joseph Sheridan. He was in the war as well, Mars. He was injured, burned. Joey was in the hospital at Tranquility Base for months then another couple weeks at the Snowfield Clinic." She pauses and fishes a handkerchief out of her handbag. "After that, he was supposed to come back to Downingtown, that's in Pennsylvania, to stay with me until he got adjusted. But the day before he was supposed to come home he sent me a message. His treatments at the clinic had been extended another month. He told me the same thing thirty days later, and again, and again. I was furious at the delay and called the clinic to, I don't know, lodge a complaint. Except when I talked to the doctor he told me..."

She breaks down in sobs, so I finish her sentence for her, "Joey had already been released months ago." She nods and looks up at me sheepishly. I take the opening and set the hook draping my arm around her shoulder. "We get a lot of veterans round these parts. They come back through the Labyrinth over in Beta and don't usually go that far, there's plenty of off-base housing in Gamma and Delta. There's something they like here, something in the air or water, something important, something more important than home."

That's when the waterworks start in full force. "Can you help me Noone?"

I nod. "Did your brother ever mention anyplace he liked in the area a bar or restaurant maybe?"

She tries to dry her eyes. "He mentioned a bar once, Volume I think it was called."

"That's down by the Crevasse; I've been there once or twice." I feed her half-truths. I don't want or need her following me around.

"Did you serve in the war?"

I lock her eyes with mine. It's a question she shouldn't have asked but now that it's been broached I have to answer. I roll up my right sleeve. She tries to turn away but I grab her by the back of the head and force her to look at the pale chitinous thing that the war has left me to use as a hand.

Lora gives me a wad of cash to get me going and I send her back to her hotel in Alpha. The bar she was talking about is on the other side of town, five minutes if I take the Labyrinth. I hoof it down the road and let the cool twilight of the midday sun seep into my senses. It's a long walk and my steps echo across the cyclopean basalt blocks that make up the roads and walls of the ancient city. The streets are crowded but the Progenitors built their thoroughfares wider than men, so I'm able to weave through the mob with ease. I grab something that pretends to be coffee and something that is supposedly ham, cheese and egg in a wrap. I try not to look at either. I think it's real meat. The eggs are pale green. I've eaten worse.

Club Vulthoom occupies what remains of a warehouse in the shadow of the Tau Airfield. The building has seen better days and fewer rats. Officially it's a private club, a members-only place. Unofficially it caters to military vets, particularly former POWs of the Martian Conflict. The bouncer is 400 pounds of Inutos with a mass of pink tentacles for a left eye that vibrate furiously as I come through the door. He grunts as I stroll down the stairs, a subtle warning that he doesn't want any trouble. I'm not looking for trouble either, but my hand instinctively slips inside my coat, finds the holster under my arm and takes the safety off the Skorpion flechette.

The bartender has a drink made for me before I even reach the bar. It's early; the place almost empty and I get a moment to soak in the red sandstone floors and the Aihais stone carvings that decorate the wall. On stage Lysandra is going through an old standard, The Hiding Box, warming up for her main show later that night. Her voice is haunting, and the way she holds the antique microphone, the way she caresses it with her hands and that husky voice, she makes every man fall in love with her, at least for the thirty minutes it takes to complete her set. She finishes and pauses in a romantic, dramatic sort of way, kind of sad, holding the microphone like a long-lost lover. You could almost think she's normal, one hundred percent human, but then she comes off the stage, that long silver gown with the deep V cut heading right toward me, the illusion is gone. She glides across the floor fluidly, like a snake. No human woman should be able to move like that.

She sidles up to the bar and calls for a drink. She's sending all the signals that tell me to leave her alone, but the bar is wide open and she's right next to me. "What do you want Noone?" Lysandra is hooked into some of the best gossip feeds in the city and for the right price she'll do a different kind of singing. I gave her a look like I'm hurt. "Oh please," she sneers. "You never come to see me unless you want something." She turns and makes sure I notice her assets. "It doesn't have to be like this Noone. You've been coming around here for three months now. You're not exactly bad looking. We could have some fun."

I dodge the proposition, knowing full well that the club owner had his eye on her. "What do you know about a guy named Joe Sheridan?"

She looks stunned for a second and then chuckles. "You're looking for Joey? Seriously, who put you on that rabbit?"

I finish my drink. "His sister is worried."

"I am sure she is. We all worry about Joey, but he made his choice and he has to live with it. That includes not coming back here, not ever."

"When was the last time you saw him?"

She turns away frustrated. It seems I've struck a nerve. She has that look women get when they are trying to keep a secret but really don't want to. "Last time I saw Joey was four months ago. He was staying at Carter House over in Beta." She pushes away upset, if she had feet and legs I'm sure she would have just stomped away, instead she glides away on thousands of miniscule ampulla.

The Grays catch me on the street, their star-shaped Elder signs backing me up against the wall. Lieutenants Zadok and Jude, detectives or what passes for detectives in this town. Honest, as far as military police go. They cuff me without offering any explanation, and I know better than to ask any questions. They drag me down the tube to the nearest Labyrinth station. The gatekeeper rises as we stumble in, his coal sack black robe covers his face and makes any kind of empathy impossible. When he stands he's bent over and his torso seems impossibly long, like a lizard without any forelimbs. Something unintelligible emerges from underneath the cloak, something I've heard a thousand times and still cannot understand. In response to his vocal incantation the Labyrinth gate pulsates open. I have a quick rush of adrenaline as panic rises up out of my gut. Jude pushes me forward and my flight reflex kicks in. There's a flash of shadow and something large connects to the back of my skull before everything goes pear-shaped.

It's the same dream I always have. We're about twenty minutes into the Labyrinth, on our way to the base at Olympus Mons. Lieutenant Kemp is yelling at us to pick up the pace and the guide, a low level gatekeeper, keeps furiously waving us forward. Sloane stumbles over Luther and the whole platoon erupts in laughter. It's so loud no one notices the Aihais that rounds the corner and lops off our guide's soft pulpy head while burying a knife in the Lieutenant's back. The unit scatters for cover, which there isn't much of in the cold energy maze that exists in the in-between space. In mere moments I'm alone and moving at a break neck speed down corridors of cool white light. My heart is pounding and my lungs burn. This place, it wasn't made for men, there's too little oxygen, and no real directional cues that our senses can latch onto. I spend hours trying to follow one strategy or another in a useless attempt to find a way out. Panic sets in and with it disorientation or perhaps it's the other way round. I ration my water, but it runs out anyway and I collapse in a heap of well-trained desperation.

Voices, sourceless and inhuman, stalk down the corridors, then shadows, long thin shadows that stretch down the endless corridors, come closer. I raise my weapon, as the three Martians, the Aihais and their guide calmly, slowly surround me. When they take my weapon I don't even resist. They say things to me, but I don't understand. They take me to Mars. The gate is old, five-fold design which makes it Progenitor made. Intel had said that all the Progenitor gates on Mars were inactive. I adjust to captivity easily. I drink the crimson tainted water and eat the dry fungal fruits that my captors grow in the shadowy rock crevices. I'm not the only prisoner. There are other men, but they haven't adjusted as I have and most die of heat stroke. There are other prisoners... things that are not men; Moonbeasts, which hop about and bleat incessantly; Lemurians with black staring eyes; and whistling semi-vaporous things with wings and claws, like a fusion of a sponge with a lobster. And of course there are shoggoths, roiling protoplasmic things that hurt to look at and devour anything at random.

I learn the language of the Aihais, just snippets really, enough to get by. I learn their names, their customs. I adjust, adapt, and conform. I survive. In time, I kneel before the great seed-like idol that represents their bulbous predatory plant god. And when the time comes, I take the knife they hand to me and I draw it across the joint between my arm and forearm. Slowly at first, then faster, sawing through skin and muscle, until finally I am furiously digging through connective tissue and bone. I don't even scream until the seed-idol cracks open and black tendrils explode out, engulfing my former arm and dragging it back where thorn-like teeth hungrily devour my still twitching fingers.

The scream translates from dream to reality, from past to present, and I wake up in a cold-sweat bolting from wherever I am. It's a short-lived panic. Jude backhands me across the mouth and I tumble back into the cold steel chair with a trickle of blood running down my lip. The room is sparse, cold, cliché, everything you think an interrogation room should look like.

My wandering thoughts must have shown up on my face because Jude gives me another backhanded slap to bring me back to reality. "Tell us about the girl."

I wipe the blood and spittle from my chin and flex my jaw back and forth. I'm giving the eye and I can tell I'm pissing him off. "Did you have one specifically in mind?"

He pulls back to take another cheap shot but a voice from the shadows stops him. "That's enough." Zadok and Jude step aside as Detective Warde comes forward. His voice is effeminate, and he walks with a certain swish that is magnified by the movements of his trench coat. A triangular metal plate covers the right side of his face from the crease of his mouth up over his eye and into his forehead. There's no hole for his eye, but just looking at where it should be makes my head ache.

"There's no reason to be abusive Mr Jude. Noone is going to give us his full cooperation. After all, he's only been in business a few months now, and I'm sure he wouldn't want to risk losing his license."

I take the flimsy photo he shoves at me, its grainy, typical coroner stuff, but there's no doubt about whose face it is. "She came to me earlier today. Told me her name was Lora Melisande, wanted me to find her brother Joey Sheridan." I toss the photo onto the table.

"She wanted you to find Joe Sheridan? She said she was his sister?" Warde looks incredulous. "Are you sure?"

I fumble around in my coat and come up with the wad of cash she gave me as a retainer. I wave it playfully, "Sure enough."

Warde walks away from me obviously frustrated. His hands go to the back of his head as he circles round the room frenetically. He's thinking about something, trying to figure out how much I know, how much I need to know. And what he's willing to tell me.

Suddenly a switch goes off and he's in my face, so close I can feel the heat coming off of his ocular implant. "You listen to me Noone. This woman, Lora Melisande, she had your card in her purse. We found what was left of her down in Rho. Someone took a liking to her and spent a good amount of time skinning her like a cat. That, by the way is police business, none of your concern. Now, I am going to lay out some real simple logic for you. Missus Melisande is dead, you've got no client, and that means you've got no reason to go looking for Joe Sheridan. Drop it. As far as you're concerned Joe Sheridan is dead, doesn't exist, never existed to begin with." He grabs a small plastic bag from the table; it has my business card in it. He opens it, takes the card out, and tears it into pieces. "You never worked for Melisande, never met her. You've never even heard of her. She's like Sheridan she never existed to begin with. You got that? Lora Melisande and Joey Shoggoth... Sheridan they never existed."

I play it coyly. "Sure," I tell him, "I get it. I'm off the case. I don't even know what case you're talking about."

They dump me back on the street. My right arm hurts at the joint where I stop being human. I pop a couple of my pills and wait for the rush to wipe out the dull ache. In fifteen minutes I'm back in form and looking for a way down to Beta. It's late, and all the legitimate rickshaws have all gone home for the day. I look at the few sketchy conveyances available to me and decide to head down to the waterfront.

The Erebus River is clean; it smells fresh, real, human, or at least not inhuman. There are several small fishing boats moving up and downstream. Most of the skippers are Asian, refugees from the Lho Mon nuclear incident. I bargain a ride and some fish stew from a Tcho-Tcho who speaks enough English, to understand what I want. After we move away from the dock my host offers me some Aklo, Stygian, but I decline. I need to clear my head and psychoacoustic hallucinogens aren't going to help. The fish and shrimp stew is salty and laced with sweet Martian spices that make my mouth burn, like cinnamon and chili mixed together. The ride is calm and it lets me think about what I am about to do.

It would be easy to do what Warde told me to, and forget about the case and Sheridan and Melisande. It would probably be safer to do as I've been told, the cops don't want me involved, they're threatening my license, and I really don't have a client anymore. There's really no reason for me to be involved. Except I don't work that way, and never have. It's not a code or some moral obligation, I'm just a dog with a bone and I'm not going to be happy until it's good and chewed. Right now, I'm just setting my teeth in.

In Beta I make my way to Carter House. It's a rehab center linked to the Snowfield Clinic, a kind of halfway house for injured soldiers, or at least that's what the data blob says. I walk in through a pair of grand glass doors and even at this hour there's a receptionist. A pretty young thing, fresh, she's kind of familiar, but I can't place her. She's engrossed in some paperwork and doesn't notice I'm there until I clear my throat. She jumps back, eyes wide and voice a sputter "What're you doing h..." She pauses, never takes her eyes off me, and recovers. Her whole attitude changes and she's suddenly calm and collected. "I'm sorry; I thought you were someone else. How can I help you sir?"

I flash my credentials. "I'm looking for someone, a man named Sheridan, Joe Sheridan. He was supposedly a resident here a few months back." I think back to Warde's slip of the tongue. "Some people call him Joey Shoggoth."

Her mouth drops wide and she stares at me like a dying fish for a full ten seconds. Finally she speaks and its clear from the start something is seriously wrong. "Let me get the director. You'll want to talk to him." Then she's down the hall without another word and I'm left alone with the bowl of stale candy on her desk. She's gone for maybe five minutes, and then comes clopping back down the hallway. She doesn't say a word, just waves for me to follow her, which I do, and I end up passing through an office door emblazoned with the name of Doctor Gregory Lazaro, Director.

He's a friendly enough guy, old, maybe seventies, white hair thinning, round face, round glasses, British accent, kind of paunchy around the middle. He smiles and shakes my hand as I take a seat. "What can I do for you Mr Noone?"

I run my hand through my hair. "Just call me Noone. I'm looking for one of your residents, a vet, went through Snowfield, and was supposed to be staying here a few months back. His name is Joe Sheridan, sometimes goes by the name Joey Shoggoth."

Lazaro takes his glasses off and begins to polish them with a cloth. "You have to understand Noone, that this is technically a medical facility. Mr Sheridan, if he was here, is entitled to certain privileges, including the right to privacy. I'm sure you understand."

I lean forward in the chair and put my elbows on my knees. "Absolutely Doc, privacy, I get it. I mean I certainly wouldn't want just anyone looking at my file, medical or otherwise." I lean further forward and he quickly covers the paperwork on his desk. "Thing is Doc, I'm not just anybody. I represent Sheridan's family, his sister. She's worried, wants to make sure that he's doing alright."

Doctor Lazaro leans back in his chair and makes a tent out of his hands. "Sheridan's sister. Noone I am intimately familiar with Mr Sheridan's case. He was my patient for quite some time, we talked at length and I've seen his military records. I don't know for whom you are working, but it's not for his sister. I know for absolute certainty that Sheridan didn't have a sister in fact he didn't have any family at all." He stands up and walks around the desk. "I think perhaps someone is playing a joke on you Noone. You should go home, get some rest and forget all about Joe Sheridan and Lora Melisande."

He stops and my eyes grow wide. He's made a mistake and he knows it. I never mentioned Lora's name and he's been speaking about Sheridan in the past tense. There's an uncomfortable moment when neither of us knows what to do, then I stand up and I cross over to the desk but never take my eyes off of him. I reach out and put my hand on the file and slide it across the smooth polished surface of the desk. A small sound of opposition escapes Lazaro's throat, but I cut him off with a gesture. I rotate the file so I can read the writing on it: a single word, SHERIDAN, stares back at me from the files of Carter House.

I turn to confront Lazaro but he's not where I left him. He's right up beside me. Where did the needle come from? I dodge the attack and flip Lazaro over my shoulder and across the room. I grab the file on his desk and push through the door. The pretty receptionist gets in my way, she tries to grab the file but I yank it back from her. Pages fly out but I don't have time to gather them back up. I snatch what I can and keep moving as fast as my legs will move. I'm out on the street and down the road in seconds. In a minute I've lost myself amongst the darkened alleyways and tunnels that run from Beta to everywhere else, including Delta. In an hour I'm deep into the city, where not even the corporate spysats can find me.

It takes me another hour to make it back to my office. I come up the back way, over the roof of the neighboring building. The city follows an inhuman geometry, men have tried to make it their own, but the sheer size of it makes figuring all the angles difficult. Even from across the way I can see the pale blue light glowing from the phone that's moving about in my office. It only takes a moment of me watching to identify both Zadok and Jude. Bastards have torn my office to shreds. It's an indiscriminate search, just for show and intimidation; the only thing they're looking for is me.

I head back down to the bar. Vulthoom is crowded, full of vets drowning their pain, listening to Lysandra sing the blues. I crawl into a back wall booth and try to make myself invisible. Time blurs, and when I check the clock I find that I've been sitting there for three hours. I dig the file from Carter House out of my coat. In the dim light the smart paper gives off a soft glow. I scroll through the contents, but there's not that much to look at. I've got a picture from a military ID. Sheridan was Caucasian with dark hair and eyes that I think women like to refer to as piercing. There's a brief biography that tells me he was raised in Pennsylvania, bit of a troublemaker, but nothing too serious. Enlisted at nineteen. Recruited for Special Forces. Deployed to Mars. Two years as a POW. After that there's a psych profile that says he suffers from PTSD with a touch of multiple personality syndrome, and a recommendation that he be placed in something called Project Ymir. The rest of the files are just images.

I turn on the viewer and let the pictures run at a three second interval. It's all shit from his past: Pictures of his unit, his parents, and his dead brother, pretty standard stuff. But then as the pages of the familiar scroll past, the public becomes private and my curiosity turns to suspicion. There's a photo of Leslie Haines, the first girl he ever kissed, and a hooker he apparently slept with in Port Wallace the night before he enlisted. I slow the scroll rate down and find myself staring at images of the camp where he was held prisoner, the Aihais who held him captive, even the food they forced him to eat. It's all way too familiar. The image changes and I stab at the page to halt the progression. The final shot is in high resolution, which allows me to see everything in horrific detail. It's black, oblong and clearly alien. As I stare my arm begins to ache and the memory of what I did to myself to satisfy the inhuman cravings of the thing in the photograph, come screaming to the forefront of my mind.

A hand reaches down and closes the file before I can do it myself. It's Lysandra staring down at me with those sorrowful big brown eyes. "You couldn't leave it alone could you Noone?" She turns away. "Have you found what you were looking for?"

Suddenly my head hurts. It's a pounding insistent throb just above my eyes. "Joey Shoggoth? I haven't even started looking, not really."

Lysandra stares at me incredulously. I'm getting tired of that look. "Word on the street is that you got into a bit of a fray over at Carter House. They say the Grays are looking for you."

I stand up. I'm a little wobbly. "The Grays are looking for me; I'm looking for Joey Shoggoth; Circle of life thing really." I pick up the file and roll it into a tube. "Not that it matters really. Unless I get a lead soon I'll have no way to find our Mr Sheridan."

She reaches out and takes the file from me. "Do you really want to Noone, find Joey I mean?" I nod and she flips the file over.

There's an address written in pencil on the back, Number 5, Twenty-Third Street, Delta. I lean forward and kiss Lysandra on the cheek. "I love you," I tell her and before she can respond I'm across the bar and up the stairs.

For a sawbuck, Sheridan's landlady lets me look around what used to be his room. She's left everything as it was, hoping that someone would come to claim his things and pay the back rent. There's not much to look through, apparently never was. On the table next to the bed I find his media player. I scroll through his lists. Whatever else Joey had fine taste in music, mostly classics. There are a couple of albums by Concrete Blonde, the complete Communards, John Favorite, and two albums by Inhouse: *Five Wooden Chairs* and *Waking Juliet*. Looking at it I realize that it's the kind of stuff that Lysandra likes to sing.

Sheridan's reading list is less common. There's something called *Masterton's Concordance to the Revelations of Glaaki*, and *The Incident at Base 31* by Flyte. I check the reading log and find that Sheridan had spent a significant amount of time reading something called *Shoggothim: Morphology and Phylogeny*. I flick the icon and go to the last bookmarked page.

Following the Dwyer method we can divide the shoggothim into several distinct classes or stages. The most primitive, the proto-shoggoth, are simple constructs almost mindless and uncontrollable with no ability to form organelles or differentiate. In contrast, the ortho-shoggoth stage has a rudimentary intelligence and is able to follow simple commands and form complex organelles. The meta-shoggoth distinguishes itself by possessing near human intelligence and problem solving skills and like its predecessor is able to form complex organelles, but still lacks the ability to differentiate. The first stage of the species to show any skill at differentiation is the hyper-shoggoth, though in this case differentiation from the main corpus is often short-lived. Sustainable differentiation is exhibited by what Dwyer deemed the epi-shoggoth stage, in which significant intellect and even infectious reproduction are also exhibited. The final stage designated the ultra-shoggoth shows several retrograde characteristics. These specimens tend to be massive and sedentary, though they are capable of movement. Multiple and constant differentiations are common and often permanent with a tendency to be non-infectious. Progenitor records identify at least two such creatures by the names Ubbo-Sathla and Idh-Ya. A third individual designated Yid-Ra may simply be a variant or corruption of Idh-Ya.

He's reading really esoteric stuff, way more than what I was taught by the military. I flip through the player. Almost every book has something on the subject, and relevant passages are either bookmarked or annotated. At least now I know why they called him Joey Shoggoth, he seemed to have been obsessed with the things.

I check the built in calendar. No appointments in the last few months, before that a smattering of dates with the Snowfield Clinic. There are also a few social engagements all with one very familiar name, Lysandra.

Two hours later I'm back at Club Vulthoom bursting through the doors. The bouncer gets up, but while he's still off balance I put my heel down on the arch of his foot and shatter it. He screams and I put him down on the floor with a knee to the groin. The bartender clears the bar carrying an aluminum baseball bat. I whip out the Skorpion and put three needles into his chest. I do a quick scan and find the bar is nearly empty. The only other person still standing is the one I'm looking for.

She's at her microphone still in the same deep V cut dress as before. She looks at me with those sad soulful eyes. There's a smile, a sneer really, as she slithers over to me. "Hello Noone, I've been waiting for you."

I train the Skorpion on her and she stops moving. "You've been sending me all over town Lysandra. I don't appreciate it. You should have told me you were involved with Sheridan."

"I told you I was worried about him."

"What else have you conveniently forgotten to tell me?"

She slides over to a chair and sits. "That I loved him, still do."

I take a few steps toward her. "Where is he? Did he kill Melisande? I know she wasn't his sister. Who was she really?"

Lysandra tosses her head back and starts laughing. "You think Joey killed Lora? You really are a fool this time." She stands up and takes a step toward me. "Do you know what a shoggoths is?"

I wave the pistol menacingly. "Of course I know what a shoggoth is. I was in the war. Sheridan was obsessed with them. Sit down please."

She ignores me. "They all start out the same you know: Mindless blobs eating their way through everything organic. That's why the Progenitors kept them in great stone pits to keep them from devouring... well everything. Funny thing is, they tend to learn from what they eat. They absorb skills, intellect, memories even personalities. Usually it's indiscriminate, they take a little of everything from all of their victims and create a gestalt personality. It's all fascinatingly sinister." She slides forward, apparently undeterred by the gun. "I say usually because the boys in the white coats figured something interesting out, something useful."

She's still moving forward when I catch a sudden movement out of the corner of my eye. It's the bartender rising up off the floor hours before he should be. He casually pulls the three flechette darts out of his chest and grins evilly at me.

Lysandra starts talking and my attention is drawn back to her. "It seems that with a proper procedure, you can insert a human brain into what passes for the shoggoth's nervous system and allow it to take over. The abilities of a shoggoth under the control of a human mind, the military brass loved it. They bought it lock, stock and stinking barrow. In a matter of years there were thousands of the things, enough to turn the tide and win the war. That's when the shit hit the fan."

Somewhere along the way Lysandra and the bartender have met up and suddenly they're walking side by side, in my direction. "Can you imagine it Noone, thousands of metamorphic monsters trained to be soldiers, and no war to let them loose on. The doctors, the psychiatrists, psychologists, sociologists and metaphysicists tried their best. They tried to find a way to put us back together, but in the end the therapies only went so far, and there were always a few that just couldn't cope."

A viscous gelatinous mass flows from behind me and over toward Lysandra and the bartender. It rises up, like a bubbling fountain of filth. It molds itself, reshapes and the face of the fat bouncer re-appears atop a pulpy semi-humanoid form. The Asian face opens its mouth and speaks with Lysandra's voice. "The more extreme cases, they subject to a course of reprogramming: new names, new identities, and new memories. The treatments work, for a while at least. They haven't got it quite right yet, and invariably the old personalities resurface, struggling to come back to life."

I take a step back. "I suppose you're going to tell me that Sheridan was one of these things?"

The thing that was once Lysandra nods as her body dissolves into a mass of jelly. "So was Lora Melisande. In fact they were the same person, just different personalities."

"You expect me to believe that Melisande was Sheridan? Then why exactly did she send me chasing after herself? And why did the Grays find her, or at least her skin down in Rho?"

Suddenly the three monstrous globs are merging together, melding, and becoming a single entity. When it speaks again it does so with three voices. "A skilled shoggoths can divide itself into pieces, autonomous units that can act and think independently, at least for a while. Melisande was one of these units created by Sheridan's subconscious to try and snap Sheridan out of his latest programming. She set you on his trail in hopes that you would find enough evidence to snap him."

The shoggoths rolls toward me, I pull the trigger on the Skorpion knowing full well it won't do anything. I turn and I sprint for the door but I don't get more than a few steps before Zadok and Jude grab me and throw me to the ground.

"Ye should have listened to Mr Warde ye fool," mumbles Zadok. "We could 'ave avoided all of this."

I swing the pistol around but Jude kicks it out of my hand. I gasp and between breaths I manage to stutter out a few words. "What happens now that I've stumbled onto your dirty little secret? What's the military willing to do to keep this under wraps?" As soon as the words leave my mouth I realize something's wrong. I didn't figure any of this out. I had a few pieces, but nothing concrete. It was Lysandra who spilled the beans, opened her mouth and let the whole secret plot come out like some motion picture heavy.

Jude starts laughing. "We're not here to kill you, if we wanted to do that we could have done it years ago, the first time you went rogue. We're going to take you back to the clinic. Get you the help that you need. We're not your killers Noone; we're your doctors."

Lysandra flows around me, enveloping me in her warm protoplasmic flesh. Her touch catalyzes something and I begin to hurt. As I come apart, they come bubbling up out of the dark recesses, Lora, Joey, and a dozen others. They clamber up over my psyche and the personality that was once Noone releases its hold over my physiology. My mind and my body become soft, fluid, and protean. I try to scream but I no longer have any lungs, let alone a mouth.

As I succumb I can feel Lysandra inside me. "This time Joey you can be someone. I promise you," her voice slides inside my brain, "you'll never have to be 'no one' ever again."

THE PLAY'S THE THING

DENISE DUMARS

As was usual for a Tuesday morning in September, the air conditioner was blasting as well as it could, the tired old thing wheezing and moaning at my back making a well of cool air surrounding myself and the desk area. At the front of the shop, near the display windows, it was beastly hot.

I was keeping one eye on my favorite soap – don't you dare call it a soap *opera* – one eye on the two old bags near the front of the shop, and one eye on the manuscript I was working on. In other words, I was apparently using three eyes; believe me, I could have used four.

Doing so much at once always made me crabby. I was waiting for Kirsten to come in so that I could free up at least one eye.

The two women were looking at the Depression glass that I had stacked by the east windows. I have the best prices on Depression glass you'll find anywhere on the South Bay's antique row. The reason for this is simple: I hate the stuff, and I always have too much of it around.

The biddies were looking at two pieces of pink hobnail and chattering away like magpies. "It's too much," I heard one of them whisper; age had yet to dim my hearing.

"So offer her less," said the other, "She doesn't look like she knows what it's worth," and I bristled.

To divert myself I briefly gave my full attention to the soap. I hadn't been following the plot much lately and so tried to put the pieces together as I watched. The eccentric Oleg was staging some sort of a coup of the family business; he'd misrepresented himself to a lovely heiress and now, armed with her money, was prepared to take over the corporation. His amber eyes burned like flames; his dark hair lay in radiant waves on the shoulders of his Savile Row suit as he gloated over his victory.

The door bell jingled and I started from my reverie, almost but not quite reaching for the loaded Glock I kept in the desk drawer.

As usual, Kirsten had come in like a cyclone, dressed in an indigo sarong and a sky-blue top that left a gap between her skirt and the top's hem. Her frizzy dark hair was piled on top of her head, looking as if it had been styled with an egg beater.

"Hey," I said. "How's school?"

"Hey," she returned my greeting. "It's OK. Looks like my drama class has some interesting possibilities," she replied. The community colleges had just begun their fall semester, and as usual, it was hot as a son of a bitch.

She saw the two women with the hobnail plates. "You ladies need some help?" she asked. There are times when Kirsten is nicer than I am.

"No, no, we're just trying to decide between these two," said the one in the polyester pants and the *Jacques C. Penné* blouse. I knew where she'd gotten the blouse because I have one just like it at home in the closet. I vowed to give it to Goodwill immediately.

"Can I work on the table in the back again today?" Kirsten said to me, coming behind the desk and throwing her snack into my small refrigerator. I had hired her in part because of her passion for antique furniture; I had neither the physical strength nor the interest in the refinishing and refurbishing that she did. Kirsten was a big, strapping girl, and while her interests ran to home decor and woodworking, mine ran to books, jewelry and really strange art. All right, call it thrift store art. Be that way. I liked strange sculpture, too. My favorite piece was a Polynesian basalt figure of some hideous multi-armed god (and multi-other-appendaged, from the looks of it!).

"Looks like the monkey with four asses on *South Park*," Kirsten had said when she first saw it. I had laughed; so what if she doesn't appreciate my taste in art? She's helpful to me in many ways, not the least of which is the fact that she can lift the boxes of books that I, admittedly, can't seem to turn down.

"Yeah," I said. "Why not start there, and then later if it cools off a bit I'll have you bring up some of those books we got in last week. But give me a break first, OK?"

"OK," she said.

I rose from my typing chair and my hip joints reluctantly got up with me. I tottered into the back to the loo, muttering to myself all the way. It's no fun getting old, boys and girls; in fact, it's a fucking pain in the ass, sometimes literally.

"We need to talk about my schedule," Kirsten said when I came back.

Damn, I thought, wanting desperately to see the last few minutes of the soap. I took a furtive glance at it. Socorro had a handful of Oleg's hair and they were cat-fighting to beat the band, if a man and a woman fighting can be called a cat-fight, that is.

"I'd like to come in on Wednesdays instead of Tuesdays," she said, unmindful of the fact that one of my many eyes was on the TV.

"Fine with me," I said. "Will you still be able to come in on Thursdays and Saturdays?" I said, hating the whine I heard in my voice.

"Sure," she said. "It's just that, in my drama class, we're going to be rehearsing a play, starting next week. So I'll need my Tuesday evenings," she said.

"Great. Have you got a good role? What's the name of the play?" I asked, knowing full well that the last time I'd kept up with modern theatre, *Oh, Calcutta!* was the most daring thing around.

"Oh, it's nothing you would have heard of," she shrugged. "Some old, supposedly classic play. Someone in class called it a 'dynastic thing.' I play a girl named Camilla," she said.

"The play's called *The King in Yellow*," she continued.

Just then the Depression glass women approached the desk.

One woman handed over one hobnailed bowl. "I can't quite read the price tag on the bottom," she said. "It looks like $3.98 to me."

I squinted at it, though I could read it quite easily with my bifocals. "Nope. I'm sure that's $8.98. I priced it myself."

"Too much," she said, setting it down, and with her friend, walked on out.

"Blew another sale," Kirsten said after the door banged shut.

"Yeah. You know how I am when I get my Irish up," I said, wondering if someone named Janette Glembotski could possibly have any Irish to get up, and then wondering if I'd just made an ethnic slur. "Just do as I say, not as I do, OK?"

She laughed, and shook her head. "I mean, I don't want you to think I'm not interested in this job. The play, well, it's not like I have a great role. The best female role – the lead in the play, in fact – is for an older chick. I play her daughter, the princess."

I flashed her my skeptical face. "You, a princess?" I said. "Well, maybe Xena, Warrior Princess, but..."

"Oh, stop it. You're embarrassing me," she waved me away.

"Too late. Your outfit already did that for you," I said.

She went about her work and I, mine. Kirsten's a good egg, the best helper I've had in a long time; in fact, she's the best one I've found since Warren died.

Warren was my first assistant. He signed on right after I took retirement from the library, you know, the whole 'take this job and shove it' routine, and I was determined to pursue my dream of opening an antique shop and writing.

He was every antique store owner's favorite type of employee: he had a love of furniture and all those interior decorating accessories that I could not care less about, matched with a strong back for lifting books and other heavy things.

For six months we were both in antique heaven. He was going to college and lived nearby with his lover, David. But no good deed ever goes unpunished, or as Robert Frost would say, "nothing gold can stay".

David graduated from HIV positive to PWA (person with AIDS). Warren, miraculously enough, was healthy and virus-free. But when David died, Warren — having left a note for his parents and, thoughtfully, one for me — checked into the Hacienda Hotel in El Segundo and put a bullet in his brain.

I've never had children. I'm so impossible to live with that both my marriages ended badly. Losing Warren was like losing the only son I ever had.

After that I had a series of assistants, none of which worked out. They all ended up either quitting or being fired, usually after a lot of angry words in which I would be denounced as a witch, a communist, or a mean old bitch... all of which were more or less true.

Things were good again, with Kirsten here. I didn't care that she had piercings and tattoos and dated guys who wore their belts down around their knees, and she didn't care that I am who I am. It was a pretty good set-up, all the way around.

Bearing in mind, of course, that nothing gold can stay.

After Kirsten left for the day I got my usual jitters. What if school proved to be too time-consuming — so much so that she decided to quit altogether? I tried to banish the thought from my mind, but spent an uneasy night tossing and turning, and, worst of all, having nightmares.

One particularly depressing dream featured Warren. Now, perhaps it's my Wiccan proclivities showing here, but I sometimes believe that my deceased friends and loved ones visit me when I sleep. For years my late uncle Jacob came to me in dreams. He'd been a lawyer, and I always figured that he just couldn't resist sharing his opinions, even years after his death. Both my grandmothers visited me from time to time. But this dream wasn't like the cozy dreams of my departed relatives; this dream was a full-blown nightmare.

In the nightmare Warren was wearing a long yellow gown that looked like a cheap acetate bathrobe from TJ Maxx. He was trying to tell me something: trying mightily, I might add, but no sound came from his mouth. He was reaching toward me with outstretched arms, gesturing as if to warn me away from something. It was a repeating dream; the scene came up again and again like a skipping LP. I awoke in a sweat, full hot-flash mode.

And it seemed to me for a moment, even when I was sure I was wide-awake, that the flames of a Hell I did not believe in licked around my bed, a wall of yellow flames like the ones that had licked around Warren's bathrobe in the nightmare.

Sitting on the edge of the bed weeping, my everyday veneer of bravado peeled away, I was suddenly that thing I pity most and never wished to be: an old woman, frightened and alone; alone with a fear no loaded Glock could chase away.

* * *

Nothing much happened for a week, except that Poseidon City decided that nearby San Pedro had a good idea when they decided to keep local shops open late on the First Thursday of the month. It would be our first Thursday evening open past seven.

I had coerced Kirsten into staying even though she seemed rather tired and preoccupied because I sure as hell wasn't keeping the shop open that late all by myself. I promised her Thai food as a bonus, so when dinner time rolled around I waddled on down to Thai Gold Coin for take-out. On the way out I rubbed the head of their green plastic money-toad, hoping it would bring me lots of customers. More likely, I figured, it'd just give me warts.

When I got back to the store, the aromas of Pahd Thai, wickedly hot green curry, and mint leaves fried rice were singing me their siren song, and Kirsten was on the phone.

She turned around as I walked in. There was a look of what I can only call shock on her face. The fact that I smiled and waved the cartons at her didn't seem to ameliorate the situation any.

"No mask?" she said into the phone, turning away from me. "No mask?!" she said again, more loudly this time, and then she cupped her hand around her mouth so that I could not hear what she said after that.

Kirsten is not the kind of employee to make lots of personal calls at work.

She doesn't sit around and text like most kids. The tone of her voice and the look on her face added up to some kind of trouble brewing. All my internal alarms were going off at once; something was not right here.

She ended the call and put down the phone.

I busied myself with the food, and pretended not to have been desperately trying to eavesdrop. "Everything OK?" I asked with false cheer.

"Uh, yeah," she said, and crossed her arms and rubbed them as though she was cold. It was still in the 70s outside, even though the sun was going down. I motioned to her to come into our break room and have dinner, but instead she walked to the front of the store. She stood staring at one of my more stellar examples of thrift-store painting. It was a truly gratuitous female nude, reclining on a yellow fainting couch and wearing only a yellow feather boa; what made it especially egregious was the fact that the nude's lips and nipples were the exact same shade of shocking pink.

"I hate this thing," she said. "I can't stand to look at it. It gives me the creeps," She turned to me at last. "Can we please put it outside? For the sidewalk sale? *Please?*"

I didn't know quite what to say. This wasn't like her at all. "We can throw it out if it bothers you *that* much," I said. "It *is* pretty offensive. It's just a thrift store painting I think I traded some old paperbacks for."

She shivered as though she was genuinely cold. She came back into the break room and by the too-harsh florescent light her verging-on-ruddy face was sweaty and pale, with just two bright spots of color above her cheekbones. "Are you coming down with something?" I said. "You look positively feverish. You don't have to stay if you feel sick."

"No — no, I'll be all right. I *have* to be all right," she said, and I had no idea what she meant.

But I had the feeling I was going to find out.

* * *

I felt so bad for Kirsten. There was something indefinable that was wrong with her, and she either would not or could not tell me about it. So I thought it would cheer her up a little if I took an interest in what she was doing at school. I knew little of her parents besides the fact that she had an emotionally unavailable Norwegian father; she never mentioned her mother at all. So on Monday I called the school to find out if I could get tickets for her play. The surreal conversation that followed went something like this:

"Box Office."

"Oh, hi," I said. "I'd like to get tickets to the play your Drama Department is putting on."

"You mean the Theatre Arts Department?"

"Sure. Whatever."

"Would you like tickets for *Twelfth Night*, which starts in December, or our Spring musical, *Little Shop of Horrors*?"

I was confused. "I thought there was another play being staged. *The King in Yellow*, something like that. My assistant attends Poseidon City Community College and she said her drama class was rehearsing it."

"Um... haven't heard of it. Perhaps it's something being studied by an individual class."

"Yeah... I guess that must be it."

"Sorry I can't help you. I only have the two plays listed this term."

"Yes, well, thanks anyway," I hung up. What the hell was going on?

On Monday, the day before my work week began, I went out for afternoon tea with my old friend Moira. We usually did the witchy things together. Moira is a hoot. She has carrot-red hair going grey which she wears long and wild. She likes garnets and chenille sweaters and wears a lot of silver Celtic-knot jewelry. I, as usual, wore Ryka tennis shoes and a hand-painted t-shirt with my 'relaxed-fit' jeans. Over the itty-bitty sandwiches, scones, and pastries that my arteries were hating me for, we kept up a steady stream of gossip and solved all of the world's political problems — if — anybody had bothered to listen to us, which they hadn't.

"How's the book coming?" Moira asked when I wasn't looking.

My mystery novel was plodding along, as it had been for... how long now?

"OK," I said.

Moira, not too mindful of her own cholesterol, was eating what was left of the Devon cream with a spoon when I bit into the last of my triangular sandwiches. This one had snow-white bread and a candy-pink filling.

I was expecting — what? Strawberry cream cheese? Marshmallow? Even pimento would have made sense but in fact the sandwich tasted like fish. Just like a tuna sandwich.

"What the hell is this?" I said.

"I was hoping you'd tell me," said Moira. "I thought it was salmon mixed with cream cheese at first but look at the color. It's not right. It's too artificial."

"Doesn't taste like salmon," I said and I should know, having lived in Oregon for a time with my first husband. I stared at the thing and the color of the filling reminded me of something. Then something very interesting happened.

The hard drive of my wetware began grinding away like the aged PC I typed on at the store. Files began to open in my memory. Glass planes slid apart and smoke and mirrors revealed what was truly behind the magician's tricks.

The sandwich that looks like one thing, and tastes like another. The psychotic break, where the patient has a totally inappropriate reaction to a stimulus, *because the sandwich looks like one thing and in fact tastes like another.*

No mask.

No mask.

If I heard what Moira said after that it went in one ear and out the next without even pausing to eat up a few bits of read-only-memory.

When I got home I dashed to the magazine rack and tore into all those *Antique Traders* and *Writer's Digests* I'm going to read some day. Somewhere on the rack was a schedule of classes for Poseidon City Community College; I may not remember much but I remembered getting one in the mail a month or so before classes began.

It was wedged between *Travel + Leisure* and *Pagans & Witches*, the magazines that I actually do read. My hands shook as I flipped through its newsprint pages looking for the Drama – I mean, *Theatre Arts* – classes.

I found the class that Kirsten was enrolled in. Under the instructor's name was the word I'd hoped not to see: STAFF.

I knew all too well what that word meant, for I'd taught a few Library Skills classes in my day, and was more than once addressed by jejune students as "Mrs Staff".

Who the hell was teaching that class, and what was he or she teaching?

The King in Yellow. "Some old dynastic thing," What did that mean? Maybe it was based on a story about the Yellow Emperor; someone who, if I remembered correctly, was a real historical figure.

I looked online and, after having found no plays based on the real-life Yellow Emperor, all I did find were a bunch of sites talking about short stories and authors like Ambrose Bierce and H.P. Lovecraft. I couldn't make the pieces fit, but I knew who could.

I called Somerset Library for the first time in a long time, and after Jenny (who answered the phone) had stopped her disingenuous gushing over how nice it was to hear my voice, I had her transfer me over to the Reference Desk.

I was in luck. Marty was there. I gave him the title and what I'd found or hadn't found and he promised to call me right back.

I puttered around and couldn't sit still. I turned on the TV and CNN said a freak downpour had caused heavy flooding on the Yangtze river, demolishing a small town; a missing Mexican drug lord had been found in, of all places, Asia's Golden Triangle of opium producers; an outbreak of yellow fever in the Caribbean had spread via cruise ship to New Orleans. There was a drive-by shooting in nearby Wilmington; the shooter could not be identified because he was wearing a pale stocking mask.

I jumped when the phone rang. It was Marty. He read me more names of writers I was mostly familiar with, then he mentioned a name I didn't know: Robert W. Chambers. Hmm. But he said he never did find the play – he only found stories that referred to it in hushed tones, giving a few innocuous-sounding lines in blank verse as representative of its content. His analysis was that it was a play that didn't exist at all – sort of like fictional grimoires: *The Necronomicon*, *The Book of Counted Sorrows*, etc. He told me about an HBO show that used it as a motif in a detective story; I doubted it was worth paying for premium cable to see it. Now I was even more confused, but I thanked Marty for his hard work. So, it was a play that wasn't a play, just something alluded to in a series of more-or-less spooky stories for the purpose of making those stories more spooky. So how—?

It looks like one thing, and tastes like another.

I had to wait until Wednesday to talk to Kirsten, and I had decided to confront her then. Tuesday night I had the dream again, but this time it was a bit different.

This time it was Warren who reclined on the fainting couch like the floozy in the thrift store painting. He looked as hollow and old as David had looked in the last stages of his illness. He wore the chintzy yellow bathrobe, and also had the canary-yellow feather boa around his neck. He sang a song and between stanzas took looks over his shoulder and out a window that displayed a night sky totally unlike the one here in the 'Harbor Gateway'. Two reddish moons rose bloated above the horizon, and a series of blood-colored stars winked on and off in a purplish sky. The song had a tune like 'As Time Goes By' and went something like this:

> The world's not what it seems,
> Cassilda's in a dream,
> If she thinks she can reach the Hyades
> > from lost Carcosa.

The mask is not a mask,
Camilla's got a task,
And she's just not up to it

     in dim Carcosa.

The lights will soon go out,
The people scream and shout,
And Empresses rise up and fall

     in dead Carcosa.

I awoke and this time I got up and turned on all the lights in the house. This was ridiculous. Warren was never into the whole drag-queen thing; he thought it was a stereotype. I felt guilty for even dreaming it. But I needed to pay attention; I still believed that he was trying to tell me something, trying to warn me even. I went to the kitchen window. Outside, the sky was just as it should be: stars were made dim and fuzzy by urban light pollution, the sky a hazy black with thin clouds lazing across the face of the nearly-full, pale golden moon.

On Wednesday afternoon Kirsten arrived, changed. Her hair was artfully arranged, with a wave of it sweeping across her brow. She went right to work without speaking. There was something else different about her, and at first I couldn't put my finger on it. Then I realized she had a new tattoo; a bit of it was just emerging from under the strap of her green tank top. I thought it was a letter at first, but finally decided it was some kind of symbol or sigil.

"Kirsten," I said. My voice sounded very thin and old in the store's dusty interior. "I wanted to surprise you and get tickets to see your play. But when I called the school they said it wasn't being put on in the theatre."

She stopped and stared at me as though I'd said I'd seen a Martian, but I continued.

"So I was wondering if maybe your teacher was holding a performance of the play just in class – what was his name again? I'm still hoping to see it if that's allowed," I said with a smile that must have seemed a rictus.

"Professor Gervais," she whispered.

"What?" I said, the sound of my own heart pounding in my ears so loudly I couldn't make out her words.

She stood up from behind the bureau she'd been refinishing, and suddenly I was aware of how much taller and stronger she was than I. "His name is Prof. Gervais," she said. – "My instructor," she said, and took a step toward me.

I took a step back.

She lowered her eyes. "I – I don't think that would be such a good idea," she said in a flat tone. "Coming to see the play, I mean," she continued, and I missed the bubbly, goofy Kirsten I was used to. She turned back to her work, and I gathered my courage.

"You have a new tattoo," I said.

She spun around. There were tears in her eyes. "Oh, Janette," she said. She wiped her eyes and the hair came away from forehead for a moment, and I thought I saw welts there, as though something very hot had rested there and blistered the skin. My stomach roiled.

"I want you to understand. I want to tell you – but I can't. I—" she shook her head, unable to go on.

"It's just a play, Kirsten," I stammered, afraid. "It's just a class. If there's some weird psychodrama going on in there then I think you should drop it. You can always take another drama class. Hell, you're not a drama major. It doesn't matter, you..."

She cut me off. "And what would you have me do?" she said, the words very un-Kirsten-like, her expression changed. "Cassilda wants to hand the diadem to one of her sons, but *I* know that the throne must be held by a woman, as it always has been. Camilla needs to be the next Empress; the dynasty must remain with the women. Certainly *you* of all people can understand that."

I understood nothing. She continued.

"I tried it on. I *wore* it – I wore the crown. Don't you see? No one thought I could do it – I surprised them." She was smiling and then held the hair away from her forehead for me to see. I could see plainly that something shaped like a crown had burned her.

She came around the side of the bureau. "You're right, though. This charade must end. Gervais will see the truth or I will make him see it. It's all there – all there in the play," she said, walking toward the front of the shop. "I *will* make him see. The King – the Pallid Mask – they can all be held back. Damn the Hyades! Carcosa will not fall." Her fist came down on the top of a glass display case, and I jumped, expecting it to shatter. Her eyes glittered.

"Please, Kirsten, I don't understand. What's going on?"

I followed her to the front door, though I admit to being a little afraid. She started to open the door, then stopped, and turned around.

She threw her arms around me. "If only Camilla had a mother like you," she said. "You'll know if I succeed. I'll send you the sign," she said, hugging me hard, then walking on out the door.

I never saw her again.

* * *

I called the college on Friday. The Theatre Arts Department swore that there was no instructor – not even a part time, temporary one – named Gervais. I gave them a line of bull I knew they'd swallow until they gave me the name of the instructor who had ended up teaching the class on the days and time Kirsten had said the class met.

It took several tries before I got hold of him – teachers are not often in their offices these days, especially when they're as dilapidated as the offices at Poseidon City Community College, but eventually I caught him in, one Mr Avila, Adjunct Instructor of Theatre Arts.

He was willing to talk to me – especially when I told him I'd taught Library Skills there a few times.

He said he wasn't supposed to give me any information, of course, but that a 'Kirsten Pedersen' was on the opening day roster, but she never did show up for class, so after a week he dropped her. Then I asked him if he knew a drama professor named Gervais. He said he didn't, but then again, he didn't know who had originally been hired to teach the class. It turned out that whoever had been hired to do so never showed up, and the college had called Avila in a panic as a last-minute replacement.

I picked up the phone a hundred times that week, but never called her. I mailed her a check, and it didn't come back in the mail, but I kept checking online and it wasn't cashed, either.

(Nothing gold can stay).

Now, I firmly believe in staying friends with one's exes. One reason is that they sometimes had helpful relatives. My second ex had a brother, Julio, who was a Harbor Division Sheriff's Deputy. I called him and told him what I could about my missing employee, and gave him her address. He said he'd drop by her place when he had a chance. Of course I could have gone by there myself, but I was a coward; if there'd been foul play, I couldn't bear to see it.

A couple of days later Julio called me. Her apartment at the address I gave him was front and center. He knocked on the front door but no one answered, and from what he could see through the windows someone had lived there recently, judging from visible indentations on the carpet, but it was clear that no one lived there anymore.

"Look, Jan," he said, calling me 'Jan' because that's what his brother Eduardo had called me, "The neighborhood where you have your shop isn't that great anymore. Ever think of just selling the stuff on Ebay? I mean, it's not like it used to be around there."

I thanked him without telling him that I didn't need his patriarchal advice, but the truth is, he was right. Antique shops were closing, even in Lomita and Torrance. Near me they were being replaced with 'vaping' places, massage parlors, and head shops. People from up on the 'Hill' wouldn't be inclined to come down here to go antiquing any more after seeing those places.

I had to beg, plead, and overpay my nephew to come in on the evening of my last First Thursday. Very few people visited my shop; most were young people who had come out for the free wine and cheese at the few galleries and artists' lofts that remained. They'd step in, giggle at the thrift store art until one of them saw the Polynesian idol, then they'd duck out, whispering amongst themselves. No one bought anything, and my blasted nephew didn't help at all but just sat on a high stool out in front texting. However, he knew enough about computers to help me once I made my decision to close the place for good.

I also had to pay him too much when he set me up to sell stuff online, and he took his own sweet time doing it. If it had been my only income, I'd've starved to death. I also lost money on the furniture because I couldn't move it myself; I'd let other dealers give me pennies on the dollar to buy it and haul it away to their own shops, some of which were in much tonier neighborhoods.

In a way it was better. I didn't have to keep one eye on the door all the time, and most of the soaps that I had enjoyed got canceled; I guess people watch 'reality shows' instead. All of this meant I could pay more attention to my writing. The Glock went in my small but extremely heavy fire safe; I'd never really felt comfortable with it around. I had more time to see my friends, which I cherished; Moira had passed away suddenly from a previously undiagnosed heart ailment, so my time with friends and relatives became more precious to me.

On one of the last days I was open I was boxing up the hated Depression glass when I noticed a young man walk by, a bit of a tattoo visible below his t-shirt sleeve. I ran out the door.

I realized that I didn't know what to say, so I said, "Hey, hi, I just wondered if I could see your tattoo."

He turned around and knitted his brows, probably thinking I was just some crazy old woman, but he stopped and pulled up his sleeve. He was Asian, and sure enough, the tattoo turned out to be a Chinese character. I'd seen this kind of tat on kids of all ethnicities before, of course, and now that I could see it better, it had really nothing in common with the strange symbol or sigil – if that's what it was – that had been Kirsten's new tat the last time I'd seen her.

"Hey, that's cool," I said, sounding like an idiot. "Have a good day." He turned and walked away without a word.

I haven't had a dream about Warren in a long time, but I did have one about Moira. In the dream she was attempting to try on a hideous mustard-colored dress in a Rodeo Drive boutique that in real life would never have carried our sizes or catered to our budgets. It had a wavering, indefinable print the color of goldenrod cardstock. She was complaining about trying to get the dress down over her hips. I kept squinting at the pattern on the fabric, but it shifted and squirmed like a living thing and was never clear. I woke up feeling very old, and got dressed and went to the local track where I could walk while buff guys and skinny women passed me by at a high lope. I tried to decide whether there was a sign or a sigil in the dream, but try as I might, I couldn't figure it out.

It looks like one thing when it's really another.

(Nothing gold can stay).

I keep waiting for a sign.

THE ELDRIDGE COLLECTION

WILL MURRAY

The package was intercepted in Kingston, Rhode Island.

It had been overnighted from Toronto via Worldwide Express. The red and white Worldwide Express jet was tracked en route by an orbiting Zircon spy satellite under the direct control of the Department of Defense's National Reconnaissance Office.

A Worldwide van left Timothy F. Green Airport trailed by a bronze Ford Taurus. It was blocked on Route 138 by a yellow Checker cab. Out of the cab popped a short, dusky man in a severe black suit and tie, showing a leatherette ID case in one hand and a 10 mm Delta Elite automatic in the other.

The van driver hit the brakes, thinking, "Highjack!"

The Taurus sheared in on his left, blocking him from exiting his vehicle. A cadaverous man in severe black slapped an ID against his window and shouted: "Exit your vehicle – now!"

The Worldwide courier driver came out quietly, hands raised.

"Department of Defense. You have a pine crate on board," said the tall man in black.

"Crate? I don't remember any—"

They threw him to the ground, cuffing his wrists behind his back. He lay prone, and the pair went in the back and carried out a flat wooden box, like a compact pallet.

"Oh, that. That's not a crate. It's a—"

"Shut up!" snapped the short dusky man.

He shut up.

They took pry bars to the sides of the flat wooden box and, with a screech and squeal of agonized nails, uncrated a canvas painting encased in cardboard and bubblewrap.

"What do you make of it?" the short one asked the other.

"Looks like the Big A."

"That's my read, too."

"Damn!"

They re-crated the painting and carefully laid it in the taxi's trunk. The cab scampered off on smoking tires.

The driver of the Taurus came back, uncuffed the courier and set him on his feet.

"You have been a participant in a sensitive Department of Defense operation. This encounter did *not* happen. You never saw us. Your supervisors have been briefed. You will say nothing to them or anyone else about what went on here."

"How do I know you're not—"

"Or I can just shoot your Goddamned eyes out here and now."

"I'm cool with this," the driver said.

He was still shaking twenty minutes after the Taurus sped away. Nobody ever asked about the missing crate, and he never brought it up, either.

* * *

The safe house could have existed only in Rhode Island. It was a dull red Colonial on Church Street in downtown Newport. The paint was peeling on both sides. The owner had had the frontage refreshed with a duller shade of colonial-era red, but had neglected the sides – probably on the theory that the adjoining houses pressed too close to warrant cosmetic paint.

Del Justice parked the Taurus out front and went in the side door. Osorio's cab was nowhere in sight. Good.

The painting lay on the kitchen table, still encased in rough hard pine. Agent Justo Osorio was on the wall phone, talking to Washington.

"The destination address is the Malbone Museum, Touro Street, Newport, Rhode Island. No, I never heard of it. Look it up."

Osorio nodded when he saw Justice walk in.

"They're running the address on the waybill," Osorio said.

"Right."

Osorio gripped the ivory phone handset until his dusky fingers almost matched the plastic. Then he said, "Okay. We'll handle it from here." He hung up.

"It checks out," he told Justice. "A private art museum. Established 1971.

Oriel Malbone, curator. He's in the database as a low-level dabbler."

"Figures."

"I guess we're going to have to go in."

Justice nodded. He picked up the heavy wood crate and set it against the silent refrigerator. Carefully, he lifted the canvas out of its pine sheathe.

The painting was an 11 × 14 oil. It might have been new, it might have been old. The colors were bright. The image was garish.

The canvas showed a fragment of interstellar space, framing a vortical disturbance within which squatted a sultanic potentate laughing uproariously as faceless things spun and whirled in orbit about him, piping on flutes composed of snowy quantum stuff.

"Azathoth, or I'm Wilbur Whately's demented second cousin..." Osorio muttered.

Justice nodded. "Yeah. And it's an Eldridge for certain. Look at those frenzied brush strokes."

"No signature."

"He never signed his work. Check this out."Osorio's finger indicated a scarlet circle centered in the upper portion of the image area. The circle was not integral to the image, but superimposed over it.

"What do you make of it?" he asked.

"Can't say. A circle. A zero. Maybe an alchemic symbol. I'm rusty on my hermetics."

"Me, too. How's your Astrology?"

"Crappy. I was born on a Mercury retrograde. I can't remember all those trines and occultations and afflicted planets."

"Wasn't there a white numeral 1 on the Nyarlathotep canvas that got away from us in Milan?"

"Not confirmed that it was a 1. Might have been a capital letter I, or the Roman numeral I. The lab said there was no way to differentiate between the two without contextual references."

"Zeroes are Arabic. I'd say this is an O and the Nyarlathotep thing was a Capital I."

"If we knew what old Esau was trying to paint when he committed these bastards to canvas, we'd have an inkling."

"But we don't. I guess we just go in and see how much of the Eldridge Collection is in that museum."

They checked their weapons, stowed the painting in the basement and claimed the Taurus.

* * *

The Surveillance and Interdiction van was already on station when they pulled up to the museum, an imposing Greek Revival building with a broken pediment over the pillared portico. It was a UPS van with one visible added feature: a small turret on top that housed the upper lens of a periscope.

Justice got the van on his cell phone.

"What have you got?"

"Damn place is choked with Eldridges," came a hoarse voice.

"Christ! You positive?"

"Of course, we're not positive. That old goat never signed his work. But I see a Cthulhu, a Yog, and a flock of—"

"Damn it. Don't invoke major entities on an unsecured line."

"—Night-gaunts. I mean, N.G.s."

"How much of the collection do you figure is inside?"

"We count at least thirty canvases."

"Good Christ! Do you think we could be this lucky?"

Justice turned to Osorio. "Intel has it the Eldridge Collection is being reassembled canvas by canvas. Now we know where they're all landing."

"Yeah. But not why."

"So we go in and we find out," Justice said tightly.

* * *

They rang the bell. It was a black push-button set in a brass plate, vintage 1933 judging from the tarnish. The door sported a row of leaded-glass fan lights.

An elderly man with a face like a dried turnip opened the tall oak-panel door. He might have been a mummified sea captain of the 1800s with his thinning goatee. He started in surprise.

"Yes?"

"We're patrons," said Justice.

"Viewing is by appointment only."

"We'd like to make an appointment," said Osorio.

"Now," said Justice.

"For now," added Osorio.

"Impossible. Arrangements are made by telephone only." The panel began to close.

Justice inserted his foot in the door, and Osorio his service weapon in the old man's face.

"Oriel Malbone, you are under arrest for the illegal importation of banned engineries of magic," warned Justice.

They urged the man in, walking in tandem with his retreating steps. The door closed shut.

* * *

In the camouflage van, the surveillance team waited tensely.

Three minutes and twelve seconds by their synchronized watches, Osorio came out. He looked dazed, and he was wearing the wrong tie.

In the van, the agent at the periscope murmured, "Something's not right…"

"What's that?"

"Osorio's wearing Justice's tie."

"So?"

"And his shoes. Take a look yourself."

It was worse than that. Osorio stumbled to the curb. They ran to his side. Up close, they saw the truth – the unbelievable truth.

"Oh, God. It's Justice."

"Are you blind? It's Osorio."

"It's Justice. Look at his wrists. Pale as muslin. It's Justice – but he's wearing Osorio's head."

A moment later, Osorio stumbled out, looking at the world through the stupefied eyes of his partner. His head did not exactly sit on his neck properly. It was too thin. He looked like a pinhead. And there was a clear neckline demarcation where dark skin turned pale.

An ambulance was called. They loaded the two twitching and flopping agents onto gurneys. Osorio's head came off during the procedure, leaving a nubby stump like a pink matchhead.

Justice's head rolled off the other body en route. They were pronounced E.O.A. – Ensorcelled on Arrival – and quietly euthanized by lethal injection.

The Malbone Museum was sealed off, its lower windows spray-painted black so that no one could see out – or worse, no agent could look in and risk having his sanity compromised. And the Cryptic Events Evaluation Section of the National Reconnaissance Office settled down for what looked to be a long, grim siege.

* * *

Word reached CEES operative James Anthony in Washington, D.C. Section

Head Morand walked into his office, shut the door and broke the news.

"We've isolated the Eldridge Collection, or most of it. Justice and Osorio succumbed in the line of duty. Never mind the grisly details. It's your assignment now. You'll be partnering with Itri."

Anthony blinked. "Itri. Who's he?"

"She. Gina Itri. Boston office. Cartomancy Division."

"A Tarot reader! I have to team up with a fucking pasteboard princess? No damned way."

"This comes from the top. Itri's already on station. You'll liaise with her in Newport."

The file landed on Anthony's desk. Clipped to the folder was a plane ticket to Newport. Anthony noticed it was one way. The Cryptic Events Evaluation Section of the National Reconnaissance Office stopped wasting money on return tickets after Agent Irby disappeared in Moodus, Connecticut, and was later found embedded in a 125-year-old swamp maple as if it had grown up around his undecayed remains since Teddy Roosevelt's day. They never explained that one.

* * *

Anthony spent the flight reading the file. Esau Eldridge, 1904–1961. Double Scorpio. Commercial Illustrator. Painted bookplates for privately-printed grimoires during the 1930s, then moved on to gallery art. His work shocked postwar America, which preferred the safer styles of Rockwell and Lovell. The works that leaked out of Eldridge's Smuttynose Island lighthouse garret were bad enough, but rumors abounded they were merely discarded rejects from his magnum opus, a series of paintings depicting the Great Old Ones and their remorseless train. No one knew their purpose. But upon Eldridge's death, his acolytes and rivals descended upon the isolated New Hampshire island and spirited away the collection piecemeal. That was in the pre-NRO days when Cosmic Countervailance was a Secret Service responsibility. After Dallas, NRO was formed and tasked with that mission.

There followed a kind of internecine war between rival Cthulhu worshippers, all vying to reassemble the complete collection. It was nothing less than a Mafia-style power struggle conducted with demons and grimoires instead of hit men and firearms. Bodies turned up in inexplicable places, unaccountably violated. Canvases materialized and dematerialized like wavicles in the quantum matrix.

That disturbing pattern was what had brought in the Cryptic Events

Evaluation Section. For better than two decades, they chased Eldridges, sometimes capturing one, but always losing them to counterforces, sometimes in the form of turncoat dark agents.

Now the paintings were being reassembled in one locale. It was a golden opportunity to seize and quarantine the entire problem.

"But we still don't know what Eldridge was up to," Anthony muttered as the 727 dropped its gear on approach to T.F. Green Airport.

* * *

Anthony expected an aging hippie in her 40s. Gina Itri was a feline redhead who looked like a cross between Fran Drescher and a moderately high-priced call girl. She smoked like a Black Mass. And she had a mouth on her...

"I'm Itri. Arts and Crafts. Cartomancy Division," she said in a smoky voice.

"Anthony. Intelligence and Enforcement. South Boston?"

She nodded. "You're good, for a non-intuitive."

"I got no use for Tarot. I'll say that up front."

"Fine," Itri said, reaching into her handbag. She pulled out the Thoth deck, secured by a black silk ribbon. That told Anthony she was a bitch on wheels. The Thoth was a man's deck.

She started running cards on him. That was another thing Anthony hated about Tarot readers. They couldn't take a leak without consulting their cards.

"First," Itri said. "I'm not a mechanical reader. I'm intuitive. In a tight spot, I'll do a one-card pull. But I don't read spreads. I'm not into relying on Chaos Theory."

"Right, right," he said impatiently.

"Aries?"

Anthony sighed. "Yeah."

"I always nail the sun sign. Moon in Capricorn, too. Divorced. No kids. I can see we're going to get along..." she said acidly. "I'm a Leo, Moon in Scorpio."

"I don't give a rat's ass for Astrology, either."

"In that case, you can do all the shooting. And dying."

"That's my job..." Anthony said tightly.

She nodded. "I've looked over the seized Azathoth. That's a zero painted at the top. That makes the device on the Nyarlathotep canvas a Roman numeral I for sure."

"The cards tell you that?"

"Yes and no." She held up a card. It showed a yellow-faced green demon or devil. It was labeled The Fool. A tapering scarlet nail touched a zero set in the top border. "Note the zero."

"Noted..."

"This is the first card in the Tarot Deck, The Fool." She cut the cards blindly, exposing another card. It was titled The Magician. "This is the second card. Note the I."

"I don't have time for this..."

"Stuff it. The Cthulhu painting glimpsed through the Malbone Museum window had a number on it. Guess what number?"

She cut the cards while Anthony frowned darkly.

Up came a card called The Hierophant, the number was V.

"Not—"

"The Fool is Azathoth, the so-called Blind Idiot God. Nyarlathotep is The Magician. Even a stiff like you would get that. And Great Cthulhu is The High Priest, or Hierophant. Want me to spell it out for you in Braille?"

Anthony stiffened. "Eldridge was painting a Tarot deck..."

"Eldridge was painting the ultimate Tarot. Maybe the original Tarot. No one knows where the Tarot comes from. Most of the decks that come down to us descend from Medieval Italy. They're unrectified, that is, incomplete. And pretty harmless within their limitations as focusing tools for divination. But there's an old theory the Tarot is Egyptian in origin, and it's based on the Book of Thoth." She fixed him with her magnetic brown eyes. "Thoth...Azathoth...Yog-Sothoth...is any of this sinking in?"

Anthony felt the blood drain from his face.

"How bad if the Eldridge Collection has been reassembled?" he croaked.

"No one knows. But we have the Azathoth painting, so we know Malbone hasn't got a complete deck yet."

Itri flipped up another card.

"Take a close look at the Magician," she said.

Anthony did. It showed a brass goblet with rather phallic attributes rampant against a creepy gray backdrop. "Are those tentacles in the background?" he asked.

"Coiled tentacles. The Thoth Tarot was envisioned by Aleister Crowley and executed by Lady Frieda Harris in the 1940s. It's thought Crowley was attempting to recreate the original ultimate Tarot deck. But he got hung up in the process. Crowley identified with The Magician. Couldn't figure out what magician to use. He ran Lady Frieda ragged painting different interpretations. Just after he produced a limited edition deck in 1944, Crowley died. The Thoth deck remained a rarity until a mass-market edition was released in 1969. By then, no one connected it with the Great Old Ones and their spawn. This is believed to be Crowley's preferred Magician card. It has *Necronomicon* written all over it."

Anthony regarded the image floating before his eyes. As he watched the tentacles seemed to... writhe.

He slapped the card aside, saying, "Get that thing away from me!"

Itri smiled. "Interesting. You have some latent ability."

"All right. You've done your part. Now I have to find a psychically secure way into that damned museum."

"The cards will lead us."

"Not on your—"

"Unless you want to drive home with someone else's head."

Anthony grabbed his neck. He felt a tightness there. He swallowed his objections.

"You lead. I'll follow."

Agent Itri smiled. "I like a man who understands who's holding all the cards."

* * *

They took up a position behind the Old Stone Mill in Touro Park. It was an eight-legged cylinder of heterogeneous native stone fenced off by wrought iron. Blank windows were set high up at regular intervals like empty-socketed eyes.

"What is this thing?" Anthony asked, looking up warily.

"No one's sure. Some claim it's of Norse origin. In Benedict Arnold's will, it was listed as a windmill."

"So it's just a windmill..."

"That's what Aquidneck Islanders believed until they found its double under thirty feet of water off Brenton's Point."

"I hate elder artifacts..."

Itri was running cards. She started with the Waite deck, clicking through them until she came to The Devil, a rather hairy bat-winged Satan perched on a block of base metal, to which were chained a nude man and a woman, both in attitudes of passive thrall.

"Look familiar?" she asked.

Anthony regarded the card. "Vaguely," he admitted. "Can't place it, though."

"Remember the Cthulhu canvas? It's nearly the same posture."

"Mother of God. You're right!"

"This confirms my college thesis. The Tarot descends from knowledge psychically apprehended by Egyptian Cthulhu-worshippers."

"Miskatonic U?"

Itri nodded. "Where else would I get a Masters in Applied Cartomancy?"

"I say we burn the damned building down. End this right here."

Itri shook her long red hair. "Can't."

"Give me one sound reason. And don't consult the damned cards."

"Reason one: We don't know how many amateur magicians, adepts, cartomancers, or whatever have Eldridge photographs in their collection. We need to record and archive every image in the rectified deck, or look forward to wasting the next 500 years confiscating and burning every Cthulhuvian canvas that comes to light."

Anthony sighed. "Point taken. What's reason two?"

"Reason two is if unrectified decks are out there, the only counterforce is a partial deck under Department of Defense control." She lit up a Marlboro. "Not to mention reason three."

"Which is?"

"I want a crack at working this complete deck myself."

Anthony shuddered. Southie women. They were as tough as advertised.

Itri blew gray tendrilly smoke. "Okay, here's the way it reads to me. Malbone can't see out his windows, and we can't look in. He's got at best a partial deck, while I have Rider-Waite, Crowley's Thoth, and if events get really sticky, a Xultun deck. That just about levels the playing field." She looked at him pointedly. "You man enough to back me up?"

Anthony silently popped his belt buckle and thumbed the reservoir last replenished on Ash Wednesday. He traced a five-pointed star on his forehead, jacked a fresh round in the chamber of his service weapon and nodded wordlessly.

Itri led him to the cellar entrance. It was a galvanized steel hatch, padlocked. He picked it in thirty seconds and threw the hatch, then they descended. The plank door at the bottom of the short wood steps wouldn't budge.

"Padlocked," he hissed.

Itri ran through her Rider-Waite. "No, just a hasp."

Anthony reversed his pick. The other end was a sharp punch. He dug the tip into the soft wood around the painted-over hasp strapping. When the point scraped hard metal, he put his weight into it. A slow screech of metal declared that he had popped the hasp.

The door came open. Itri cut the cards, saw The Star, and seemed satisfied.

"The easy part's over," Anthony muttered as he stepped into the crepuscular gloom. An ancient coal furnace blew hot air, throwing angry orange light. The light showed the dusty orb web blocking the angling stairs to the upper floors.

Anthony advanced, one big hand lifted to swat away the drooping strands.

"Don't touch it!" Itri hissed. "Early warning webbing. I ran into one of these in a 300-year-old grist mill in Foxfield, Mass."

Anthony froze. He saw the spider. It looked dead. On closer inspection, its resemblance to a spider was more general than specific.

Itri took a piece of tissue, masticated it into a soggy ball in her mouth, then spit it into the web. The spider scuttled from its hole, sinking fangs into the moist morsel.

It sizzled and fell, a sputtering cinder that stank of burnt tar.

"Holy water gets them every time..." said Itri, clearing the web away with a dusty ski pole.

"Holy...?"

"I gargle the stuff before every operation."

Anthony followed her up the steps, weapon at the ready.

"Holy water never works for me," he said.

"Not against major entities. But the minor ones really bought into that old good vs. evil modality."

* * *

Oriel Malbone sat in a throne carved from a single block of imperial jade, his smoldering eyes fixed upon a crystal ball upheld by the inverted talons of an Arabian Roc.

The UPS van was still parked across the street, regarding the building with its primitive ground glass lens. No doubt the now-blackened windows were laser-miked for sound. It was getting so that science was catching up to sorcery...

A faint vibration caught his attention. He looked to his left wrist, where a thin strand of spider silk vibrated. It went limp. The cellar web had been breached. Good. Just as the card had foretold.

Rising, Malbone laid six oversized pasteboards in a circle around his booted feet. Fixing his eye on The Elder Sign card, he stepped in a slow circle until he had addressed all six cards three times three.

Then the hardwood floor began to melt under his feet like so much hot molasses, swallowing his feet...

* * *

Itri was picking her way from the kitchen to the cramped angular hallways with their unhappy carvings. There were no doors, making their stealthy progress smooth and silent.

They encountered the first Eldridge at the terminus of the main hallway. It was a massive black canvas, fretted with watery greens and grays that limned a shuddering stone structure.

"R'lyeh," Itri hissed. "The Tower. It always signifies disaster."

"We gotta walk past it to..."

"Waite isn't helping." She switched to the Thoth deck. "Okay, just follow in my footsteps. Don't deviate."

Itri walked toward the painting, holding to the middle of the hardwood floor.

Anthony followed. At one point, his foot slipped and his straying toe encountered empty air. He strangled his curse.

"The floor's an illusion," Itri called over her shoulder. "Only this middle section is real."

"Why didn't you say so?"

"Didn't want you losing your water. I partnered with an I&E stiff in Ubar."

"Ubar?"

"Irem to you. A sand gulper jumped out of a dune and swallowed the lower half of his body."

Anthony nodded. "I knew him. Hurley. Heard he ate his own gun."

"That was the story I&E put out to save face. Truth is, I put him out of his misery with his own weapon. The big baby kept blubbering."

"Bitch."

"What's that?"

"I said witch. You're into Wicca, right?"

"I'm part Gypsy."

"Same difference."

The hallway negotiated, they came to a large room paneled in old teak and ebony dominated by a brick fireplace. In the center sat a jade throne facing a crystal ball about the size of a console television.

Anthony approached the crystal gingerly. "What's with the oracle?

Malbone's a cartomancer, right?"

"Divination is divination," Itri said. She stopped dead when she spotted the six cards lying flat on the floor in a circle. Her brown eyes fixed on one card, which looked like a Yin-Yang sign as if it were some kind of symbiotic Siamese creature. "Eldridge knew his stuff. The Lovers card is Nug and Yeb."

"Nug and who?" asked Anthony.

"Two of the most obscure yet potent of the Old Ones. If Eldridge painted them from life, he was communing with the highest universal powers in existence."

Itri picked up the cards, extracted an equal number from the Thoth, discarded them, and whispered, "Let's get moving."

"What are you doing?"

"Building a rectified ultimate Tarot," she said.

They worked from room to room, Itri consulting her cards before turning each corner, Anthony jumping in ahead, Delta Elite ready to fire. They encountered no one.

The walls were covered in canvases, all hung in heavy ornate gilt frames. And all arranged in orderly numbers. All they had to do was follow the numerical progression to explore the collection and take stock of the museum's holdings.

They came to a card displaying a congeries of bubbles floating in a void.

Itri extracted the Nine of Disks from her Thoth deck. Labeled Gain, it showed a dismal blue, green, and gray mélange of floating spheres. The resemblance of the two designs was unmistakable.

"Which proves what?" Anthony asked.

Itri moved on until she came to a canvas that could be only Great Cthulhu. He squatted on a block of some base metal, batwings outspread, one hand raised, facing the viewer. Chained to the block were two headless humanoid beings.

Itri pulled her Rider-Waite and, without deliberately appearing to select a card, revealed The Devil. Its pose was identical to that of Cthulhu.

"There's no question now. Every Tarot descends from a proto-Tarot predating the earliest known decks. This is the original book. This is the key to everything, and Eldridge managed to recreate it through God knows what occult medium."

The progression took them to a winding staircase the newels of which were carved in the traditional Kingsport motif. They went up, their feet staying on the fuzzy brown runner to muffle any sound. It felt as if they were walking up a long, dead tongue.

"Check it out," Itri said, indicating a canvas depicting a black faceless bat-winged creature rising into a moonlit night clutching a naked man and woman by their stomachs. "The Death card is a night-gaunt."

"I hate the Death card," Anthony said.

"It's not what you think," Itri returned. "Only an amateur reads the Death card as Death personified."

"Looks like Death to me..."

"Amateur."

Reaching the top step, they found themselves facing a gilt-framed painting that looked weirdly familiar. A tall grayish cone of a creature squatted on eight elephantine legs, looking out in eight directions with an equal number of blank orbs.

"What the hell is that?" Anthony said.

"Shoggoth."

"Damned if it doesn't look exactly like that stone tower across the street."

"I was thinking the exact same thing."

"Aren't shoggoths amphibious?"

Itri nodded. "That might explain the waterlogged stone tower, too. They're petrified shoggoths. Could also explain that Nazi sub that went down near here during the Big One. A shoggoth got it."

The second floor split in two directions. Every wall was hung with Eldridges. There were only two doors, both shut.

Itri ran cards on the south door, nodded, then performed the same operation on the north door.

"Bedrooms. Empty," she said.

"Secret panels?" wondered Anthony.

She ran along the deck, stopped at The Hermit.

"Plenty of them. All empty."

"Malbone's gotta be somewhere in here."

"I don't see him in the cards..."

"Dammit, we should be looking behind every door, not in your damned deck," Anthony hissed.

"Feel free to waste your time," Itri said acidly.

Anthony hit the north door. It popped inward when his shoulder struck it. A bedroom. The south door opened on a mirror image bedroom. The last of the canvases sat over each four-poster bed. A row of high vaulted windows looked out upon Touro Park and its strange sentinel of stone.

Itri was tapping one toe impatiently when Anthony rejoined her.

"Satisfied?" she asked.

"Yeah."

"Taurus ascendant?"

Anthony frowned darkly. "You tell me…"

"Something in your chart made you as stubborn as a bad smell."

They discovered no missing canvases in the Minor Arcana. And only one in the Major Arcana.

"Only The Fool is missing," Itri said grimly.

Anthony nodded. "Azathoth. And we have that covered."

Absently, Itri dropped a card. Her hand snagged it before it hit the floor. She looked at it. "The Moon," she said thoughtfully.

"So what? You dropped it by accident."

"Nothing in the universe happens by chance. I wonder what this means…" Itri looked up. There was a box-frame hatch directly over their heads. "Boost me up," she said.

Holstering his weapon, Anthony made a basket with his hands. Itri stepped into it. He lifted her up. She slapped the hatch door up. It fell back, and she pulled herself up and in.

Anthony drew his weapon again and waited tensely. Minutes crawled by. The shoggoth in the painting seemed to be staring at him like a deformed owl at a mouse.

"Itri!"

No answer.

"Itri!"

Her face appeared in the hatch, wearing a wide red grin. She flashed a fan of cards, saying "Jackpot!" then disappeared.

When her legs reappeared a moment later, Anthony reached up to catch her about the waist. Her feet hit the hardwood flooring with a single click.

"What'd you find?" Anthony demanded.

"Malbone's printing press and photographic equipment. And all these." She flashed a fat deck of cards. "Rejects and castoffs, but they're good enough for government work."

"How many?"

"No time to take inventory. Okay, let's go."

"Go where?"

Without answering, Itri ran down the steps. Anthony followed her to the room dominated by the crystal ball. She took up a standing position before it, peering deep within.

Catching up, Anthony asked, "I thought you—"

"I minored in scrying at MU, okay? Now get your ass out of my light."

Anthony retreated to guard the door.

Itri leaned into the crystal. Her supple body stiffened. "Don't look now, but I found our wayward wizard. He's at the safe house. Nice I&E security, by the way."

Anthony rushed forward. "Malbone?"

She turned. "Once he has the Azathoth, he's on his way to a complete deck, minus my six."

"And you have just what – how many?"

Itri said nothing. She was thinking. Quietly, she went picking through her composite deck, an admixture of Thoth and Cthulhu cards. Pulling six, she laid them in a circle before the crystal ball. They were the six she had found originally.

"Let's see if he comes back..."

"Back?"

The floor began to run and congeal. A face like a jaundiced carven turnip lifted out of the cold molasses morass. The eyes were wide, but unseeing as if tranced. Tucked under the set beard-feathered chin was the upper portion of a starry canvas bearing a blood-red zero.

Anthony stepped in, leveled his Delta Elite at the rising head. "I'll take that."

Itri beat him to it. She wrested the canvas from Malbone's trance-stiff fingers, spun away with it.

Anthony tracked the exact middle of Malbone's rising forehead with a steady gun hand. When the floor solidified under his settling boots, vision returned to the old magician's faded agate eyes. His dry lips formed a malevolent orifice.

Anthony said, "Oriel Malbone, you stand accused of trafficking in forbidden engineries of magic. It is my sworn duty to dispatch you from this Earth."

Anthony's finger squeezed the stainless steel trigger. The weapon popped, jumping in his hand. Malbone's head jerked back on its age-wattled neck. Gunsmoke obscured Anthony's view.

He turned to address Itri. She wasn't there.

"Where..."

A cold voice behind him intoned: "Not so quick, my uninitiated pretender to power."

Anthony whirled. Oriel Malbone stood there with his deck held before him arrayed in a short fan, a bloodless blue hole in the center of his forehead closing like a meaty iris.

Anthony opened fire. The weapon shook and smoked, creating thunder in the room. Hot rounds chipped jade fragments off the Oriental throne. Struck once, the crystal ball shattered into clear chunks and powdery glass particles.

Yet Oriel Malbone stood unharmed, protected by nothing more substantial than a fan of Tarot cards...

A cold fear creeping into his bones, Anthony began backing out of the room, calling, "Itri! Agent Itri! Damn it, where are you?"

Floating down the stairs came a smoky taunting laugh.

"Last one into the attic eats the Death card..."

"Damn that mouthy bitch!"

Malbone was advancing now, eyes wild, his parched lips peeling back from yellow peg teeth. He was running cards, their faces directed at Anthony as if to ensnare and confuse him.

Every round Anthony sent his way veered in midair to ricochet into teak paneling. The automatic soon ran empty, slide freezing into the locked position.

Malbone cackled a thin laugh as Anthony expertly ejected the empty clip and slammed home a fresh one. He resumed firing.

"You waste your time," Malbone taunted. "I am protected."

He revealed the Yog-Sothoth card. It seemed to pulse and shift its bubbling congeries of alien spheres.

Anthony picked his shots. A round seemed to bounce off the old wizard's skull, to gouge a decorative rosette. Another smeared a leaden brushstroke along the fireplace lintel. Anthony began seeing science in the misses, geometry in the ricochets.

At the door, he dropped into a marksman's crouch and blazed away at an imaginary spot to the immediate right of Oriel Malbone's coldly advancing form.

Bullets rained on the fireplace, knocking over brass andirons and fracturing brick. Some ricocheted. One found a soft spot in Malbone's lower spine. Wearing an expression of shocked astonishment, Malbone stumbled forward, cards fluttering all around him like tired origami bats. He clutched at them wildly.

Anthony lunged, stepping on a thin wrist so hard bones snapped. The wizard howled in pain. He let go of a fistful of pasteboards. Without hesitation, Anthony aligned the Elite's muzzle with Oriel Malbone's yawning mouth.

Two rounds fragmented the old wizard's head in a brutal echo of the shattered crystal ball. The thin body collapsed, one yellowing claw crushing a lone card.

Anthony plucked it free, saw it was a night-gaunt – the Death card – and got down on his knees to collect the rest of the deck.

When he had them all, Anthony gave the jittering corpse an angry kick and went in search of Agent Gina Itri.

Reaching the second-floor landing, he located her. A fitful green light came down from the attic hatch. It repeated.

"What the hell..."

Accompanying sounds told him an ordinary photocopier was in operation.

"Damn! Itri! Get down here!"

Her voice came back, distracted and brittle. "Hold your horses. I'm almost done reducing Azathoth to card size."

"That is a direct order. You are not authorized to—"

"Bite me, okay?"

The photocopier went silent. Attic flooring creaked under a shifting human weight.

Anthony looked at the cards in his hands and felt a chill touch his bone marrow. Between them, they had a full Tarot. And for the first time in his life, he began to wish he'd studied the damn cards.

Itri's voice was thin when it next sounded. "Get ready. I'm coming down."

Anthony took up a position on the top of the staircase, Delta Elite sighted on the square ceiling hatch. When Itri's oval face appeared, he said tightly: "Drop the cards ahead of you, Itri."

"What are you afraid of?"

Anthony's voice was flat and expressionless. "You."

A silence. Then: "All right. Here they come..."

A single card dropped down, fluttered momentarily, and made a sharp midair veer.

It sliced through the automatic's muzzle like a guillotine. The fore part of the weapon hit the floor with a clank!

"Jesus!" Anthony said, recoiling.

The card lay on the floor. It was The Shoggoth. Anthony's eye went from the card image to the original painting framed on the wall just beneath the hatch. The card sported a vertical black line – a printing or photocopying defect. It seemed not to matter because Itri's voice lifted in some guttural prehuman chant and—

Abruptly, the shoggoth in the painting turned to petrified rock. Its weird blank orbs melted into empty stone sockets.

And outside, coming from the direction of Touro Park, came a plodding thud-thud-thud-thud of dull, elephantine feet.

"Itri, what the hell do you think you're doing?" Anthony shouted.

"Seizing my rightful power. No one has ever wielded the ultimate Tarot. This is the dream of every cartomancer since Bonifacio Bembo painted the original medieval deck. Waite tried, but he got tangled up in useless Jungian archetypes. Crowley came close, but he put too much faith in modern science. Eldridge succeeded only to die just as he finished his masterpiece. His bad karma is my glory."

"Renegade. You've gone renegade!" Anthony said heatedly.

"Your word for it, not mine. I had it up to here with I&E stuffed suits like you looking down your long noses at my gift. I don't owe the agency anything."

"You know the building is surrounded, Itri."

"And you know I can drop through the floor to Paris or London any time I damn well want," Itri fired back.

"But you won't until you have the rest of Malbone's deck. Come down and get them."

The dull thudding of heavy feet was drawing near.

"I don't have to," came the smoky laughing voice from the attic. "Reinforcements are coming your way."

Anthony was not a prayerful man. But he made a sign of the cross. He couldn't see what was bearing down on the house. He didn't need to see it. The stony thing in the painting gave his imagination all it needed to fill in the pieces.

"Last chance to surrender," Itri warned. "Before your brains get scooped out like seeds from a gourd."

Anthony's teeth squeezed tight. "You—"

"I think the word you're groping for is bitch. Or do you mean witch?"

"Take your damn pick..." Anthony growled.

"Trade you card for card. No? Try this one."

Another card fluttered down like a falling leaf. A night-gaunt. The Death card. It slid along the floor and kept sliding, homing in on James Anthony like a flat speedy cockroach. It sliced the heel off his left shoe, then came back for the right. Anthony dodged it. The pasteboard continued after him. He stepped on it. Hard.

Under his surviving shoe heel, Anthony felt the card tug and tug stubbornly. The damned thing was not giving up. He relinquished pressure long enough to bring his heel up and down with crushing force. That momentary lapse was his mistake. The card zipped free, pulling Anthony's foot out from under him.

He landed on his backside. Eyes widening, he looked for the fugitive night-gaunt card. Where was it? Where the hell did it go?

He understood he was sitting on the card too late. He discovered himself skidding along the polished hardwood floor into the north bedroom where the row of high vaulted windows framed a two-story-tall cone of dull gray matter which regarded him with blank orbs like polished ivory balls.

The glass broke inward, impelled by an extrusion like a gray clay limb.

And over his shoulder, Anthony heard a mocking voice say, "I'll take that from you." Nimble fingers extracted the last of Oriel Malbone's Tarot deck from his bone-and-sinew vise of a hand. The nails were scarlet, as if enameled in blood. He caught that much out of the tail of his eye — but the thing in the window continued to hold his frozen attention.

"Only an amateur reads the Death card as Death," Gina Itri was saying. "But only a fool ignores the inevitable. *Ciao*."

Anthony opened his mouth to scream as the blunt extension reached in to envelop his head. He never got out a single sound.

As the world turned black to his eyes and cold to his brain, Agent James Anthony had time to process a final strange thought: Shoggoths tasted exactly like dead wet clams.

Then his pressure-stressed skull cracked while a cold gray mass slipped down his gullet to fill his lungs and stomach with the dead weight of unliving alien matter.

* * *

The Cryptic Events Evaluation Section of the National Reconnaissance Office that day declared the Malbone Museum a Compromised Site and burned it to the ground after the sun had gone down.

By that time, they knew it was too late. For the shoggoth had retraced its leaden steps to Touro Park and resumed its petrified state and stance.

The body of the late James Anthony was discovered at the foot of one of the eight arched feet, his corpse intact, but his head encased in stone as if integral to it. They separated what could be buried from what couldn't. They never explained his fate, either.

When the charred remains of the Malbone Museum were later combed over by a CEES Contamination and Containment crew, they found only blackened gilt frames where the 78 paintings of the Esau Eldridge collection had hung. They were declared officially destroyed. Oriel Malbone's black vitrified bones were ground to powder and scattered off Brenton's Reef.

No trace of CEES Cartomancer First Class Gina Itri was ever uncovered, but in the Washington offices of the agency, her file was quietly transferred from Personnel to the Known Collaborators database.

No matter how many times they moved the file, the photograph kept reappearing in Personnel, one brown eye closed in a knowing wink.

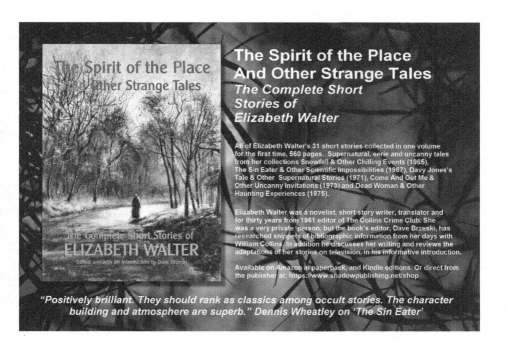

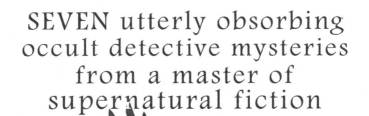

MR NOUSEL'S MIRROR

MICHAEL KEYTON

I remember pausing, the tall medieval lines of the car park on my left; to my right the King's Head, a late Victorian hotel: red bricks, deep windows and sandstone sills laced in grime. Facing me were the grey ruins of Newport castle. I paused, an instant longer, content to allow the thoughtless bustle pass me by. A wind, cold and gritty, scattered paper across the pavement, causing my eyes to water and fading everything into a washed-out blur.

I checked the map once more, then retraced my steps, stopping before a narrow street that ran down the side of the market. The street was strangely silent as if for some reason people chose to avoid it, perhaps had good reason to. I shivered, sensing that it wasn't the kind of place to linger when darkness fell. Though I walked slowly, my footsteps seemed abnormally loud, almost as if the enclosed space were savouring the sound, savouring my presence. Then I saw it, a tiny arcade to my left, an alley, a winding thread, grimy and underused.

Unobtrusive doorways, silent in dust, appeared on either side of me, and before each one I paused, studying signs, fading labels or any other indication as to what the rooms above might hold. A door that had once been painted green came into view. It was half-open, and below a knocker cast in the form of a seedy-looking lion was a small brass plate. Mr William Nousel – Optics.

I sighed then in some relief, and cautiously walked up a flight of grey wooden stairs. They led to a landing and four facing doors, all but one of them closed. I hesitated, resting my hand on a crudely carved balustrade and stared at the one partially opened door. It was barely ajar, its rectangular silhouette outlined in a thin seam of light. Someone was on the other side, listening, and I wondered whether he had picked up my footfall in the alley, perhaps even the street beyond.

"Mr Nousel?" The question was accompanied by a tentative knock.

"Mr James. Come in. I've been expecting you." There was relief in the voice, even perhaps eagerness that caused me again to hesitate. I pushed the street-map deep down into my pocket, and tightened my grip on a neatly furled newspaper. It was an instinctive gesture, as if the baton shaped paper might in some way serve as an explanation, or subliminal threat. The thought made me grin. I clutched it firmly and opened the door wide.

The room beyond was bathed in a golden light and belonged to a different age. It exuded careless opulence, shabby, scholarly even arcane. A large Persian rug almost hidden by books, strewn at random or arranged in towers like termite nests, seemed curiously dominated by a figure hunched expectantly in a chair too large for him. I stared at Mr Nousel's bone white face and the unnatural brass appendages that looked as if they were glued to his eyes.

A gentle cough prompted me to speak. "I was intrigued by your advert, sir."

"Ah, the *Beacon* – you will have come from Monmouth, then." Mr Nousel stared at the paper for a moment or two. He raised his head, until the two small brass cylinders were aimed directly at my face. Though highly polished, they looked strangely crude and yet imbued with the minute and subtle craftsmanship I had learnt to associate with the early eighteenth century, perhaps earlier. And then, to my unease, I became aware of Mr Nousel's eyes staring out from them, like a pair of large and blue exotic fish.

"Sit down, sit down." Mr Nousel gestured towards the fire as if suggesting immolation was just the thing on such a cold and blustery day. I edged round books that seemed to be teetering in stasis and dust; there was a sense of tracing time through a labyrinth, the unstable towers now resembling wind-torn buttes as they picked up the glow from the fire.

The chair faced my host, but was positioned closer to the hearth, forcing Mr Nousel to turn ever so slightly. The effect was off-putting. The brass eyepiece gleamed, and ruddy shadows flowed from his waxen face as if they didn't belong there. Eyes that had only a moment ago appeared as large cobalt fish had been replaced by two tiny red flickers, simulacra of the low burning fire.

Mr Nousel leant forward and smiled. "I am selling everything; everything," he repeated. "Books, everything in this room, the room itself, if that's what you want." He paused, his smile for a moment sardonic. "And these of course." He tapped the metallic appendages that covered his eyes. I wondered how easily they might be detached. "The Alchemical Lenses; John Dee's last and greatest secret."

I gazed absently across the finely panelled room, glancing once or twice at this or that pile of books, noticing, that for all its subtle richness, the room itself possessed only one tiny window, and that it looked out upon a yellow-brick wall, built only inches away. I kept my voice even, tried to restrain an almost overpowering sense of excitement.

"John Dee, you say." I looked with polite interest at the two cylinders that seemed to grow almost organically from Mr Nousel's head, and which were pointing at me now like two tiny brass cannons. "They look of later workmanship."

Mr Nousel nodded approvingly. "So, it *is* the lenses you are after." He sighed, a strange sound of relief and regret. "And your surmise is correct. They were fashioned some years after Dr Dee's death."

I leant back in my seat, demolishing an adjacent tower block and causing me to wonder whether all of them were attached to each other by a finely spun web of air, and whether very shortly they would all proceed to tumble like synchronised dominoes in a Japanese-run tournament. I raised an eyebrow in way of apology, but my host appeared not to have noticed. Cautiously I repositioned myself, trying once more to disguise any show of excitement.

Ten years or more of study, hunting down every antiquarian reference, every church-yard clue, the thread growing gradually stronger, the scent more intense, so that towards the end I was occasionally prone to the uncomfortable feeling that I was being reeled in; the predator become the eager fish. And now here they were, within arm's length, a mere grasp away. I wondered how much he wanted for them, and whether it would not be easier just to take them. Then I realised the old man was still talking.

"You see both Dee, and later Ashmole of course, believed in angels, faeries, the otherworld, call it what you will." Mr Nousel sighed. "Only much of Dee's work vanished in flame, and even more of his work perished by virtue of being buried... for safe-keeping"

"Sir Robert Cotton dug some of it up I believe."

"Some of it, sir, some of it." Mr Nousel chuckled. It was a grim sound. Like a mole briefly amused by a worm's repartee. "But you must remember, Mr James, that a mere breath of wind separated alchemy from sorcery, and for one you could be burnt."

"Hanged," The correction was gentle, reflexive. Mr Nousel seemed unperturbed. He waved a hand as if swatting a fly.

"Even so, the most secret part of his work was retrieved, as Dee intended, and was passed down and talked of – discreetly, amongst friends and those who followed similar trails. Ashmole knew of it as, too, did Newton – along with his colleague John Wickens."

I chose my words carefully. Don't give too much away. "I have heard of Wickens. He died, I believe, at Stoke Edith, a few miles or so north of Monmouth."

Mr Nousel nodded as if the news in no way surprised him. "Ah, the by-ways of Monmouthshire, a natural haunt of alchemists and recusants." He looked up sharply, his glasses twinkling in the light from the fire. "Men who strived to reach other and better worlds."

"As do we all," I said.

He looked at me and licked dry lips. "The magical tradition is powerful, though secretive, and it always exacts a price. Even Sir Isaac cavilled at that – in the end."

"Newton was a great explorer, he dabbled in alchemy, I know." I was finding it increasingly difficult to wrest my gaze far from Mr Nousel's bone-white face.

"Dabbled! Dabbled, you say." Mr Nousel leant further forward. "Sir Isaac Newton walked a very thin line, young man. On the one hand he ran the risk of offending the leading alchemists of his day; they were right to be suspicious of him, right to suspect that he would steal their credit. On the other hand he couldn't afford to offend religious conformity – nor the university authorities that patronised him."

"So what did he do?" And when do we get down to talking money? Impatience began to taint a natural interest in the lenses' provenance. I stared guilelessly at the old man, restraining the impulse to just reach out and wrench the alchemical eye-piece from his wretched face. No, no need for that; besides, I knew there were still secrets yet to be voiced; secrets perhaps as vital as the eye-piece itself.

"Newton realised that so long as he didn't actually publish the darker side of his research there would be little if any recrimination; but his experiments continued alongside more orthodox research in to such things as the nature of light." Nousel paused, as if somehow he had just given me a clue and was waiting for it to be taken up.

"So, when Newton would wax lyrical about how light could be manipulated into its various colours then made to converge back into its original whiteness…"

Nousel nodded. "He was also exploring the possibility of its opposite, something more than the mere absence of light."

"Black light, you mean?" It was the wildest of guesses, or else the room and its occupant was slowly, subtly re-configuring my mind. I wondered how much the old man already knew, or sensed about my intentions.

Mr Nousel smiled. "Black light, a nonsense in how we see things I know." He tapped his eye-piece, "but not impossible. You see, both he and Wickens speculated on the nature of the space that separated the colours; both of them believed there was more behind what our eyes allow us to see."

An image came suddenly into my mind, causing me to shudder. Something I had read at school. "He nearly blinded himself – Newton. I read that somewhere."

"On more than one occasion. Staring into the sun in search of perfect blackness." Nousel coughed as if he had just made a joke and was pleased with it. "In his notes he described it as a study in eye fatigue. Again, some time later he proceeded to press a bodkin deep between his eye and its bony cavity. Pressing it just behind the optic nerve and analysing the black and white circles he could create by varying the pressure. Curiosity, Mr James, and a peculiar sense of duty."

Mr Nousel spoke slowly, clearly sensing and enjoying my evident discomfort. "In the end, however, Newton found his fame in more orthodox pursuits. It was the incomparable Wickens who built upon the dreams of Ashmole; Wickens who explored the clues that Dr Dee had made obscure. John Wickens who manufactured these." He tapped the strange spectacles once more.

"And you would sell them – to me?"

Nousel sighed, again with that strange mixture of relief and regret. "Are you a dutiful man, Mr James." He didn't wait for an answer. "Come back tomorrow and we might agree a price."

I stared into the bone-white face and knew that I would. The face was expressionless, putting me in mind of a gambler saving his best card until last.

As I stood up to leave, I spotted the mirror behind me, just to the right of the door.

* * *

That night I dreamed of the mirror. I remember walking towards it, knowing that should I see my reflection, I might never wake up. To my relief the mirror was black; it reminded me of an oriel window looking out upon a starless night. As I walked closer, the mirror thickened into something gelatinous and black and I sensed in it the reptilian, the cold, unblinking stare of something on the other side. The feeling was so strong I imagined I saw it coiling towards me, and then the picture fragmented into the sinuous writhing of what looked like coffin worms. Only as I approached did I see that they were in fact women, white and naked and extending back into the mirror as far as the eye could see. They looked upon me with eyes that were both languorous and bold, and I wondered what further marvels lay beyond.

I returned early the next morning, a cheque neatly folded in my middle pocket, confident that come what may a transaction of one kind or another would take place; and then I wondered what Mr Nousel would do with the money.

The street seemed even more silent that morning; my footsteps a little louder. As I passed the various doors, I pictured a Mr Nousel, sitting patiently behind each one, all of them waiting to make a sale.

But Mr Nousel's door was open; even the seedy lion appeared to be smiling at me today. I stroked the tarnished knocker almost proprietarily and marched briskly up the grey wooden stairway.

"Ah, Mr James." The greeting was warm, the fire just a little warmer. As I walked in, I became aware on an intense fragrance like that of an orchid coming into bloom. And then I remembered the mirror. My glance was casual and brief, necessarily so, since most of my attention was focussed on manoeuvring past the random columns of books. I noticed that, as in my dream, it offered little in the way of reflection; the smell, too, seemed to be coming from that part of the room.

"Sit down; sit down."

The old man had cleared a pathway through the maze of books separating the two chairs: a sign perhaps that he, too, was eager to get down to business.

"I would like to buy it from you." I waved my arm carelessly across the littered study, trying to convey an air of the omnivorous collector. "Everything in fact."

"Even the mirror?"

"Especially the mirror." The answer seemed to come from nowhere, as if my mind somehow sensed more than it could shape into words. I remembered the dream and knew that both the mirror and the eyepiece were fundamentally linked. Even so, it had been a mistake to sound so eager.

Was I really prepared to pay more than was needed? Mr Nousel smiled, and I noticed that the two brass cylinders gleamed even more brightly than the day before, as if the old man had polished them especially for the occasion.

"It will not come cheap," Mr Nousel said, as if somehow guessing my thoughts. "None of it will; but let me tell you more, and then you can tell me whether you are still interested."

"You said that they were manufactured by Wickens and that he in turn was working on principles established by Dee." I paused, largely for effect. "And now you seem to be hinting that the eye-glass is somehow linked with the mirror standing behind me." I glanced round at the dense pool of blackness defined by a tall rectangular frame. "In any event I will make you richer than any man needs to be in order to have them both."

"Along with their history of course," said the old man imperturbably. "Or else you may be buying more, or less than you expected."

Curiosity helped curb my impatience. I was about to buy a secret, something that would shake reality into fragments. I wondered how and why it had been kept a secret for so long and why, now, the old man was about to sell it.

"You see," Mr, Nousel continued. "John Dee questioned what Newton would later seek. What else might be seen if light could be refracted through the Philosopher's Stone?"

"The Philosopher's Stone." The neutral tone failed to disguise my disappointment. He'd be talking about Dracula next, the Da Vinci Code, Harry Potter. I closed my eyes, examining the possibility that I had just crashed into yet another dead end. It was irrational I knew, to have pursued almost obsessively the workings of minds such as Ashmole, Wickens and Dee, and at the same time to hesitate over one of their central beliefs.

Mr Nousel chuckled. "I see the phrase creates doubt. The magic shatters about you; the power of words, eh."

The power of words indeed I thought, angry at my own irrationality. How many times had I argued that magic might contain answers to abstruse quantum puzzles? It was all a matter of words. Scientists conjectured extra dimensions but had as yet found none, for all their talk of high energy and short-distance observation. Words. Our reality was probably little more than a fluke, a tiny three-dimensional pocket inside a universe of infinite variants. And inside this room was the alchemical secret that would reveal what science couldn't. Believe it, believe. I believed and smiled, and thought of Tinker Bell, dying in an airless vase.

"Something amuses you."

"I'm sorry. Truth sometimes wears unfashionable clothes, I know."

"Words date, the truth does not – quite so." Mr Nousel leant forward. "And have you in your studies come across the 'Prospective Stone'?"

"I have heard of it."

"Only our old friend Elias Ashmole writes about it with great enthusiasm; great enthusiasm. Through it he believed it would be possible to discover any person—" Mr Nousel raised his face to the ceiling, giving me the distinct impression that his eyes were closed, and that he was quoting directly from pages seen only in his head. "—in any part of the world whatsoever, although never so secretly concealed or hid in chambers, closets or caverns of the earth. In a word, it fairly presents to your view even the whole world, wherein to behold, hear, or see your desire. And yet this I assure you is not in anyways necromantical or devilish; but easy, wondrous easy, natural and honest."

I regarded the optical device greedily. "The Prospective stone is incorporated in that?" I tried to make a joke. "Beats Google Earth, or anything the Americans have."

"Oh, it's more than that, Martin," Mr Nousel said gently. "It is much more than that." He raised his hands to his face as if about to take the device off, then thought better of it. He tapped it instead. "Here, light is refracted through *two* stones, subtly cut and layered in most ingenious ways. You will have heard, too, of the Angelical stone, Mr James, or else I suspect you would not be here now."

I nodded, content to be silent. The time for pretence was past. The wizard Dee had talked with angels, but he'd always wanted more, and here in this room was what he had striven for but never lived to see: entrance to their world.

"It is the stone that Wickens and Ashmole valued above anything else, and as I said, they discovered clues to its making in Dee's most secret writings."

"Only Ashmole died."

The bone-white face nodded. "But that unsung genius of the alchemical art, John Wickens continued the work, at first in collaboration with Newton then later alone in the obscurity of Stoke Edith." He tapped the eye-piece once more. "And here you have the two stones, translucent and layered, catching light and unseen worlds in the most subtle of prisms."

"The Angelical Stone," I whispered.

Nousel smiled, as if the two of us were just then sharing a glass of the world's finest wine. "Something that can be neither seen, felt or weighed; a thing less visible than air yet possessing great power—"

"—Affording sight of Angels... the power of conversing with them in dream and revelation. Yes, I have read of it. But the mirror – what about the mirror?"

"Ah, the mirror you will see soon enough, but as to what you will pay—"

"I will pay what you ask."

"You may change your mind."

Something in his tone made me uneasy. I remembered a circus, a five-year-old boy, and how a clown, hideously white and bald with black painted eyes had pushed his face close to my own and pushed out his tongue. I had screamed; I remember my father laughing.

Mr Nousel didn't laugh, but he frightened me more. "Wickens found something he shouldn't."

"The mirror..."

"Less a mirror than a window that can never be shut." Mr Nousel lowered his head as if the eye-piece had become suddenly heavy. "It is why he made these."

I turned, staring into the mirror I'd dreamed of that night.

"In it is magic, pure and evil. More than our world could hold." There was a curious longing in his voice as one already seduced.

"I don't understand."

"I am 'A Watcher' Mr James, as you will be. My eyes veil the window, engages the rift. It feeds on my mind, and is unaware of any world beyond."

"The finger in the dyke... but why?" I stared around the room, realising again how small it was.

"The mirror is addictive. What might occupy a world captures a mind. It quickly discovers what you most desire... and satisfies. And when there is nothing else there, it takes you."

"You want to be taken?"

"Oh, yes, I want to be taken."

"After a new 'Watcher' releases you..." I wondered how many there'd been. "You could just smash it."

"And create a hundred thousand windows." He smiled sadly. "Are you having second thoughts?"

Yes, yes, I wanted to run... and yet. "If you're so desperate," I nodded at the mirror. "Why sell it?"

"You mean give it away?" The smile turned sour "Sometimes I think it is the mirror that chooses... it senses the curious."

Mr Nousel pulled himself to his feet and brought his face closer. "But do you believe in duty, Martin? Duty. Do you believe in that?" Slowly he raised both hands to the gleaming brass, and even more slowly tugged, stretching unnaturally white skin until I half expected to see it tear free from the bone. There followed one final soft, reluctant squelch as the eye-glasses released their hold on long dead flesh.

For one horrible moment I didn't know whether to retch or scream. I turned, determined then to flee the room, but caught sight of the mirror and knew then I'd been caught.

"Mr James." The old man sounded as if he were in pain. His head was bowed and he held the magical artifice in both hands like a vassal to a king. "Take them before it's too late."

Too late – what did he mean? I hesitated, turning instinctively towards the door as the old man looked up. There was a whiff of corrupted flesh, a smell like that of very old meat. I glimpsed ruined eyes, thin, like tiny blue maggots wriggling frantically; things seeking the dark.

"What do you mean, before it's too late?"

"The lenses, they need a host." The old man spoke in short, measured gasps; he was staring at the mirror like a man about to jump from a very high building.

"And you think I want to pay its price?"

"Yes," he said, "I do. You have spent your life searching for this, Mr James. And now you have found it." Mr Nousel's voice softened. "Dee's Angelic Realms." He pushed the eyepiece closer to my face. "Your every desire satisfied. Take them. The price is what you are prepared to pay." His tone became intimate, like a salesman closing a deal. "Just try them, look into the mirror and then tell me you're not interested."

"You mean I can take them off as and when I please?"

"Oh yes, Mr James, as and when you please."

I took the eyepiece from him and brought it slowly up to my face. The polished brass retained a lingering smell of rotten meat, forcing me at once to hold it at some distance from my nose. It was as I was fishing out a handkerchief from an inside pocket that I heard a soft mewling sound. I looked up to see Mr Nousel slowly careering round the room, whimpering like a kitten in pain. Both hands were fixed to his head and he was shaking it slowly from side to side.

"Mr Nousel!" Books tumbled in ruined piles as the old man weaved his way clumsily towards the gloomy mirror. The thought came from nowhere. Smash it! Smash it! As for the eyepiece – I looked at the finely engineered brass in horror and disgust and felt my face convulse at the thought of what being a 'watcher' entailed. I reached for one of two paper weights resting on a small table; then looking up, froze.

The old man had reached the mirror, was touching its surface, was walking through, the blackness closing in around him like ink, or fine silk. I caught a glimpse of Nousel's half turned face, twisted in longing and lust, saw his lips move, "They're waiting for me," the syllables disappearing like bubbles in a pond. And then I heard a faint, high pitched scream – of ecstasy – or fear, followed by silence.

I leapt towards the dark mirror, causing books to crash in all directions. I hurled myself at it with force, confident that I too, would pass through into what lay behind. The glass should have shattered. Instead it held firm, and however hard I pushed and poked or prodded there seemed no evident entry through it into another more exotic world. However hard I stared, and from whatever angle, it offered nothing but the dimmest reflection, as if it had sucked up all the light in the room, and enough was enough.

Then I regarded the brass eyepiece. It dangled loosely in my hand, its gleam an enticing wink. I stared at it for a moment or two longer. A decade of research, obsessive at times, reduced to this: revulsion and temptation, fear and desire. The mirror looked back at me, as if somehow it knew what I would do.

Decision made, but not knowing whose it was, a fearsome thought possessed me. Even if I stopped the horror beyond would I in turn become part of it, my mind and soul consumed until like Nousel it snapped me up as a dry little fly? I wondered whether this was the fate of every 'Watcher'. Were we making it stronger, our sacrifices ultimately in vain?

My lips were dry as I made my way back to Nousel's chair; my legs warm jelly.

The mirror's smell had become more intense, filling the room with a perfume of rose and rotten meat, and its glass rippled then slowly bulged, as though the thing behind had sensed an open door.

I held the eye-piece firmly and raised it to my head.

FALLOUT

D.J. TYRER

"You are familiar, of course, with Operation Totem," stated C as Harms took the seat opposite.

The grey-suited agent nodded. "Indeed. I reviewed the security arrangements at Windscale where the plutonium for the tests was produced. They took place at a site code-named X200, otherwise known as Emu Field, under the supervision of Sir William Penney. A success, as I understand it."

"Good man. Those are the bald details. What has been kept under wraps, even from many involved in the project, is the unusual dispersal of the cloud. The plumes rose higher and were carried further than the boffins expected, due to unexpectedly high winds."

"So much for science," shrugged Harms, who had a low opinion of scientists and researchers.

"Not quite. We believe that the winds were not natural."

"The Soviets?" He had heard that they were indulging in weather manipulation.

"No. At least, we do not believe so. It is suspected that the test... disturbed something."

"Sir?"

"The site was picked by a pundit named Bresslaw, who had identified anomalies in the region. He passed his suspicions to Penney who agreed the detonations: regular munitions, initially, then nuclear weapons."

"I'm not sure I understand, sir."

"I am not sure I do, either, if I am being honest. What I do know is that, after the fallout, the Australians have ordered a halt to the detonations. Naturally, it has been decided to ignore their concerns and proceed in secret. Unfortunately, Professor Bresslaw has vanished and the higher-ups are in quite a tizzy about it all. They have demanded that I put my best man on it and, as he isn't available, I've decided to send you."

"Very droll, sir."

C slid a manila file across the desk. "You can read up on the professor, his colleagues and his disappearance on your flight to Australia. You leave immediately. And, no heroics..."

* * *

The file had certainly helped to pass the time during the flight, despite failing to elucidate anything about Bresslaw's curious disappearance. If one discounted his recent obsession with detonating a seemingly unimportant patch of desert, there was nothing odd about him. He was no turncoat, nor a Turing. In fact, if anything, he was too good to be true – sober, punctual, hardworking, happily married. The only blip on his record, very nearly half a century before, was a vague reference to some minor scandal in his undergraduate days that seemed unlikely to explain his going missing.

According to the report, Bresslaw had been involved in surveying the area and had flagged it as anomalous for reasons unexplained. He had been vocal in calling for the detonations and had helped oversee them. With the official moratorium on testing, he had been left behind with a skeletal staff at Emu Field to carry out a third and final nuclear explosion. However, according to reports from the site, he had begun to act erratically – sleepwalking, talking to himself, making errors in his calculations – for none of which any precedent existed. Then, finally, he had vanished. Which was what had brought Harms here, to this expanse of dry, flat clay and sandstone.

The long flight from England terminated at Darwin, in the north of the country, where a private plane had been chartered to carry him across the red, desert heart of the island-continent to the landing strip near Emu Field.

As the plane descended, he realised that the landing strip lay in what clearly had been a lake bed. He commented to the pilot on that.

"Yup," said the pilot in an accent that owed more to Yorkshire than the antipodes. Obviously, they were keeping the locals out of the loop entirely. "This entire area was rich with water, millennia ago. All gone. No idea if anyone knows why. All desert now."

Harms shrugged that away. He had long since learnt to put aside anything, no matter how interesting, that did not directly relate to his mission. Distraction had an unpleasant tendency to be a prelude to death in his line of work.

Something else he needed to put to one side was the fact that his welcoming committee, such as it was, consisted of an attractive blonde woman of about thirty wearing a practical, yet daring, pair of khaki shorts and matching jacket, sitting at the wheel of a pockmarked, sandy-coloured jeep.

"Agent Harms?" she asked, her voice rich with 'jolly hockey sticks', and he nodded. "My name is Doctor Haley, but you can call me Alison. If you hop in, I'll drive you back to our base camp."

As they drove away, she described how a freak windstorm had devastated their original base of operations and the village that had housed the workers prior to the test-field's official abandonment, forcing them to relocate to a series of tents and prefabs further south.

"It's all very peculiar," she finished. "There seems to be no reason for the high winds, yet the area is plagued with them."

"Artificial?" That was what C had said.

She shrugged. "Bresslaw thought so, and there's no other explanation I can think of. Are the Russians to blame? Is that why you are here?"

"We don't know, to be honest. Bresslaw's vanishing act has got the bigwigs in a hugger-mugger, so I'm here to see if I can find him, or what happened to him."

The camp was a ramshackle affair of tents and lean-to structures with a prefab building at its heart surmounted by a series of aerials.

"Here we are, I'll find you a tent."

He had never enjoyed sleeping under canvas. "Sounds great," he deadpanned. The still air of the camp was a miasma of stale sweat and field latrines – it was unpleasantly like being back in the army.

"Dump your stuff in here – we're pretty informal. I'm afraid we don't have too many home comforts, having been officially disbanded. Our resources have been directed towards the provision of fissionable material. I hope you enjoy beans and chips."

He didn't reply as they were being joined by the other personnel in the camp. There was an Indian in a dark Nehru suit, an old, large man with huge muttonchop whiskers and an unsuitable tweed outfit and no hat, a half-dozen engineers and a red-bearded man dressed in khaki shorts and toting a Sten gun.

She introduced him to them and vice versa. They, of course, had been informed that he would be coming and he, in turn, was familiar with each of them, having been furnished with their files. Redbeard was in charge of security – Andrew Ross by name, a veteran of the Long-Range Desert Group; it was Ross who had prepared the report on Bresslaw's disappearance. The man with the muttonchops was Professor Tolhurst, Bresslaw's deputy and, now, de facto head of the project. He appeared every inch the crusty old academic. The Indian went by the name of Doctor Krishna Nair. Harms had little respect for the people of the subcontinent, but, according to his file, the man was a genius, a world-renowned atomic expert who had advised Oppenheimer on the Manhattan Project. That raised certain questions about where his loyalties might lie.

"So, you're going to find ol' Bresslaw for us, eh?" boomed Tolhurst.

"That is correct, sir. I will need to speak to you all about him and what has been going on down here."

"It's all in my report," spat Ross.

"Yes, it is comprehensive." That was pure flattery. "But, I am sure you appreciate my need to go over everything myself. I will also need you to show me around the area. But, first, I really need something to drink and forty winks..."

* * *

Suitably rested, Harms started his investigation as the sun began to wane.

"Tea or beer, I'm afraid," Alison apologised as he joined them in the tent where one of the technicians was busy cooking-up a basic supper.

"The sacrifices we make for Queen and Country," he commented, accepting a bottle from her and taking a long pleasurable sip. "Once we've all eaten, I'll speak to you and your colleagues about the missing professor."

Although chips and beans were not what he favoured, the smell of them cooking did, at least, do something to conceal the unpleasant smell that clung to the camp, and his stomach was growling with anticipation at being filled at last.

"I don't know if anyone will be able to tell you anything useful," Alison replied swigging her own beer. "He was acting a bit odd before he vanished, but, mainly, was keeping to himself."

"Were you close?"

She blushed slightly, telling him more than her words would admit. "Fairly. He was like a father to me."

"How about the others?"

"You mean, did they get on alright with him? Sure, I guess. Mostly, he worked with Tolhurst. He and Doctor Nair were distant. He wasn't too friendly with Ross, thought he was ignorant and coarse."

"No problems?"

She shook her head. "Not that I can think of."

The other staff were beginning to drift in and the technician announced, "Chow's up."

Conversation was subdued, but Harms couldn't tell if it was just his presence that was to blame or something else, as there was tension in the still evening air. Perhaps it was the heat; even with the blazing sun finally dropping below the horizon, the ground was radiating the stored heat of the day and would continue to do so for some time, before succumbing to the chill of night.

He had just begun to ask questions about the missing professor when winds began to whip up after a day of utter stillness.

"A lovely breeze," he attempted to alleviate the tension, but the winds clearly had the others concerned. "Oh, come on, it's just a breeze!" he exclaimed at their panicked expressions.

"You didn't experience the winds that destroyed—" Alison started to say, only for the wind to whip the tent away from the ground so that it stood upright like a sail, flapping noisily.

Then, as suddenly as the winds had come, they were gone.

"What the hell was that?" he demanded as they fought their way out from underneath the fallen canvas.

"Your guess is as good as mine," spat Ross, his voice fragile with bravado.

"We do not know, young man," admitted Tolhurst, "but we believe that it is a force defending this place against us. It is what we are trying to destroy."

"Bresslaw knew," stated Alison.

"Drove him mad," agreed Tolhurst.

"A force?" Harms felt stupid for asking. "You mean it isn't a weapon?"

"Not of man," Krishna Nair told him, his face a mask. "Perhaps, not of this world."

"Really?"

The Indian responded with a slight smirk but said nothing.

As the technicians set about restoring the camp to order, he asked the professors to join him in a prefab building that now sagged alarmingly.

"I need you to tell me exactly what Bresslaw said, no matter how insignificant. Also, what is your plan now that he is gone?"

Tolhurst shrugged. "There was a strange rock formation on the shore of one of the dried-up lakes that dot the desert. Bresslaw seemed to... well, he seemed to think that it was some sort of city. He never said what he thought that it contained, but whatever he told Sir William Penney, they certainly took his claims seriously."

Nair steepled his fingers. "The Mahabharata and Ramayana speak of ancient civilisations – and, there are others, almost unrecorded, of even-greater antiquity. Do you know what Doctor Oppenheimer said to me when we watched the detonation of the first atomic bomb? He quoted to me the Bhagavad-Gita: 'If the radiance of a thousand suns were to burst at once into the sky, that would be like the splendour of the mighty one.' That was no mere poetic flourish, but a memory of a civilisation as great – greater than – the one that exists now, and which possessed destructive powers comparable to atomic weaponry."

"If you say so." Really, that just reconfirmed his low opinion of the man – educated, but still a mere step away from primitive superstition.

Nair's neutral expression seemed to twitch for a moment. "Oh, I know what you think of me – a savage in a suit. You forget that India was civilised and practising science whilst your precious Rome was but a handful of lowly huts and your ancestors grubbed for survival in untamed forests. The memories of the subcontinent are longer than most, Harms."

"So, what? Are you saying that Bresslaw had you bombing a primordial nuclear power?"

Nair gave the slightest of shrugs. "I merely remind you that æons of history have passed that, now, are unknown to man and that, here and there, remnants survive that might be stumbled upon by the ever-curious race of man."

"Right."

"Bresslaw certainly seems to have believed something like that," Tolhurst interjected, "and Penney seems to have believed whatever he had to say. Certainly far enough to hand him three atomic bombs."

"Oh, yes; you have one left?"

Alison nodded. "If the winds are anything to go by, the first two were unsuccessful. The city, or whatever, was levelled, but still they blow. One more try..."

"How?"

"The bombs," Tolhurst explained, "were delivered in a tower-mounting. As it would seem that they failed to penetrate into... well, whatever is down there, for the final detonation, we intend a subterranean blast – there are plenty of cave entrances to choose from."

"The problem," Alison added, "is the disruption that the winds cause, but we are finally just about ready..."

"Tomorrow or the day after," Nair confirmed.

"Well, you deal with that and I will look for Bresslaw." Harms wasn't sure how to take their speculations. He knew the Agency had files on some quite frankly bizarre cases, but such claims as these seemed to be castles built of smoke.

His statement was the cue for them to drift away to their beds. Alison was the last to leave.

"Bresslaw knew what he was doing," she told him.

Ignoring the challenge in her tone, he asked: "How did you come to be here?"

"You mean, what is a nice girl like me doing in a desert like this?"

"Something like that. You seem rather young to be a Doctor — what are you? Thirty?"

She laughed in reply. "You should know better than to ask a lady her age."

"Oh, I thought you were a Doctor?"

"Alright, I will give you that, Agent Harms. Add a few years to your guess and you would be right. I was something of a child prodigy and my uncle made sure I got a good education and every advantage that money could buy."

"Well, it obviously didn't go to waste. You wouldn't be here if you didn't know your subject."

"Oh, I am one of the best. But, Bresslaw, he *is* the best — and, he is the only one who understands what is really going on here. That is why we need him back."

"I'll do my best. Good night."

She was a distraction he could well do without.

* * *

There was something very wrong with the scene that lay before him. Vast towers like termite mounds of immense size rose above a lush green landscape of unfamiliar plant life from their place on the shore of an azure lake. Beyond them, twin suns bloomed into existence, casting the scene into stark silhouette, before descending, almost lazily, into the lake, plunging the scene into an impenetrable darkness.

* * *

Harms woke with a start. It was still dark and, now that the heat had dissipated, as chill as it had been in London. Unlike that which had consumed his bizarre dream, this darkness was not total: moonlight filtered around the canvas flaps of the tent to give his surroundings a numinous quality.

"You alright?" a voice asked him from just outside the entrance to his tent. Alison. She had put him in one beside hers. "I heard you shout."

"Bad dream."

Pulling the flap back, she stepped inside. "Me, too."

"Sorry?" he asked, sitting up.

"Bad dream. I had one, as well. That was why I was awake to hear you." She sat down on a folding stool.

"I think Nair's bluster got under my skin..."

"You dreamt of the towers and the two suns, didn't you?"

He didn't answer, just stared at her, then, finally, nodded.

"Bresslaw dreamed of them, too..." she left the rest of that thought unsaid, then added: "He called the city Alchera."

"Alchera?"

"An aboriginal term, I think. A place existing in dream."

"Have any others shared it?"

She shrugged. "I think so. Not all of them sleep too well, but nobody really wants to talk about it. We haven't really discussed any of it, not till you arrived. Too much like talking about madness – especially since Bresslaw..."

Harm nodded his understanding. "What causes it? Is it something in the air; something from the atom bombs?"

Alison shrugged again. "Could be. Could be the strain. The after-effects of an atomic blast is one of the things we have been studying here, in addition to our real mission."

"I suppose the awesome power of the atom is enough to give anyone nightmares."

"Well, there was another quote that Oppenheimer took from Hindu scripture."

"Really?"

"Yes, when he saw what he had wrought, he thought: 'I am become Death, the destroyer of worlds.' It is the power of Death that we wield, like children playing with a new toy..."

* * *

Harms watched Alison, her fellow scientists and most of the technicians depart in the direction of the lakebed aboard two jeeps, a half-ton truck and two flatbeds, one carrying the framework for the modified launch-tower and the other the bomb and detonation mechanism. He and Ross would be taking the third jeep and searching for the missing professor. Having learnt of Bresslaw's dreams, he had a suspicion that, in the grip of some madness, he had gone in search of the city of his dreams. With the inspiring formations largely obliterated by atomic fire, he had either just wandered off into the depths of the desert, searching fruitlessly, or else had made his way into the caves nearby. The former possibility offered little chance of them locating him prior to the detonation of the bomb, so they would take the latter option and hope that they could find him in time.

"Ready?" asked Ross, who had fetched the jeep. "Oh, and don't forget to wear a hat. There's one in the glove compartment, if you need it."

Harms had been given a safari suit accompanied by a wide-brimmed straw hat with a band of faux zebra-hide. He didn't like it – to him it seemed more like a film costume than a real outfit – but it was the best option available.

"Remember," Ross went on, after Harms had climbed aboard, "the detonation is timed for the mid afternoon and we need to do a perimeter search before hand, so we have to be back at the jeep by midday. Spend too long in the caves and we risk being blown to kingdom come."

"Right, let's get on."

* * *

The trip to the caves was uneventful, if bouncy and dusty. Rather than interfere with the placement of the bomb – Harms assuming that, if the professor was in the vicinity of the chosen cave, the others would detect him – they headed for a pit amongst the fractured bases of stone towers on the edge of the blast zone, broken but not obliterated. At this distance, Alison had assured him, his brief exposure to the radiation would not be too dangerous. He had smiled grimly at the 'too' – dangerous, just not 'too' dangerous. Nice. Give him a good, old-fashioned bullet with his name on it, rather than all this mumbo-jumbo of atoms and primordial cities.

With the help of Ross, he attached the rope to the jeep's towbar and lowered it into the darkness of the pit. A slight breeze made it twist like a serpent for a moment and he felt a chill run down his spine, despite the heat of the morning sun beating down on him. Then, all was silent and still.

"Here," said Ross, handing him a hard hat with a small electric lamp mounted on it, the word shattering the eerie silence and making him jump.

"Thanks. Make sure you keep an ear out for me – I might need you to haul me out of here in a hurry…"

"No worries. Just remember that we have a deadline – most literally, if you are hanging around when the bomb detonates…"

"Got it." Harms took a firm hold on the rope and swung himself over the lip of the deep chasm. Tilting his head downward, the wan beam of light failed to find the floor. He hoped he would have sufficient rope.

Finally, after what seemed an unpleasantly long scramble downwards, the rubble-strewn bottom of the pit came into view and he gratefully set his feet back onto a solid surface. He appeared to be in a circular cavern, partially buried under rubble, disturbingly like a basement level: he shied away from any thoughts that implied that what had stood there had been anything but a natural rock formation. About the only positive aspect of his descent was the cool air of the subterranean space compared to the heat of the desert.

Curious petroglyphs painted in long-faded yellow ochre were daubed upon the walls – triskelion-like symbols, abstract ones that put him mind of the caduceus; curious clusters of dots, five in number, like the points of a pentagram, that came in threes; strange troy-town-like swirls; handprints; and what might have been figures, like women in long yellow gowns. Clearly, the local aboriginal people had regarded the site as one of some importance and decorated it in some primitive rite. Yet, for reasons he could not place, the petroglyphs seemed to convey some deeper meaning than he would like to admit, and he turned away from them as quickly as he could in search of an exit.

Something with too many legs skittered across the floor past his feet.

He spotted a way out, partially collapsed, but still passable, and squeezed through it. Beyond the rubble fall, it opened up to a more usable width.

Having wandered through several more chambers and numerous twisting passageways, he was becoming more and more convinced of two things: firstly, that the site was not as natural as he had hoped, and that, secondly, he was not going to find the professor. Glancing down at his wrist watch, he decided that it would be prudent to return to the initial chamber before he became lost. Maybe he could look elsewhere quickly before abandoning the search altogether.

Turning, he thought, for just a moment, that he heard something moving in the darkness behind him. A soft breeze caressed his skin.

"Is there anybody there?" he called.

Silence.

Then, the slow rise of a wind down the corridor until it came like a scream, tugging wildly at him, then suddenly, it ceased and all was silent and still once more.

He stood for a moment, straining his hearing, fearful of what he might hear, yet nothing more happened and he cautiously made his way back towards his entry point.

"You down there?" he heard Ross's voice calling down to him.

"I'm here! Help me up!"

"What was that wind?" Ross asked as Harms was hauled out into the light. "It came screeching up out of there like a banshee out of hell!"

Harms shrugged. "I honestly have no idea. It whipped round me, then was gone..."

Gratefully, he seized a bottle of water offered by Ross and slurped it greedily down.

"I want to try another cave," he said, although he wasn't really keen.

"Well, we don't have long... There're some more a little way to the north of here that you could try. The wind sometimes blows there."

"Let's try them," he agreed, climbing aboard.

The other caves were in an area of high ground that afforded them a view of the lakebed and the circular region of vitrified ground that marked the centre of the atomic blast. If any rocky towers had stood there, the explosion had obliterated all trace of them. Those that had stood beyond the actual blast had been reduced to jagged fragments. He wondered how many millennia of erosion and earthquake they had survived only to be levelled by man. Had they stood there for millions of years as the continents crept slowly to their present positions? He found such thoughts almost inconceivable. Best to leave such ideas to the boffins and keep his focus on the here and now.

From their vantage point, they could make out figures in strange green rubber outfits moving about the blast site and operating a crane over a fissure in the glassy ground.

Ross fished a pair of binoculars out from under his seat and surveyed the scene.

"Looks like they have almost got the bomb deployed," he informed Harms. "Better hurry this up – we've got plenty of perimeter to cover."

"Sure." With the cave mouth he had chosen sloping gently down into the earth, entry would be pretty straightforward. It also raised the possibility that Professor Bresslaw had come this way.

Facing southward, the cave had received some of the nuclear flame, vitrifying the rock surface so that the beam of his helmet-mounted lantern reflected strangely across it and he found his feet slipping on the smooth surface.

Deeper within, the atomic scarring slowly faded to reveal more of the yellow ochre art. He wasn't sure if it was the chill of the cave or the nebulous unpleasantness of the images that caused him to shiver, but he was in half a mind to retreat to the baking surface when he spotted a prone figure lying half-propped up against the cave wall.

"Ross!" he called up. "I think I've found him – I need a hand with him!"

Bending to check, he confirmed that it was the professor and was surprised to see that he was breathing, albeit very shallowly. For the want of anything better to do, he rolled him into the Coma Position and waited for Ross to slip-slide his way down to join him.

"Yes, that's the professor," Ross confirmed. "Lucky for him he passed-out here in the cool – out there he would have been long dead. Still, he's probably dehydrated. Should we give him some water?"

"We can try... Help me to sit him up..."

Together, they raised him into a sitting position and pressed a water bottle to his lips. It seemed to have some effect as his eyes flickered slightly, but he didn't waken and they were forced to drag him up out to the jeep.

The rays of the sun, however, did have an effect: Professor Bresslaw lunged upward from where they were attempting to lay him in the back and he suddenly shrieked that the suns were burning him.

"Must be going ga-ga," commented Ross as they attempted to restrain the struggling man. "Better get him back to base."

Harms didn't reply, but the plural made him wonder if he was reliving the dream that he had shared.

Although speeding southward, they had to make a wide circle around the blast site. All the way, Harms was forced to hold the raving man down in the back seat to prevent him from jumping out. He was half-thankful, half-frustrated that he was unable to make much sense of Bresslaw's babbling. The references to plural suns, something about unholy winds and the word Alchera repeated over and over again like a mantra.

"Absolute nutter," Ross commented after one particularly harsh bump threw them all around and sent the professor into new heights of wailing.

"Try to get us there in one piece!"

Eventually, the ride came to an end as they drew up outside the camp's first aid tent. Between them, they manhandled Bresslaw inside and laid him upon a field cot before Ross took the jeep to patrol the perimeter and ensure that nobody had wandered into the danger area.

The professor seemed to have grown calm since their return and Harms left him in the care of one of the remaining technicians whilst he set off in search of something to eat and drink.

* * *

The team who had been installing the bomb returned shortly after and he noticed that they had returned with one less jeep and one man carried upon a makeshift stretcher.

"What happened to you?" Harms asked, walking over to intercept Alison and hand her a beer.

"Oh, there you are," she exclaimed, taking the beer and pausing to savour a long draught. "A... freak wind overturned one of the jeeps. It also wrecked the launch tower we built over the cave entrance, but we replaced it without too much difficulty." She sank onto a nearby crate with a sigh. "The detonation should occur in..." she checked her watch, "... half an hour."

"I've got some good news: I found Bresslaw."

"You found him? Where? Where is he?"

"Yes, in a cave to the north of the blast zone. He's in the first aid tent, if you want to see him."

Even before he had finished speaking, she was on her feet and rushing to see her mentor.

The moment she entered the first aid tent, Bresslaw began to rant again: "There are dragons in the earth, Alison! Horrific beasts that drive their unholy winds before them! They came from the stars – down – down – down to Earth! They were bound, but never defeated – not even by the twin suns that blossomed above Alchera and turned the lake to dust! Alchera was their home and they rise again to claim it! Not even the cleansing fire can cleanse their taint! They shall rise again!" Then he sank back onto the bed, eyelids drooping and panting heavily.

"Wow! That is far more coherent than he was when we found him!" Harms exclaimed.

"He was probably severely dehydrated," she observed, pausing to check his pulse and examine him. "To be honest, I'm surprised he looks this well..."

"He was down in a cave."

"Ah, cool and dark."

"Uhuh. I didn't realise your doctorate was in medicine."

"Very funny. I did my bit during the war, as a nurse, out in north Africa – I could tell you stories that would make Emu Field seem like The Strand – before I returned to complete my studies. I know my way around a bed pan, I assure you," she added with a grin.

"So, what do you think of Bresslaw's ramblings? He kept repeating Alchera over and over on our way back here."

Alison shrugged. "Alchera is clearly the... city or whatever it was. He seems to be saying it was built by little green men from Mars." He could hear in her voice a false bravado, that she was desperately trying to mask her uncertainty with jokes. He could imagine that this was what had been inculcated in her from an early age, the hallmark of their class: stiff upper lip and a wry sense of humour would see you through anything from the Blitz to The Bomb.

"Not so much little green men... more monsters, like something out of that film, what was it called? *The Thing From Another World*, or out of a horrible myth."

"Does that make me the damsel in distress?"

"I hope not – I don't know how to slay a dragon!"

That lessened the tension a little.

"I don't know," he went on, after a pause. "This Alchera term has me thinking. You said it was a place in a dream...?"

"Something like that. Do you know anything about the Aborigines and their myths?"

He shook his head. "I can't say I know too much about our myths, King Arthur and the like, let alone anyone else's..."

"I've read a little about them and he," she nodded at her mentor, "told me more – he is an avid amateur anthropologist. Fascinating." He wasn't sure if she meant Bresslaw or the myths. "They believe in a sort of dream reality in which myths play out repeatedly, forever renewing the world. I think Alchera is a term for that reality or a place within it."

He nodded. "So, it is possible that he is not, actually, talking about the physical world, but something that exists in a dream state, something not quite real, or, at least, not outside our dreams."

She held up her hand, almost as if she were in class, seeking permission to speak. He paused and nodded.

"As I said, the Aborigines speak of the events in the dream world as repeating again and again for infinity, with no beginning and no end."

"You've lost me."

"I mean – they don't just think that their legends happened in the distant past, they think they are still happening now. It is as if we thought King Arthur was still actively seeking out the Grail somewhere right now."

"Right, I follow that, but I'm not sure I see where you are going with it."

"Neither am I, if I'm honest. I suppose what I am saying is that whatever happened here in the past is still happening in some sense."

"In our dreams?"

"Perhaps. Maybe what we dreamt is like a film playing over and over again. Perhaps even our presence here is just playing out something that has happened before…"

"Very astute, Doctor Haley," interrupted a familiar voice. It was Professor Nair. Harms was surprised to notice that Doctor Bresslaw seemed to shudder at the sound of the man's voice. "In India, it is believed that time is, indeed, cyclic, repeating through a series of ages. The exact details of events that occur will, of course, be different but, it is thought, the overarching trends during the course of history are ever the same. When the stars are right, the gods will awaken to walk the world, and, at other times, they are absent, the wheel of time ever turning, alternating between the two conditions."

"Um, right, thank you…" Harms wasn't certain how to take that, beyond feeling slightly unnerved by his words.

"As you say," Nair continued, "it seems likely that, once, atomic weapons were used here – and, now, we are repeating what was done before."

"So, how does the story end?" Alison asked.

"It does not end – it repeats forever."

"For us, I meant."

"Oh, only time will tell…"

* * *

It was time. Any moment now, the bomb would detonate. Aside from Bresslaw, who was still lying, semi-conscious in the first aid tent, everyone at Emu was gathered on the northern side of the camp, waiting to view the explosion.

Harms had asked if it was safe as Alison handed him a bulky pair of goggles.

"Yes. We are outside the blast radius – you might feel a little warm and there will be a shockwave that will stagger you slightly, but nothing worse than that. The flash will dazzle you for a few minutes, but there is no permanent damage at this distance. The goggles will protect your eyes from any dust and the radiation. The fallout from the blast – that is the dust and the debris – should fall to the north-east of the blast site, so we will be safe. It is the fallout that carries the real danger at this distance – breathe it in and who knows what damage it might do. I sure don't – we are still studying the effects..."

"Well, I hope you are right about the rest of it."

"Heh, so do I! I suppose you could say that it is a case of 'live and learn', but, really, if we get this wrong, it is more of a case of 'die and someone else learns'..."

"Thank you for the reassuring thought..."

"Right. Any moment now..."

"And if it doesn't work?"

"Well, eventually, somebody gets the short straw and has to take a stroll into the blast zone and see what went wrong... Not a popular task, as I am sure you can guess!"

"Like picking up a dud grenade only to discover it isn't a dud?"

"Exactly, except this does more than take your arm off..."

"Detonation in T-minus ten," called Professor Tolhurst.

"Here we go," nodded Alison.

"Nine.

"Eight.

"Seven.

"Six.

"Five."

"Behold the glory," said Nair.

"Three."

"Of the soul—"

"One."

"—of the Universe."

A blinding flash suddenly seared across Harms' vision and, for a moment, he panicked that Alison had been wrong about the effects only being temporary, but, then, he saw the rising mushroom-like plume of cloud on the horizon. It was an awe-inspiring, if horrendous sight to behold. Harms had seen more than his fair share of death and destruction, but being this close to an atomic explosion was unlike anything he had experienced.

"Beautiful," he heard Doctor Nair murmur as he gazed at the plume in rapture. Harms was not sure whether he could disagree with the sentiment; the cloud did have a certain, terrifying beauty to it...

Then, he heard the gasps and realised that something had gone wrong.

Even to his untutored eye, it was clear that the cloud was not holding the usual mushroom shape that had become a symbol to millions. It was beginning to blur on its edges, lose its definition, as if it were being shredded by a powerful wind. A ribbon of swirling ash seemed to be forming about the main column as if something were dragging the rising dust and smoke in its wake. Although a little like a tornado in form, it reminded Harms of nothing so much as the caduceus-like glyphs he had seen in the caves. The words of Professor Bresslaw stirred in the back of his mind as the serpentine nature of the coiling ribbon of ash put him in mind of a dragon, as if some primordial beast had been awakened by the blast and taken flight in a rage.

"Do you see that?" Alison whispered, dumbfounded.

He just nodded, staring at the roiling column. For reasons he could not quite grasp, he felt that the glyph-like form of the cloud was not some random quirk, but held some terrifying deeper meaning. He was glad he could not quite grasp it.

"The doom of Alchera falls upon us!" Bresslaw cried, emerging to join them.

"Oh, get him inside," snapped Ross at one of the technicians, who seized the babbling professor and hustled him back inside the tent.

But, the distraction was only momentary – the cloud had ceased climbing upwards and had begun to surge outwards, collapsing into a fast-moving dark wall that was coming their way.

"Cover your faces!" he heard Tolhurst shout, his voice rich with panic, but barely audible over the approaching roar. From what Alison had told him earlier, he understood the danger that the fallout posed.

"This can't be happening!" He only heard Alison's cry because she was right beside him, practically shouting in his ear. The roar was growing louder.

He felt Alison grab onto his arm and pull him towards the nearest tent, seeking what little cover was available.

Looking back as they reached the tent flap, he thought he could see *things* writhing in the approaching darkness, half-seen and ephemeral, yet horrible. Ross was standing at the edge of the camp, yelling his defiance at the storm and firing wildly into the cloud with his Sten gun; he disappeared a moment later as the cloud enveloped the camp. Suddenly, they were inside the tent, the canvas proving a flimsy shield, smoke and dust bursting in behind them. Grabbing a sheet from the nearest bed, Harms thrust it over his face and just prayed that it would soon end.

It didn't; it seemed to keep going on and on, dust pouring in as if they were caught in a sand storm. Terrible winds howled around them and tore at the tent, stripping away at what little cover they possessed, exposing them to the gale raging through the camp.

Grimly, desperately, he and Alison clung to one another as the wind tugged at them, eyes closed, their breaths seeming to be sucked from their lungs, leaving them gasping. They could hear nothing, the noise having overwhelmed their senses until it was almost as if they were in an empty void, only the touch they shared providing any reference point.

Finally, it was all too much and they lost consciousness.

* * *

Slowly, Harms' eyes flickered open. For a moment, he was disorientated, his goggles caked with black ash, but he wiped them clean and looked around himself. He was lying amidst the scattered wreckage of the camp and six inches of dust. As his memory returned, he glanced around for Alison. There was a figure sprawled nearby, but he wasn't sure if it was her at first glance due to the all-covering ash that coated faces and clothing with heavy layers.

He called her name and the figure shifted, lethargically.

Crawling over, he saw that it was her and helped her to sit up and wipe off the worst of the muck. He was coughing, but, as soon as she sat up, Alison began to hack and retch, spewing copious amounts of blackened phlegm.

"Oh, damn," she managed to gasp between torturous coughs, "this isn't good..."

They had each breathed in quite a bit of the fallout and they had also sustained numerous cuts and scratches into which it had worked its way. He had no idea how bad it was – he was not even certain anyone really knew – but, he was sure that it was not good.

A short distance away, Harms spotted a series of impressions in the deposited layer of ash, clusters of five circular indentations grouped in trios that were disturbingly similar to some of the odd markings he had seen down in the caves and gave the unpleasant impression that some sort of tripod device had touched down in the aftermath of the rampaging windstorm. A sudden surge of panic rose in him and, in a moment of madness, he obliterated all trace of the strange indentations so that he need not consider the unpleasant implications of their presence.

Coughing again, Alison whined: "There were *things* in the darkness..."

He didn't answer. He didn't want to recall the destruction that had overtaken them. A cursory examination of the area showed no signs of life, merely a collection of mangled bodies, lifeless and broken. Why they had survived, he had no idea, but he wondered whether their days were numbered. Had they been left alive as a cruel joke just to die later, or was their survival down to some mere quirk of fate or accidental oversight?

* * *

"Another G & T?" he asked, raising himself on one elbow. Alison rolled over to face him. One side of her was caked, but, this time, with silvery sand.

"No thank you," she smiled, and leaned in at him and planted a kiss on his lips. Their brush was pleasurable and well worth it as a reward for all he had been through with her.

The pilot had flown in the next morning and evacuated them. Doubtless, a clean up team had been dispatched to recover the bodies and equipment abandoned there. Besides them, nobody had survived. Of Professor Nair, there was no sign, but they held out no hope of finding him alive.

Harms had faithfully put everything in his report to C, no matter how outlandish or disconnected it might have seemed written down in black and white. He would vouch no knowledge of what they had encountered. Was it real, or was it a dream? Or, was it something in-between the two? Whatever it was, it had wrought a most devastating destruction upon them. He would leave all that to C and his boffins. He had no desire to relive the nightmare.

Allowed leave, he had taken Alison to enjoy one of Australia's fine beaches. It had taken them a couple of weeks, but they could almost imagine that none of it had happened – if only the dreams of strange towers and twin suns descending into a lake would not disturb their sleep.

"I think I'll have another," he told her, gesturing to the waiter serving their section of the shining sands. Sufficient drink helped to block the memories and numb his concerns for their future – the battery of tests they had been subjected to subsequent to their evacuation having yet to produce any information for them. As to whether the explosion had been successful, that, too, was for the boffins to ascertain, but he had his doubts. That a remote mining town was reported devastated by a freak windstorm, he did not wish to ponder. He had done what he had been sent to do and, now, he wished nothing more than to wash his hands of it.

"I love you," Alison told him.

He grinned back at her. "And, I love you, too." He had a feeling that they could have a fine future together. If they had a future. Maybe he would retire from the service.

"Here you are, sir," said the waiter, handing him his drink.

Harms savoured the beautiful view as he took a sip. Life was good. Behind him, the trees rustled in the breeze. The waves were being whipped up by the wind and a beach umbrella tumbled across the sand into the water.

"Wind's picking up," the waiter observed, walking away.

DREAMLANDS DETECTIVE

CARDINAL COX

Back when alive I was a private eye

Then somehow into the Dreamlands I fell

Some dog-headed ghouls would not let me lie

So inducted me into this weird hell

I have chased cat burglars in Ulthar and

Solved the theft of Kuranes' moonbeam crown

Back street gnolls have felt the weight of my hand

Men of Leng still whisper of my renown

New case though into which I've stuck my snout

All started when I found Mnar's grey stones

My ability I've started to doubt

This gives me a strange feeling in my bones

The clues all point to something very wrong

Makes me feel as though I do not belong

Some doozy of a dame knocked on my door

Needed a guy – Randolph Carter by name

All a distraction but what was it for?

I hate being a pawn in someone's game

The Sarnath Shantak – mentioned by a snitch

A strange statue that was lost for ages

This ju-ju was all making my fur itch

Like I'm ink on someone else's pages

Back-room hop-joints – wharves of the Endless Sea

Got to walk hot Illarnek's dusty roads

Searching for clues wherever they might be

Word was I was target of the men-toads

This was all trouble, and I was in deep

Could see it would lead straight to the big sleep

I'm caught in the court of the chartreuse king

Help for their pleasure – guess what that might be

Offers a deal, don't want me to sing

Got to do a job before I am free

"Take a scroll to Kadath", oh, is that all

Only gods get to go to that far place

"Yeah, well, you're part dog, so got to play ball"

Says the royal with a mask for a face

So I swaps the scroll for something with runes

When they cast their spell it's under their throne

Give gatekeeper paper – night without moon

Demon turns up – I hear a distant groan

No telling how many times I can die

Back when alive I was a private eye

EXILE IN EXTREMIS

PAULA D. ASHE

From: DDennis@reviledmag.com "David Dennis"
To: ELLE@abyssus.net "ELLE Unknown"
Subject: Re: Priest of Breathing Piece
Date: 9.25.XX at 9:13am

I'm gonna skip any and all pleasantries since the police are getting involved. Jesus. Who knew a weird little story about grave-robber barons of suburbia would turn into a fucking manhunt for Cay Castleton III? I won't insult you by asking again if the story's true; our fact-checkers verified everything a week before the story went live. I think I'm just writing that out again to make myself feel better. I guess when I imagined some creep paying another creep to 'resurrect' his dead wife, I just figured it was some anonymous nobody. Not the heir apparent to the Castleton empire. Like, what the actual fuck is happening in this town? How'd you even come up with the idea for this story?

Anyway, it's nothing too serious at this point, just thinly veiled threats about subpoenas and warrants and other shit. Since I have no 'identifying information,' about you other than your email address and Venmo account, you shouldn't be bothered. I just wanted to give you a head's up since they're asking a lot of questions about you and your sources. I shouldn't mention this but I'm sort of freaking out.

Dave

David Dennis
Managing Editor
Reviled Magazine

From: ELLE@abyssus.net "ELLE Unknown"
To: DDennis@reviledmag.com "David Dennis"
Subject: Re: Re: Priest of Breathing Piece
Date: 9.25.XX at 11:22am

David,

Thank you for your message. Feel free to share the audio files and/or transcripts of my interviews should the police request them.

As to your question, I ply my trade in revealing the depraved. Nothing surprises me anymore, especially when it involves sex and conservative politicians. I did a piece for another underground publication a few years ago about a (male) state senator (a real Family Values type) who was found dead beneath a (male) putrefying corpse. The kicker? The corpse was tumescent inside the senator. EMTs had to... separate them. The rumors spanned everything from True Detective-like occult conspiracies to an underground market in cadavers for closet cases ('no homo' if the other dude is dead, right?). To this day – I monitor the outcomes of every story I write – nobody has yet provided a solid explanation about how a carcass managed to get inside the senator's estate, bedroom, bed, and body. Real-life rapist zombies sounds like just the sort of story *Reviled* readers would love, does it not? Sadly, my connection to that story is no longer speaking to me.

As for answers, I have none. None that would make reasonable sense, anyway. I wanted to find out more about the spate of break-ins at St Julian's Cemetery. I initially presumed some impoverished junkies were bribing their security staff. When I realized all the break-ins were at mausoleums, and the bodies themselves (three at that point) were gone, I had to use some unorthodox methods to track down the sorts of people who would be in the 'female corpse recirculation' racket. It should not surprise you that there are many. What caught my attention was that the people responsible for the abductions were formerly betrothed to the remains. They did nothing to hide their tracks, aside from paying in cash, which is also traceable if one has the necessary skillset to do so. Thankfully (I suppose?) my methods are the kind that law enforcement have no mind or use for, so I am not concerned there. In fact, Cay Castleton Cubed has only been mentioned in the comment threads of the article and the police have been rousting those folks ever since. It is not their fault that Castleton's tragically deceased ladylove was found decomposing in a squalid flat in Kedger's Point, propped up in their nuptial bed with glistening cat entrails dangling from her Botox-injected lips.

You and your publication are fine. Do not let the police scare you with their bluster. I can assure you, there are far worse things in the world, in our own backyards even, than bureaucrats with badges.

There is someone in our city called the 'Priest of Breathing' who is somehow convincing otherwise rational people he alone can revive their loved ones from the dead. If it is any consolation, I have not slept much since penning this story.

ELLE

From: SLim@reviledmag.com "Scott Lim"
To: ELLE@abyssus.net "ELLE Unknown"
CC: DDennis@reviledmag.com "David Dennis"
Subject: Police Investigation Protocol
Date: 9.25.XX at 1:13pm

Hello Elle,

I'm Scott Lim, President and CEO of Reviled Media. Your story, " 'Til Death': Inside the Real-Life Resurrection Cult in Anchorite City," has become quite the viral sensation! I wanted to touch base with you to establish a protocol for the police investigation that has resulted in light of the publication of your article. As you know, all contracted journalists sign a waiver indicating should a police investigation arise as result of their work, they will cooperate fully with any and all law enforcement in perpetuity. After 31 days online, we're at 212M views and counting. Reviled mag's V=R (views equal revenues) platform means that you've been receiving significant payouts for your article, and we wish you your continued success.

As a friendly reminder, the contract you digitally signed also states that in order to continue receiving those payments, you must remain in good standing with our company and in order to remain in good standing, you will cooperate with any criminal or civil investigation that results from the publication of your work. I understand that the nature of your story is such that the anonyminty of your sources is critical, but remember that you are representing not just your integrity, but the integrity of the Reviled Media Network. I'd be happy to discuss this matter farther at a mutually agreed-upon time. My personal cell number is XXX-XXX-XXXX.

Sincerely,
Scotty

Scott Lim
President and CEO
Reviled Media Networks

From: ELLE@abyssus.net "ELLE Unknown"
To: DDennis@reviledmag.com "David Dennis"
Subject: FW: Police Investigation Protocol
Date: 9.26.XX at 09:18pm

Your boss is a real asshole. Does he not use spellcheck? Is he a grown man? Is he really your boss?

ELLE

PS. I heard they found Buster Brown trying to book a private, one-way flight to Toronto. I love that he's too sophisticated to hoof it down to Mexico like a respectable American criminal. I also heard that he was a real mess. He has apparently been self-mutilating; slashes all over his body, even his face. That sound like the normal behavior of a newly married millionaire to you?

From: DaVeD@abyssus.net
To: ELLE@abyssus.net "ELLE Unknown"
Subject: Asshole Scott
Date: 9.27.XX at 10:20pm

Elle,

That's not even the worst of it. He doesn't use spellcheck because he watched a FredTalk called "Spellcheck is for Pussies." He forwarded it to all the magazine staff like we a) give a shit and b) would agree with such an assessment. The video instead suggested you get a woman to read your work and correct it for you, because "that's just one small way for men to re-assert their dominance in this backwards feminist era." Tip of the shit iceberg. And if you're wondering, yes, he's named in several sexual harassment lawsuits.

Anyway, I got an Abyssus account because I wanted to talk to you more without leaving a trail at work. Since they caught Buster Brown (full disclosure: I had to look that reference up, and no, I didn't hear about Cay being all cut up – how did you know about it and that he did it to himself?) things have calmed down a lot. Now we're debating if we should run what promises to be a sterling piece of journalism called, "Around the World in Eighty BJ's." You can guess who is in full support of it and will likely accept it, despite my many misgivings.

I'll be in touch.

Dave

From: DaVeD@abyssus.net
To: ELLE@abyssus.net "ELLE Unknown"
Subject: Re: Asshole Scott
Date: 9.28.XX at 12:34am

How did you know Kelsey Castleton was eating cat entrails? I can't stop thinking about that. You made that up right? Cause you don't like her or Cay or something? I've read like fifty-seven (no exaggeration) different news reports about the recovery of her body and nothing mentions that. Again, you don't have to disclose your sources but... the fuck, dude. I also read (on /r/AnchoriteCity) that she had drugs in her system that weren't there for the first autopsy. At first I thought it was odd that she had an autopsy but I guess when you're twenty-seven and in perfect health and keel over out of nowhere from heart failure, people ask questions. And then, if after all that you show up in some shithole tenement building looking for all the world like you've been alive or animated or some shit for the last month, people gotta find answers somewhere, right?

Dave

From: DaVeD@abyssus.net
To: ELLE@abyssus.net "ELLE Unknown"
Subject: Re: Re: Asshole Scott
Date: 9.28.XX at 2:46am

Leni Verlis and Rachelle Emerson also died of 'natural causes,' at thirty one and thirty four, respectively. All married within the last year to some scumbag golden boy. Martin Verlis and Rich Emerson made their millions on Wall Street, but Leni and Rachelle's ties ran deep here. I went to high school with Rachelle, she was a year ahead of me. She was homecoming queen. I heard she skipped two grades in middle school. We weren't friends or anything, but I knew her. In your article you mentioned that Leni's family owned a lot of real estate around here, and they do, but her mom personally ran that little Turkish café downtown. So I knew her, too. I tried to go in there this past weekend but it's still closed. Sucks, it was one of my favorite spots to hangout. Leni and her family weren't just like, dickbag gentrifiers preying on the poor. They meant a lot to a lot of people. I'm guessing you're not from around here originally, but people in the AC don't have much to be proud of. We're just a shitty little crime-ridden city at the edge of Cleveland with a high rate of sex trafficking and methamphetamine addiction. This place sucks. But we were proud of those girls. I really wish I'd pulled your story.

From: DaVeD@abyssus.net
To: ELLE@abyssus.net "ELLE Unknown"
Subject: Re: Re: Asshole Scott
Date: 9.28.XX at 4:12am

I'm trying to say that these were real people and shit like this just doesn't happen to real people. maybe I'm a 'normie' ('normy?'), but this is just some super fucked up shit and it's making me super uncomfortable. I appreciate your kind words in your previous message about being afraid of this 'Priest of Breathing' person, but I'm really starting to wonder about your 'methods' and your angle. you came highly recommended. Your clips were impeccable. How do you know shit cops don't even know?

From: ELLE@abyssus.net "ELLE Unknown"
To: DaVeD@abyssus.net
Subject: Re: Re: Re: Asshole Scott
Date: 9.28.XX at 4:32am

David,

Get some sleep. Stop while you're ahead. You don't want any part of this. Trust me.

ELLE

From: DaVeD@abyssus.net
To: ELLE@abyssus.net "ELLE Unknown"
Subject: Re: Re: Re: Re: Asshole Scott
Date: 9.28.XX at 7:39am

I can't sleep. Please just tell me what you know. I knew Rachelle. I wrote her a poem. I liked her. She wasn't into me but she wasn't a bitch about it like most girls are. I just want to know if someone hurt her. Like before she died.

From: ELLE@abyssus.net "ELLE Unknown"
To: DaVeD@abyssus.net
Subject: Re: Re: Re: Re: Re: Asshole Scott
Date: 9.28.XX at 5:49pm

David,

You have to get yourself together. If someone did hurt her before she died, what exactly are you of all people going to do about it? That is what I have been trying to tell you. Perhaps I have been too oblique so let me make it clear: stay the fuck away from this story. Stay the fuck away from Kedger's Point. And stay the fuck away from me.

ELLE

From: ELLE@abyssus.net "ELLE Unknown"
To: DaVeD@abyssus.net
Subject: A Compromise
Date: 9.30.XX at 8:02am

David,

You seem like a stupid, impetuous person and since I have not heard anything from you in two days I would like to present you with an offer: I will tell you everything I know (sans sources) if you promise to stay away from this story. I will tell you what (as far as I understand) happened to Kelsey Castleton, Leni Verlis, and Rachelle Emerson. You have to promise me that you will not try to follow up on this. I hate to do this but as insurance, if you attempt to further investigate any aspect of this story, I will let everyone at Reviled Mag, the Anchorite College alumni association, your parents (Steven Dennis SSN XX2-8X-90XX, Maureen Dennis SSN XX5-3X-27XX), brother (Christopher Dennis-Harland SSN XX9-5X-55XX), brother-in-law (Jon Dennis-

Harland SSN XX1-4X-04XX), and the entire internet, see the video I recorded via your webcam of you... vigorously watching hair porn on September 26th from 11:31pm to 11:43pm. I do not want to do this. I really don't. But I do not know any other way to keep you safe. I can defend myself in so many ways, but you can't even be bothered to put a piece of tape over your webcam while jerking off.

Obviously, I did not know that you personally knew any of the women involved. And I apparently cannot help but drop a juicy little detail whenever I get the chance. It is a problem. If we had had this conversation via your work's email account, I could have just deleted our correspondence remotely. Abyssus is impenetrable, so I am fucked. And it isn't like you'll just forget anyway. Look just please respond as soon as you get this message. I'm sure you'll be upset but I am doing this to protect you.

I don't know why either.

ELLE

PS. I am including an excerpt of the video (just fifteen seconds) so you'll know I am serious.

Attachments: DaveDMovie.mov

From: DaVeD@abyssus.net
To: ELLE@abyssus.net "ELLE Unknown"
Subject: Re: A Compromise
Date: 9.30.XX at 8:12am

You crazy hacker baitch. What the fuck? Delete that shit now or I'll call the police. You're harrassing me. Fuck!

Fuck. Fuck. Okay, I won't do anything else. Please. Please don't show that to anyone. Fuck.

Fuck I'm not even at work yet. Fuck. Please don't show that to anyone. I went to Kedger's Point this weekend. I saw some scary shit. Please don't show that video to anyone. PLEASE! We can talk if you want. I will tell you what I saw.

Please. Please. Please don't show that to anyone.

Dave

From: ELLE@abyssus.net "ELLE Unknown"
To: DaVeD@abyssus.net
Subject: Re: Re: A Compromise
Date: 9.30.XX at 9:12am

David,

I think you are the dumbest person I have ever not met. What the fuck do you mean, you "went to Kedger's Point?" Are you insane?

You're off work by 6pm, right? Download the WHOSAT app to your pc (NOT YOUR PHONE) as soon as you get home. Create an account with your Abyssus email address. At 7:30pm you'll receive a message.

ELLE

WHOSAT Application v4.5
BEGIN CHAT TRANSCRIPT
September 30th, 20XX 7:30pm – 9:12pm

ELLE: Hey.

DaVeD: Yeah hi.

DaVeD: What the fuck, Elle.

ELLE: I know. I'm trying to protect you. I was, at least.

DaVeD: Thanks. I can't believe you recorded me.

ELLE: I can't believe you leave that camera wide open on your computer. Left. Good on you for finally taping it shut.

DaVeD: Jesus, did you just check again? You know what, I don't even want to know. Fuck.

ELLE: Tell me what happened at Kedger's Point.

DaVeD: Tell me what happened to Rachelle.

ELLE: You aren't in much position to tell me what to do, David. Not to be a dick about it, but... c'mon man.

DaVeD: I don't even care about the video anymore. I just want to know what happened to her. Maybe it'll help me make sense of the fucked up shit I saw. Maybe.

ELLE: WHAT DID YOU SEE?

DaVeD: Why haven't you been out there? Seen it for yourself, Little Miss Hacker?

ELLE: Because I'm not a fucking idiot. That place... isn't safe. To put it mildly.

DaVeD: That's true. I saw... do you know what a 'shade' is?

ELLE: Like, something that blocks light?

DaVeD: No, like in mythology, I guess.

ELLE: Like the spirit of a dead person?

DaVeD: Yeah. That's what I saw. I saw shades.

DaVeD: At least seven of them. That's the best way I can describe them.

DaVeD: But they were solid. Physical. Like the faded versions of the people they used to be. They were like... strung out. And that place and the people smelled... I threw up. Twice. Gagged all the way back home.

ELLE: Can you start from the beginning?

DaVeD: I went there Saturday morning. Early.

ELLE: Did you have any weapons with you or anything?

DaVeD: What kind of weapon would I have?

ELLE: Like a gun or something? You're the white boy, don't they give you an assault rifle at birth?

DaVeD: Very funny.

ELLE: Go on. I can't believe you just walked your happy ass down there...

DaVeD: It seemed deserted at first. I took the bus. I was alone. The closest stop was like six blocks from the place so I had a nice walk through what I can only describe as AC's own version of Tartarus.

ELLE: Sometimes I forget that you majored in Classics but you always find a way to remind me.

DaVeD: You're a fucking creep. Anyway, I got to the building and... it was like... being in a warzone. Except the war had ended a long time ago. The place is uninhabitable. I'm talking windows blasted out of their casings, broken glass fucking everywhere, no vegetation, half the telephone wires were just cut in half and dangling in the streets. Dude I even saw those big rusty drums sitting on a corner with fires lit inside them. I've only seen that shit in the movies. It was crazy. I saw a wrapper for 'Mr Chuckies Burgers and Brew'. Mr. Chuckies went out of business like twelve years ago. Time had stopped there.

DaVeD: Anyway, there's a courtyard and there was this hollow-eyed cadaverous looking dude just sitting on the steps that lead back into the entry way into the building proper. I thought he was going to say something to me but I walked passed him and he didn't even fucking blink. He didn't move. And he'd shit himself. He was just sitting in it. That's the first time I threw up.

ELLE: Gross.

DaVeD: It gets way worse. His fingernails were like... at least five, maybe six inches long I thought... okay it sounds weird but I thought he was holding like, a bunch of strawberries or something. But I got closer and he was digging. Into himself. He had gouged out parts of his chest and upper arms.

ELLE: Fuck me.

DaVeD: He was staring out past me, past the courtyard, like he was staring right out of this fucking world and into somewhere else. I'll never forget what it felt like to realize what he was doing. I felt like I had fallen into someplace. Truth be told, I still feel like I'm there.

ELLE: I bet.

DaVeD: After walking past him I was in the entry way and it was all dark. I mean, there was a little light seeping from the exit at the other end, but it was mostly dark. Caliginous, even. On either side of the hall were the doors to the apartments. They were all closed. I walked until I came to a stairwell.

DaVeD: The second floor was... unbelievable. It was darker because there was no light from an open exit like there was downstairs. And there were more 'people' in the halls. A woman, I think, was sitting up against the wall at the top of the stairs. At first I could only see her body (she'd soiled herself too) and as I stepped up more and more of her was revealed. She was making like a chewing, gristly noise.

ELLE: Oh fuck you David.

DaVeD: No, you have to hear all of it. I have to tell somebody. You were right. You were fucking right and I never should have gone out there. But you owe me. So now you listen. Read. Whatever.

DaVeD: I saw her face. What was left of it. There was just...rawness and redness and a row of red-stained teeth. She had chewed off her whole lower lip. She was chewing automatically. You could tell, her movements were... mechanistic. Her arms were wrapped around herself, like she'd been cold once but had forgotten to care. There was caked blood and filth all over her. And she was staring out of the world just like that dude downstairs.

ELLE: How the fuck did you not leave after that?!

DaVeD: I screamed. Fuck it, I screamed like a girl. Anyone would have, shit. She didn't move. Didn't blink. She was gone. Everybody in that place was like that.

ELLE: How many people were there?

DaVeD: I saw seven 'people'. I think there were more, but their doors were locked. Some of them weren't. There were animal parts lying around. Carcasses chewed down to the bones. There was maybe what looked like a scalp at the far end of the hallway. Just a scalp, lying on the dirty floor.

ELLE: Fuck that. Fuck that to hell.

ELLE: Did you call the police?

DaVeD: What the fuck are the police going to do, Elle? They'd already been there!

ELLE: No, I mean, they couldn't have seen that. Kedger's Point has been condemned for years. And the reports said all the other apartments had been abandoned. The fucking building is condemned.

DaVeD: What reports?

ELLE: The internal police reports.

DaVeD: That's how you knew what happened to Kelsey and Leni and Rachelle. You hacked the police records.

ELLE: It doesn't matter, but I feel obligated to tell you that nobody says 'hacked' anymore.

DaVeD: Thanks for the tip. What else do you know?

ELLE: Let me ask you one more question and then I'll tell you everything.

DaVeD: What?

ELLE: What was in Kelsey's apartment?

DaVeD: Nothing. I mean, some shitty furniture and garbage. And a checkered blotter.

ELLE: A what?

DaVeD: Like blotting paper? For acid? There was a sheet underneath the bed. I thought it was just trash but the pattern caught my eye.

ELLE: What pattern?

DaVeD: I took a picture. I took lots of pictures actually.

ELLE: Why the fuck did... never mind.

DaVeD: KPblotter.jpg

ELLE: How'd you know it was a blotter?

DaVeD: I grew up here and there ain't much for the youth to do, so... hallucinogens.

ELLE: It's here now. I mean that's obvious but I didn't have all the pieces. I do now.

DaVeD: What? You lost me.

ELLE: I've been looking into this shit for decades. Chasing the myth. Stalking the rumors. Wait, before I tell you what I know, what happened after you left Kelsey's apartment?

DaVeD: Nothing. I mean I just left. That hollowed out guy said something to me. Or he said something out loud while I was running the fuck away.

ELLE: What did he say?

DaVeD: It sounded like "My voice is dead," or "My voice is dying," or something.

ELLE: "Song of my soul, my voice is dead." Please don't ever go back there and if you ever see that man or that woman again or anyone else from that place you run from them. Do you understand me? I'm not kidding, David.

DaVeD: Why the fuck will I ever see them again? After this shit I'll probably never leave my house.

ELLE: Good.

DaVeD: How did you know what he said? Why does it sound familiar?

ELLE: Because it's from R.W. Chambers' story, 'The King in Yellow.' It's a fictionalized, ruinous city that exists in another dimension. It's a mythos, like the Cthulhu stories, and all kinds of writers have played around with the concept.

DaVeD: So...

ELLE: Somebody, we'll call him the Priest of Breathing, made a drug that takes its users to Carcosa. Hence the name, Carcosine.

DaVeD: I don't understand.

ELLE: Yeah well there's a lot I'm pretty fucking baffled about too, but that's what I know.

DaVeD: So, that's how those girls came back? Is that what you're saying?

ELLE: Yes. I know it doesn't make any kind of sense. That's the thing about this whole fucking story. The more I chase after it the more it unravels. I'm tired, David.

DaVeD: Do you want to talk more later? It is late.

ELLE: I mean I'm tired of this. I'm tired of hunting this shit. I'm tired of living like this.

DaVeD: How do you mean?

DaVeD: ELLE?

DaVeD: Fuck did you leave?

ELLE: No, I'm still here. Always fucking here. The spider's in her web, watching everything. Look at that pattern in the blotter. Tell me where it ends and where it begins.

DaVeD: I've seen some really fucked up shit the last few days. Some weird optical illusion is the least of my concerns right now.

ELLE: Good. That's good actually.

DaVeD: How do you mean? Hang on, my phone just made a weird noise.

ELLE: I deleted the image from your phone and hard drive.

DaVeD: WHAT THE FUCK ELL GODDAMMIT

ELLE: You don't need it for anything. To keep staring at it, like I have, for as long as I have... it'll just start to tempt you.

DaVeD: Could you stop fucking with my devices? Goddamn.

ELLE: I will. Carcosine makes the living feel dead and the dead feel alive. But their appetites change.

DaVeD: What are you fucking saying?

ELLE: You said it yourself, you saw 'shades.' You were more correct than you thought.

DaVeD: I was just using that as a description. Are you serious? Those people were really dead?

ELLE: No, those people were alive and they now think they are dead. Somebody, I'm guessing the Priest of Breathing or one of his... servants, cleared those people out when the cops came. And once they left, they brought them back. Kind of them, really. Leni and Kelsey and Rachelle, those women were dead. Their bodies killed them. And their grieving husband's found something to make them seem as if they were alive. And they came back, but they came back wrong. They always come back wrong. You cannot invert the pattern.

DaVeD: Where are you? I know you're in town but where exactly? I don't like what you're saying.

ELLE: You couldn't find me even if you really tried. That's sweet though. I have some, you know? From a long time ago. I've been saving it.

DaVeD: Please don't do anything stupid.

ELLE: I think, maybe, being alive is the stupidest thing any of us will ever do. To keep at it, like somehow things will right themselves.

DaVeD: You don't have to go all edgelord on me, okay? We can talk about this some more. I can meet you somewhere. Anywhere.

ELLE: That's nice. I thought you were mad at me?

DaVeD: Okay, yeah I am but... this is freaking me the fuck out. Hard. And I don't like what you're saying.

ELLE: I don't like what I'm saying. I don't like what I know. You know how earlier you said that you'll never forget the faces of the people in Kedger's Point? That faraway look in their eyes?

DaVeD: Yeah, so?

ELLE: When you climax in that video, you had the same look on your face. We all do. Death is peace, David. Peace is death. It may look ugly on the outside, but inside, it's the only thing that calms us. That focal point of bright black at the center of everything. Maybe what the Priest of Breathing is doing is a good thing.

DaVeD: Jesus Elle. Please don't do whatever it is you're going to do.

ELLE: You know exactly what I'm going to do. Maybe someday we'll meet face to face.

DaVeD: Shit we could meet now! Please! None no one else will believe this shit!

ELLE: In dim Carcosa. Bye David.

DaVeD: Elle?

ELLE: User ELLE is no longer connected.

DaVeD: Elle?

DaVeD: What the fuck? Elle?

END CHAT TRANSCRIPT

CARNACKI: THE WATCHER AT THE GATE

WILLIAM MEIKLE

I arrived on Carnacki's doorstep in Cheyne Walk that Wednesday at the same time as Jessup. Our old friend opened the door and let us inside. I thought at first glance that Carnacki looked somewhat pale and tired, and indeed, after another fine meal, he appeared content to sit and smoke. I was rather disappointed to realize that we would not get a new story that night, for it seemed from his demeanour that something had worn him out. Our friend looked ten years older than his true age, and, in truth, it was obvious that he should have cancelled tonight's gathering for the general good of his health.

I was about to tell him exactly that when he spoke, his voice alarmingly frail.

"I wondered whether I should lock myself away and get some rest," he said. "But I find I am in the need of the company of friendly faces and stout friends, so please, chaps, indulge me. Do make sure you have your drinks fully charged and plenty of smokes at hand, for the story I shall tell is a long one, and I am sore tired so will need to take it slowly. It is also an alarming tale, and I cannot promise that you will sleep well in your own beds this night, for I have hardly had a wink myself since the events unfolded."

* * *

"It began last Friday with a telegram from Whitehall requesting that I attend a meeting at the Home Office. As there was no other explanation as to what the purpose of the meeting might be, I did not make any preparations beyond ensuring I had my pipe and tobacco with me as I made my way along the Embankment.

"I was made to wait for an interminably long time in a draughty corridor – you know how these chaps are who think themselves more important than those they serve? I was finally shown into a rather cramped little office. It had one tiny window and air that smelled like many people had been breathing it. A thin little man with pursed lips and pinched cheeks looked me up and down and sniffed, as if he had just been offered a bit of fish that had clearly gone off. I can tell you, I was jolly close to turning on my heels and having none of it, but I suppose I was just intrigued enough by the summoning to hear him out.

"His disdain for me could not have been much clearer.

" 'Before we start,' he said. 'I will have you know I have no truck with any witchcraft or mumbo jumbo. I was against involving you right from the start and am only doing this under pressure from above.'

"I merely smiled thinly across the table at him – had I opened my mouth at that point I might have said something I would only regret later. I lit up a pipe – rather pleased to find that it annoyed him slightly, and also rather pleased to note that he did not mention that annoyance. It seemed he needed my services rather more than had been originally apparent.

"Finally, after he had made completely sure that I knew he did not like me, I got his name, a Mr Gray – most apt in his case – and a reason for my being summoned.

" 'There a bit of a flap on down Kent way – some scientist Johnnies have got themselves in a spot of bother, and the man in the Ministry seems to think that you will be able to help.'

"He passed me an envelope, gingerly, as if the contents might explode in his face.

" 'All you need to know is in there. Your train leaves in an hour so you had best hurry.'

"And with that I was dismissed – he had his head down, signing interminable sheets of reports in crabbed writing, long before I turned and gladly took my leave of him. His rudeness had almost convinced me to head straight home, but the envelope had me intrigued. It was expensive paper – not the cheap stuff they generally used in these corridors – and it had been addressed to me personally, in a fine cursive hand.

"I took a seat in the corridor and quickly read it through while finishing my pipe."

Carnacki,

Sorry to bother you like this, but I have need of your services. Our research establishment at East Malling has uncovered something that I think is right up your street. The chaps down there don't know what to make of it, but I have assured them that you're the man for the job.

They know you are coming, and there is a room waiting for you at the White Lion in the village should you need to stay over.

Your ticket is enclosed.

"It was signed, simply, *'Churchill.'*

"I hadn't heard a peep from the man since that thing with the bally German spy, and there were little in the way of pleasantries or entreaties to my good nature. He had simply assumed, as was his way, that all he had to do was say 'jump' and everybody would ask 'how high?' And you chaps know me – I can be quite contrary if I feel someone is trying to take advantage.

"In this case however, I will admit to being intrigued, so an hour later was I settled in to a compartment on the train heading at some speed through South East London and down into Kent. I did not have an overnight bag with me, for I was resolute in my belief that I would be home in time for supper.

"Unfortunately things did not work out quite as I would have had hoped."

* * *

"I knew of East Malling only as a small hamlet, and a stop on the main line to Canterbury. Having never previously alighted there, I was pleasantly surprised to find it a neat and tidy Kentish town of the old style, with several inns and taverns that looked most welcoming. I was not, however, given any time to sample their pleasures, as I was met off the train by a uniformed chap, a Sergeant Masters, who, while pleasant enough, was most insistent that I accompany him immediately.

"He led me, at quite a march, some way along the railway line then down into a maze of apple and pear tree plantings until we came out to a large copse of tall beech trees. And there, in a clearing in the middle of that copse, I finally came to get some idea as to why Churchill thought I might be able to help.

"The clearing housed a small scatter of tin-roofed huts gathered around a larger building, more of a barn, in the centre. And despite the fact it was broad daylight, I saw most clearly that there was something decidedly off about the scene in front of me. It took me several seconds to spot it, then it came to me – despite it being not yet July, and it having been rather a damp start to the Summer, the trees were already showing signs of autumn colours – and in some cases the fall had already begun. There was something else too – a most distinctive rainbow shimmer, like oil evaporating on a hot skillet, and it covered the whole area. I almost tensed as the Sergeant led me forward, expecting to feel it, greasy against my cheeks, but the air seemed quite dry and warm as we approached the barn.

"Armed soldiers stood on either side of the tall doors, but did not attempt to stop me from entering – it seemed I was indeed expected.

"The inside of the barn was a flurry of activity. There did not seem to be any more military, just chaps in serious suits with even more serious expressions on their faces. All of the hubbub was centred around a contraption in the middle of the floor, a tall tangled nest of wiring, valves and coils that hummed rather alarmingly and gave off the most nerve wracking bolts of blue electricity at what seemed to be irregular intervals.

"One of the suited chaps saw me enter and came over to relieve the Sergeant of his duties. He pumped my hand most eagerly. 'Swithin's my name,' he said. 'I'll be your liaison here. I'll bet you're champing at the bit to get started.'

"It turned out that both of us were under quite some misapprehension as to the amount of knowledge the other held. Swithin believed I had already been fully briefed, which was obviously not the case. And I believed that these scientist chaps knew what they were up to. As it turned out, that was obviously not the case either."

* * *

Carnacki stopped at that point and turned to me.

"Can I bother you to fetch me a refill, Dodgson?" he said. "I'm not sure I have the energy to get up."

I did as requested, and while I was at the drinks cabinet, Arkwright took his chance to interject.

"East Malling? I played cricket there some years ago. Isn't it all agricultural research they do down that way – new varieties of apples and pears, better quality strawberries, that kind of thing?"

Carnacki smiled thinly.

"That had been my thought too," he said softly. "But I was soon to discover that I was very much mistaken."

He waited until I had fetched him a stiff brandy, downed a hefty gulp of it, then continued his tale.

* * *

"At first Swithin did not answer me when I asked the purpose of the equipment in the barn. He took my arm and led me closer to the coils and whining machinery.

" 'We believe we have discovered a way to access the most basic building blocks of reality itself – the stuff of primal creation – a gateway to the secrets of the universe.'

"I did not quite know how to reply to that; I certainly suspected it of being mere hyperbole, but it was clear that he believed at least some of what he had said. I turned my back as the contraption pulsed blue again, so intense it was brighter than the sun, even through my closed eyes. Swithin patted me on the shoulder a few seconds later.

" 'Open your eyes, Carnacki. Look here.'

"I looked where he pointed. It took several moments for my eyes to adjust to the glare, and I had to squint. Even then, it wasn't actually clear what I was observing, but there was obviously something happening.

"A tear in the fabric of space, no bigger than a sliver of fingernail, appeared in a void in the centre of the contraption and hung there. As I watched it settled into a new configuration, a black, somewhat oily in appearance droplet little more than an inch across at the thickest point. It seemed to be held quivering in mid-air by some strange force emanating from Swithin's somewhat makeshift electrical mechanism.

"It looked like an egg.

"Swithin looked like the cat that had got the cream, a broad grin plastered across his face.

" 'As you can clearly see, we have done it, Carnacki.'

"I looked at the black egg, then Swithin, then back to the egg again. The rainbow aura thickened again, dancing around the shimmering thing that hung impossibly real in the air.

" 'What in blazes is it?' I whispered.

" 'We like to think of them as soap bubbles." Swithin replied. "It is a theory that comes to us from Tesla. Reality consists of many of them – multiple, perhaps even infinite, universes, each in its own bubble, each connected by the thinnest of membranes to many of its neighbours. Glue, if you like – the stuff that holds everything together.'

" 'so what happens now?'

" 'Now we study it. Think of it, Carnacki. A whole new universe at our disposal.'

" 'And what is inside the bubble?'

" 'He laughed.

" 'That is what we are trying to find out.'

"I had another look at the egg. It certainly looked larger to me. The barn started to throb, like a heartbeat. The egg pulsed in time. And now it was more than obvious – it was most definitely getting bigger.

" 'The field boundary is collapsing,' Swithin shouted.

"The throb became a rapid thumping; the barn shook and trembled. The vibration rattled my teeth and set my guts roiling.

"A blinding flare of blue blasted all coherent thought from my head. When I recovered enough to look back at the contraption there was nothing to be seen hanging there but empty space. The black egg was gone as quickly as it had come.

" 'As you can tell, we're having a few teething problems. Mr Churchill tells us that you are just the man to advise us on the way forward.'

"I looked up at the barn roof. A glistening aurora of rainbow colour hung there, hissing slightly. A piece of rafter fell to the ground near my feet – a six inch slat of wood that crumbled into dust – and more rainbow shimmers – under the slightest pressure of my fingers.

" 'It's my advice you want is it? Then you shall have it. Raze this place to the ground. Do it now, and do it quickly. You do not know what you are playing with.'

"Of course my outburst caused quite some consternation – it was clearly not what they had been expecting to hear. I was badgered and harried until in the end I used Churchill's name again, just to get them to keep quiet.

" 'Look, I was sent here to give my opinion. I gave it. I have told you what I can do to help. The fact that you do not like what you have been told concerns me not a jot. If you have a problem, take it up with Mr Churchill. I am going home.'

"And with that I left, glad to get out from under that dancing rainbow aurora, and even more glad of a smoke in the station as I waited for a train back to town.

"And there it might have ended, had I not caught sight of two local children playing with something by the side of the track. I strolled over in that direction and looked down.

" 'It was a cat — or rather, it had been until recently. Now it was just a pitiful crumpled thing, fallen in on itself into little more than dust — a dust that sent a rainbow aura dancing in the air as the lads poked at it with a stick."

* * *

"Ten minutes later I was back with Swithin — one of the small huts in the copse of beech trees was a makeshift mess, and he was able to get me a sandwich and a cup of strong sweet tea. I'd have preferred something stronger but had to make do with what was on offer as I tried to impress on Swithin just what they were getting themselves in to.

" 'Those things you think of as eggs — or glue — or whatever the blazes you said earlier — that is all wrong. I have seen their like — or something dashed like it — before. I do not know how you have managed it, but you have clearly opened a gateway to the Outer Darkness with all your fumbling around. And like all gateways, the longer you leave it open, the more chance there is of something coming through it.'

"Swithin tried to allay my fears, and did not even seem concerned when I mentioned the dead cat at the railway.

" 'It must have sneaked in here at an inopportune moment — we have been finding dead rats these past few days.'

" 'And you do not think that is perhaps problematic?'

" 'Needs of science, old chap — and Mr Churchill's orders that we find something he can use. We cannot go backwards at this juncture.'

" 'It is not your going backwards that worries me,' I said. I believed I was starting to understand why Churchill had sent me here. 'Can you at least stop until I've had a chance to catch up with what you have done already?'

" 'No can do, old boy,' he said. 'The powering up sequence is already underway for the next attempt. You should come and watch — it's jolly fascinating stuff.'

" 'Fascinating is a word I have often used in my encounters with the Great Beyond,' I replied. 'But in this case, I believe fear would be a more appropriate response. These gateways have been closed tight for a reason. To open them without thought for the consequences is folly of the highest order.'

"My concerns continued to be waved aside at every turn, and short of beating a path back to Whitehall and demanding to see Churchill himself, I was at quite a loss as to how to proceed. My only hope was to stay close by and hope that I could prevent catastrophe, so I made my way back to the barn with Swithin. A rainbow aurora, like oil shimmering in the sun on a hot day, hung over the stand of trees, swaying in time with the waft of branches in the slight breeze. It was all very pretty, but the sight of it filled me with deep dread and I felt a shiver of cold despite the summer sunshine.

"We were just in time to see them switch on the power."

* * *

"Almost immediately a black, almost oily egg appeared in the void inside the contraption and hung in the air. It gave off a distinct hum – I felt it in my gut and jaw and with an accompanying vibration that made me more than slightly nauseous.

"Swithin had a look of relief on his face.

" 'It has stabilized,' he said, and smiled, but it did not reach his eyes and I saw that there was something else troubling the man.

" 'So let us say that I believe you, and it is indeed stable,' I said. 'In that case, what has got you so worried?'

"He sucked on a pen as if pretending it was a cigarette.

" 'I wasn't going to tell you,' he said eventually. 'It might be nothing. It was something I saw when the field collapsed earlier.'

" 'Just tell me,' I said, cold terror gripping me again. I was not at all sure I wanted to hear his reply.

" 'It was just when the field went,' he said. He couldn't look at me. 'And only for an instant. But when the field collapsed I thought I saw the egg burst. It opened out – a fine, rainbow infused fog. It seemed to swell and diminish, twice, as if breathing, and when I looked back, it was gone.'

" 'Fog?'

" 'Probably an effect of the field itself – you know, like the patterns you can make with magnets and iron filings?' He sounded like he was trying to convince himself rather than me.

" 'Anything at all could have happened – you have no conception of what lurks just beyond that boundary. We are damned lucky to still be here.'

"He looked pale, but pointed at the floating egg again.

" 'But look, it's stable now.' It sounded like a plea. I didn't listen to him. I was thinking, of the barn filling with oily, glistening bubbles. They popped and spawned yet more bubbles, then more still. They filled everything with rainbow colour, expanding through the building, spilling out into the orchards, over the railway line, engulfing everything in their path and humming along as they ravaged – there was more than the deaths of a cat and a few rats at stake here – much more.

" 'shut it off,' I said. 'Do it now, before it's too late.'

"He looked at me as if I was insane.

" 'But we've done it, Carnacki.' He pointed at a stack of batteries off to one side. An array of meters showed that the power inside them was building rapidly. 'Energy from nothing. This is fortune and glory stuff, right here; this is our place in the history books.'

" 'Forget the history books. I'll be happy to have some more history. Shut it down, before it does for us all.

"Swithin watched the meters rise for several more seconds. And finally he gave the order – whether it was because I had asked, or whether he was satisfied with his results I did not care. This time I was looking at the egg as they tried to manage the shut down.

"It was indeed too late. Far too late."

* * *

"Two eggs now hung in the void side by side, just touching, each as black as the other, twin bubbles only held in check by the forces generated by the electrical equipment. I was suddenly all too aware how fragile that field had been earlier. The hum throbbed louder. The eggs pulsed in synchronized agreement.

" 'Do something, Swithin, before it's too late.'

" 'I'm trying,' he said, pulling out copper wire and untwisting valves to no apparent effect. The throb from the field went up a notch until it felt like being inside a vast kettledrum beaten by a manic giant.

"Four eggs hung in a tight group, pulsing in time with the magnetic throb. colours danced and flowed across the sheer black surface; blues and greens and shimmering silvers that were now all too familiar.

" 'Shut it off,' I shouted. Swithin had stopped trying to pull out wires. All his attention was on the chamber in the void as each of the eggs trembled and calved.

"In the blink of an eye there were eight.

"The crystal valves howled in anguish. I was vaguely aware of Swithin attempting to connect yet another battery to the system, but I was past caring, lost in contemplation of the beauty in front of me.

"The eggs calved again, and again.

"Thirty two now, and they had started to fill the barn with dancing

aurora of shimmering lights that pulsed and capered in time with the vibration and the whine of the valves. Most of the scientist chaps took this as their signal and beat a hasty retreat, but Swithin was made of sterner stuff. He stepped closer to the calving eggs.

" 'Carnacki!' he shouted as he tried to disconnect the system. 'I need you.'

"Sixty-four now, each a shimmering pearl of black light.

"The colours filled the barn, spilled out across the floor, crept among the rafters, danced in my eyes, in my head, all though my body as I felt a flicker of memory. A hundred and twenty eight bubbles hung in the void – and I realized they formed an image I had seen before – in the Sigsand MS. Just as suddenly, I knew exactly what was happening, and I felt a fresh twinge of fear – and not a little awe.

"At that same moment Swithin pulled the remaining wires out from where they were attached to the batteries. The drone faded to a whisper, the drumbeat slowing and diminishing, leaving us in almost complete silence.

"The eggs had already calved into two hundred and fifty-six. The void was filling fast, threatening to spill over into the barn itself which shook and quaked, sending fine dust falling all around us.

"A crack ran through the wall to my left, and two of the large battery cells on the far side fell over. There was a sudden burst of colour; red, blue and shimmering silver filled my head.

"I blinked, looked back, and the eggs were gone as quickly as they had come – there was only the empty containment chamber. But the damage had been done. The crack in the wall widened. A portion of the roof collapsed, fell to the floor and immediately disintegrated into dust. Swithin and I looked at each other, then made for the door.

"We only just made it in time. The whole barn was coming down around us. We burst through the door together, reducing it completely to dust and splinters in the process. We emerged into sunlight, blinking, as the barn caved in on itself at our back.

"A pall of dust rose up from the ruined building. I might have been the only one that noticed, but it did not disperse in the breeze – instead it seemed to thicken somewhat. A rainbow aura hung above the beeches for a long second, breathed, twice, then seemed to fall to the ground to be swallowed into the earth."

* * *

Carnacki stopped again, clearly showing signs of some fatigue. I fetched him some more brandy, and he got a fresh smoke lit before continuing.

"That was it, for Friday at least. I was hurried away from the area by the same Sergeant as had shown me in earlier, and within the hour was on a train back home, arriving just in time to fall into bed and a troubled sleep full of dreams of rainbow dancing colour and bursting eggs.

"I checked the early papers on Saturday to see if there were any reports of anything untoward in Kent, but all seemed quiet and I heard nothing more about the matter... until Monday morning. I was sitting in my library, perusing the Sigsand and contemplating several diagrams I had found there when there was a knock on my door. It was Swithin, and he looked as sick as any man I have ever seen.

"He only just managed to walk the short distance from the door to my library, and fell in a heap in the nearest chair, clearly exhausted. Despite the fact that Monday was one of the warmest days of the summer so far, he had wrapped himself up inside a voluminous overcoat several sizes too large for his frame, and he looked like a child, sitting there in my chair lost inside his parent's clothes.

"Indeed, he looked so ill that I broke out the Scotch, which he took to readily despite it not being long after ten in the morning. After he had downed a goodly quantity his cheeks took on some colour and he seemed to have the strength to talk.

" 'I need you to come back to Kent with me, Carnacki,' he said.

" 'Give me one good reason why I should,' I replied.

He stood, somewhat shakily, dropped off the overcoat and undid the cuff of his shirt.

" 'No, you do not understand. I really need you,' he said. He rolled up his sleeve. The arm he exposed wasn't just an arm. 'I guess we didn't get out of that barn fast enough.'

I saw tendons and flesh through a hand-sized translucent area. It looked almost opaque, and grooved, as if it had melted then reformed. There was a soft appearance to the flesh that I did not like the look of at all – it reminded me all too much of some of the manifestations of the Outer Darkness I have encountered on my various adventures.

" 'Whatever was done is not over,' Swithin whispered. 'Lights have been seen in the sky over the orchards. The trees, the fruit, the very ground itself are all sickening. And we are all sorely afflicted – all of us who worked on the machine.'

"At that Swithin fell silent, as if unable to continue.

"In truth I did not need much explanation, for I could imagine it all too clearly in my mind's eye. And my morning reading had only confirmed the seriousness of the situation to me.

" 'I shall need Churchill's help,' I replied. 'For what I have in mind is beyond my own means.'

"Swithin looked up at me, tears filling his eyes.

" 'I am to get you anything you need,' he said. 'Mr Churchill has already given the order.'

"I told him what I would require. He had a small military truck waiting in the street and one of the two men inside was dispatched off toward Whitehall with my procurement order for delivery, post-haste, to Kent. I had the driver pack my defences in the back of the vehicle then it took the two of us to lift Swithin in to the passenger seat. I had to keep him upright most of the way as we headed at some speed through South London and out through Bromley, heading once again for East Malling."

* * *

"Swithin looked like he might lapse into unconsciousness at any moment, so I tried to keep him awake by summarizing what I had found in my library. I don't know that he heard more than the half of it, but talking it out did a great deal to get the matter straight in my own mind. I have told you already that I recognized the cluster of black ovals that formed in Swithin's contraption, have I not? Well now I had more – I had a name for the phenomenon, one that is as old as mankind itself.

" 'People have long searched for a way through to the other side – whatever their idea of that other side might be. It is only logical that over the course of those long millennia, from primitive tribesmen, through great civilizations and all the way up to your most recent forays, that some have succeeded, in some small part. The gate is there for any that want to look hard enough. And yesterday you found it, and opened it, just a fraction. Part of our place here, our Microcosm if you like, has no doubt gone over there to the Great Beyond – just as part of something from that side has seeped over here – and you yourself are feeling the effects.

" 'The Outer Darkness would quickly surge through all these gateways – were it given the means to do so – but there are checks and balances in all nature, and it is no different with the gateway itself. I recognized the configuration of your hanging eggs from something the Persians discovered nearly three thousand years before you – now there is some history you should have considered – they called it Darbān and it is the source of many legends that follow over the centuries. It now has many names. You may have heard it called The Opener of the Way.

" 'My hope is that just as it opens, so it may close. But that is something that remains to be seen. If the gate has been opened too far, it might be too late to ever close it again, and the sickness – your sickness – will spread and fester and darkness will once again cover the face of the earth. We can only hope we are in time.'

" 'We did not know,' Swithin replied in a hoarse whisper. 'How could we have known?'

" 'You could have asked me. And you should have razed it to the ground when I said so. Now we may be too late.' "

* * *

"My suspicion that we were too late was reinforced as we arrived in East Malling just after noon.

"Even for a small village in the rural heartland, it was far too quiet for a Monday lunchtime. The inns and taverns lay empty and nothing – not even a sparrow – moved on the streets. A Canterbury train flew past as we reached the junction but if it was meant to stop, the driver had decided to ignore it, and barrelled through at some great speed, as if afraid to hang around too long in the vicinity. The air felt too hot, too dry, and everywhere one looked, one saw the instantly recognizable shimmering rainbow aura.

"Had we had the time, I might have stopped and investigated further. But I had no doubt that the shrubbery in the gardens, the trees and the hedgerows, possibly even the people themselves wrapped up abed, would be slowly crumbling down into a fine dust that would soon be subsumed into the dancing rainbows as it spread – and fed.

"I saw more signs of the spread of the malignant influence as we made our way through the maze of orchards. Every tree was withered and twisted. Rotting fruit hung in oozing pustules, dripping globs of pus to a dry dusty ground that sent up puffs of rainbow dust in reply. A glance in the side mirror showed that even our own journey down the track was sending up clouds of the dust, glittering rainbows rising high in the air kicked up by our wheels. I urged our driver to make all haste for the copse of beeches, and he did not have to be asked twice.

"Two more army trucks waited for us just outside the ring of beech trees – Churchill had made good on my offer, and indeed the supplies had made better time than us. Several bemused squaddies shared a smoke and cast worried glances at the treetops where the rainbow aura hung and shimmered in a huge, ever shifting amorphous bubble; it almost seemed alive.

"I wasted no time in getting about my preparations. I had the squaddies help unload the two trucks – one of them contained the heaviest duty diesel generator available and fuel to run it, and the other contained as much electrical wiring, and as many coloured crystal valves as could be found in the limited time available.

"You see, I hoped – it was my only hope – to pit my colour theory against the opening gateway, to send a message to the other side that we were not prepared, that that gate must be shut. I only hoped that someone – or rather something – might be listening.

"I also knew that setting up my circle outside the beeches would be futile – rather than fight against something, on this occasion I had to focus on containment. I had the men set up a great pentacle of the coloured valves, with the ruin of the collapsed barn smack in the centre. Such was the size of the thing that the wiring had, of necessity, to be threaded between the trunks of the trees, the pentacle encompassing most of the area of the copse.

"Swithin, despite a growing lethargy and despair, managed to cannibalize a deal of electrical equipment from the other huts. He came up with a rather ingenious set of switches for controlling the crystal valves – a method I indeed hope to be able to use in future adventures – and finally I was able to pronounce that we were ready.

"It had taken most of the day – the rainbow aura had thickened overhead, and hummed slightly, glowing bright against a sky that was dimming as dusk fell."

* * *

Carnacki paused again.

"And now we come to it, gentlemen. So if you'd like to refill your glasses for the last time – and if Dodgson would be so kind as to oblige me again – let us get to the end of this remarkable tale, while I still have the energy – and the inclination – to see it through."

Once more I did as requested, pouring Carnacki a very stiff brandy, for he looked like he might need it, being as drawn and haggard as I have ever seen him. I was thinking on his description of the man Swithin's illness as I sat back in my chair and waited to hear him out.

He took some time getting a smoke lit, and sipped at his brandy before starting again.

* * *

"As you have probably gathered, I did not have a great deal of hope of any success. I sent the squaddies away – there was no sense in exposing them for any longer than was necessary. Swithin refused to leave with them.

" 'This is my mess, in the main,' he said. 'I intend to see it sorted, whatever it takes.'

"We stood side by side, smoking a last cigarette as the light went from the sky. The rainbow aura danced overhead, hissing slightly, almost singing as I threw the switch and turned on the pentacle. My colours, a wash of blue and yellow, filled the glade and overhead the aurora dimmed, and seemed to shrink.

" 'It's working,' Swithin said, although I was by no means certain of that.

"Seconds later what appeared to be a thin fog started to rise from the ground all around where the barn had collapsed, glowing faintly and pulsing in time with the thrum and hum emanating from the pentacle.

"Swithin pointed at his little box of switches.

" 'What now, Carnacki? How is your colour theory going to work?'

" 'We must attempt to nullify the rainbow – as you know, colours can either work together, or cancel each other out – let us see how a hefty dose of blue does against it.'

"I flicked the switch that Swithin had indicated controlled the blue end of the spectrum. The crystal valves flared, white, blue then white again, so bright that I had to avert my gaze. The pale glow in the fog inside the pentacle took on a blue tinge. Sparks flew, like arcs from a Van Der Graaf generator, making the hair on my arms stand on end. The very ground around us started to buck and sway.

"I flicked a switch to add more yellow.

"The fog immediately thickened and became almost palpable.

" 'I think you've got it, Carnacki,' Swithin shouted.

"Even as he spoke a black tear opened in the air above the ruins of the barn, accompanied by what sounded like the ripping of paper. A singe black egg, no bigger than my thumb, hung there.

"The egg quivered, a rainbow aura danced over it, and ever so slowly it became two, oily sheen running over their sleek black surface. They hummed to themselves, a high singing that was taken up and amplified by an answering whine from the crystal valves.

"As two eggs became four, the whole copse rocked from side to side in rhythm.

"The dance had begun."

* * *

"Eight black eggs hung impossibly in the air above the ruined barn, oily and glistening, thrumming in time with the vibration from the pentacle that was getting ever louder, ever more insistent. I had to resist a sudden urge to start clapping in time to the beat.

"Thick fog glowed in an aurora of rainbow colour and swirled angrily in the darkened grove of beeches, but whatever the pentacle was doing to contain it seemed to be holding, for now.

"Eight became sixteen, and thirty-two seconds later, clustered in a tight ball that spun lazily in the air. The beeches themselves were changing too — the trees had become noticeably thinner, almost translucent and swirling rainbow fog clearly moved through them. They thinned further, almost ghostly now, then vanished completely until there was only the dark ground and the darker eggs hanging over it — sixty-four now, and singing louder.

"The dust and ash in the blasted earth where the barn had been started to tremble and shake, then, as if taken by the wind, rose in a tight funnel spiralling up toward the hanging eggs, faster and faster still. The eggs sucked up the material and sang louder, as if requesting more.

"I felt them suck at me too, and had the pentacle not been in place I think I might have been taken — and gone almost willingly — to whatever was on the other side.

"There were too many eggs to count now — into the hundreds for sure. They almost filled the space in the pentacle, their song rising higher, the beat and thrum of the rhythm filling my head, and the dancing rainbow colours filling my eyes with blue and green and gold and wonderment.

"My whole body shook, vibrating with the rhythm. My head swam, and it seemed as if everything melted and ran. The scene receded into a great distance until it was little more than a pinpoint in a blanket of darkness, and I was alone, in a cathedral of emptiness where nothing existed save the dark and the pounding.

"And then there was light.

"I saw stars — vast swathes of gold and blue and silver, all dancing in great purple and red clouds that spun webs of grandeur across unending vistas. Shapes moved in and among the nebulae; dark, wispy shadows casting a pallor over whole galaxies at a time, shadows that capered and whirled as the dance grew ever more frenetic. I was buffeted, as if by a strong, surging tide, but as the beat grew ever stronger I cared little. I gave myself to it, lost in the dance, lost in the stars.

"I don't know how long I wandered in the space between. I forgot myself, forgot Swithin, dancing in the vastness where only rhythm mattered. I may even have been there yet had Swithin not brought me back. He had me gripped by the shoulders and was screaming into my face.

" 'Fight it, Carnacki. Fight it man. I need your help.'

"It was that simple request for humanity that brought me back – back from a place where humankind was as insignificant as one of the motes of dancing ash from the ruined barn. Although when I managed to focus on him, I could see that Swithin was now as far gone from humanity as the stars among which I had been dancing. His head looked misshapen and deformed, as if his brain had grown too large for his skull and was threatening to expunge itself. His hands had taken on a peculiar flipper-like aspect, as had his feet. The left one in particular bothered me – it had thickened and hardened into black cuticle. It looked like it wanted to become a claw. What is more, wet-mouthed suckers ran, not just over his torso but up and down both his arms.

" 'I don't have much time, Carnacki,' he said – even his voice was going, barely more than a throaty gurgle. 'We can finish this – I think. It calls to me, and I must go to it. But when I do, when the way is opened – then you shall have your chance. Watch closely – and take it. Do not falter or flinch – it might be the only chance we have.'

"He motioned me forward and pointed at a knob on his box of tricks.

" 'Turn that full clockwise when I tell you to. It will amplify all the valves at once – a full blast with everything we've got,' he said. 'And follow my lead.'

"He left my side and went to stand at the edge of the pentacle then, without a pause, stepped inside and quickly moved to the centre where he raised his hands until they seemed to be engulfed in the mass of the eggs. I could hardly see him inside the swirling aurora of dancing colour.

"The eggs danced faster – thousands of them filling the pentacle and the whole area above me with song and dance that I had to fight to resist. Swithin sank his hands completely into them.

" 'Now,' he shouted.

"I turned the knob to its full extent.

"The myriad of eggs popped, burst and disappeared as if they had never been there at all. Dancing fog swirled, a dark funnel that brought a howling, screaming wind that threatened to throw me to the ground.

"Swithin screamed.

"Everything went black as a pit of hell, and a thunderous blast came down like a hammer from above, driving me down into a place where I dreamed of empty spaces filled with oily, glistening bubbles. They popped and spawned yet more bubbles, then even more, until I swam in a swirling sea of colours.

"Lost."

* * *

"I woke in the dark, lying on a bed of withered dry leaves under a star filled sky.

"There was no sign of Swithin, nor of any of the eggs. We had succeeded – Swithin had gone through – and the Keeper of the Gate had closed the way behind him. When I looked into the centre of the pentacle I saw only rubble and dust – and as I was about to turn away a dim rainbow aura, already fading, sinking into the ground.

"I walked out of those blasted orchards and made my report to the Sergeant in charge of the squaddies who were gathered at the railway station. I left them to the clean up and took the first available train home to seek out the nearest bottle of Scotch and get closely acquainted with it. I did not look back and I shall never return.

"I am sorry to say that I cannot promise the same for that blasted rainbow aurora though."

* * *

Carnacki sat back and tipped down the last of his brandy, his tale clearly done.

But that was not the end of the evening – not quite, for when Arkwright asked after Carnacki's health, our old friend did not speak but rolled up his sleeve.

His inner forearm seemed to have been melted and reformed, the skin being thin, almost translucent. When he held his arm up to the light we all saw it – the faintest of rainbow shimmers, like oil evaporating in hot sun.

"It improves," Carnacki said with a thin smile. "As will I, in time. But I shall never eat another apple out of Kent – and neither should you. Now, out you go."

I watched the trees carefully all the way home along the Embankment, but thankfully I saw only darkness, and the clear bright stars of our own night sky.

THE PERILOUS PEREGRINATION

A EUGENE ANGOVE ADVENTURE

TIM MENDEES

January 7th, 1939:

Holding his breath, Doctor Jason Blackburn quietly opened the door to his sleeper compartment and slipped out into the corridor, melting into the shadows between windows. Rectangular shafts of lambent light cast by the gibbous moon gave the darkened passage an almost abstract beauty. After once again checking that his assistant, Ruby Radcliff, was sleeping soundly, he pulled the door gently closed. Stifling the *click* of the latch with his gloved palm, Jason finally exhaled and a grin spread across his weathered features. His pulse was racing... he loved this part.

The LNER's flagship locomotive, The Flying Scotsman, rattled and shook as it crossed the rolling hills and valleys of lowlands Scotland. Jason's furtive eyes darted left and right as he checked that he was alone. Satisfied, he put on his shoes and crept down the corridor, wincing slightly with every footfall. In not wanting to risk waking Ruby, he had stood on her hat-pin with his stockinged foot, the fact that he didn't yelp with pain was a testament to the man's grit.

Tiptoeing past the other compartments, he listened for any activity, all was silent. As he'd planned, the other passengers appeared to have either gone down to the dining carriage for supper at midnight, or were getting spruced up in the WCs beforehand. Feigning illness so he and his assistant could retire without scrutiny had been a stroke of genius. The salacious tongues of the other passengers had been wagging ever since they had arrived at the archaeological dig in the woods near Gabhar Vale. Every man and woman on board was aware that his and Ruby's relationship wasn't purely professional, so they were guaranteed to believe that their withdrawal was simply a gossamer-thin ruse to sneak in a bit of clandestine rumpy-pumpy. Jason smiled, there would be time for that later, right now, he had a job to do.

Experiencing a slight pang of guilt as he pulled open the door at the end of the corridor and stepped out into the night, Jason thought again about the task in hand and quickly shook it off. He didn't particularly like deceiving Ruby, but needs must when the Devil drives. The icy Scottish wind bit at his ears as he passed between carriages and slipped into another sleeper car. Nobody was allocated to this one, so he relaxed somewhat. Aside from the eight other passengers, there was only the driver, stoker, a cook, a waiter, and a guard on board, and they were all down the opposite end of the train. He was anticipating plain sailing from that point onwards.

Quickening his pace, Blackburn made his way past the compartments, pausing briefly to mop his brow with a monogrammed handkerchief. Despite the cold, he was sweating profusely. Adrenaline always had that effect on him and he could detect its metallic sharpness in the back of his throat. He was going to need a stiff drink or three once the deed was done. Upon leaving the carriage, he skipped over to the baggage car with renewed vigour, his task was nearing completion.

Lighting the oil lamp that hung on a nail by the door with a *Swan Vestas*, he illuminated the cluttered compartment. The eggy smell of sulphur mingled noxiously with the musty aroma of things long buried. Crates containing stones covered in strange carvings and bizarre pictographs were piled high against the scratched wooden panelling. While the rest of the train was somewhat salubrious, this car would have been much more at home coupled to a freight locomotive. Clearly, the fastidious cleaning regime only reached those parts of the train open to the judgemental eyes of passengers.

"Where are you, you little beauty?" Blackburn purred, stroking his pencil moustache with a thumb and forefinger. Sweeping the lamp left and right, he looked for a crate that he had covertly marked with a series of notches around the lid. He'd been careful to make them look like the marks a crowbar would leave, but he would know them anywhere.

"Ah," he exclaimed in triumph, spotting the crate over in the far corner.

"There you are, you cheeky little minx."

Stepping over piles of camping and digging equipment, Jason clambered over to the crate and placed the lamp on the floor to its left. Looking around for a handy tool, he spotted a rusty crowbar leaning against a selection of grubby shovels. Slipping the flat end under the lid and putting his weight on the other end, he prised the lid open just enough to slip his hand inside. He had packed the crate himself, and ensured that what he desired was situated right at the top. Grinning to himself, he pulled out the cold stone artefact and slipped it into his pocket.

"Got you," Jason smirked, unaware that while he had been busy, someone had come silently into the carriage behind him. As he removed the crowbar and began to replace the lid, a shadowy figure walked up behind him, arm raised...

There was a dull *thud* as a heavy object was brought down with brutal efficiency on the back of Jason Blackburn's cranium. The force of the blow was sufficient to split his skull and drop him like a sack of spuds. The would-be thief fell forwards, his head striking the floor next to the lamp. His prolonged death rattle extinguished the flame and plunged the carriage into darkness...

* * *

Eugene Angove's bushy eyebrows knitted together as he tried to stab a pea with his fork, the sway of the train had the small green vegetable rolling back and forth on his plate, mocking his attempts. In the end, it all became too much, and he squashed it flat in a fit of pique. "Bloody peas... who in their right mind decides to serve peas on a moving train?"

His faithful valet, Hampton, smirked as he poured his employer another glass of *vin rouge*. "Perhaps the cook is a sadist, Sir?"

"You know, Hampton, old chap, that wouldn't surprise me one little bit on this trip," Eugene made a sweeping gesture towards the rest of the dining cart. "I've never met such a rum bunch."

Hampton looked around discreetly, though he hated to judge on appearances, Eugene wasn't far off the mark. At the far end of the room were a red-faced military man and his valet. Next to them, a rotund elderly nun chatted animatedly with an enormous Sikh. Finally, sitting alone with a table covered in notes and maps was the refined Professor Mirabelle. Conspicuous by their absence were Doctor Blackburn and his glamorous assistant, Ruby Radcliff. "It certainly is a motley collection for an archaeological team, Sir... I must say, I'm surprised that you agreed to get mixed up in all of this."

Eugene shovelled a dollop of mashed potato and horseradish sauce into his maw and chewed. He let his fork *clatter* to his plate and tapped his bulbous nose with a pudgy forefinger. "I have my reasons, Hampton. Let's just say that, Miss Stephenson made me an offer I couldn't refuse."

"Ah," Hampton nodded sagely, he could tell by the glint in his employer's eye that vast sums of cash, or something he could sell for vast sums of cash, were behind his enthusiasm. Normally, Eugene wouldn't touch anything to do with the Order of Tamesis with a ten-foot pole... not after all the fuss over the Black Stone of Tsathoggua. It probably helped that Edith Stephenson recruited him and not her adoptive sibling, he always did hold a candle for her, he would have told Algernon to go and whistle...

"After all, it's a simple enough job," Eugene continued, sloshing more wine into his glass. "Escort a bunch of academics, religious types, and some buffoon from the Army, up to the back end of beyond and keep an eye on them while they escort some kind of Pagan bauble back down to London. Once it's safely in the vault of the British Museum, job done." He paused to lean in conspiratorially. "Between you and me, Hampton, I was treating this trip as an opportunity to sample some of the local whiskey!"

"Really, Sir, I hadn't noticed," Hampton rolled his eyes as Eugene roared with laughter, his employer had certainly taken advantage of that opportunity. On their first night in Gabhar Vale, Eugene had guzzled so much of the local tipple that he'd ended up having to be carted back to his tent in a rusty wheelbarrow. He'd been worse than useless for the next two days, forcing Hampton to do all of the supervision while Eugene lay on his bedroll, groaning and complaining about the profusion of midges.

"Well," Eugene smiled with satisfaction at a job well done. "The item in question is safely on board the train... I can't see how anything can go wrong now... No, For once, I think this is easy money."

As Hampton opened his mouth to tell Eugene not to jinx things, the door at the far end of the carriage burst open, startling the nun. It was Ruby Radcliff, white as a sheet and visibly shaken. "Come quickly, Doctor Blackburn has been murdered!"

* * *

"Well, Hampton... that'll teach me to keep my ruddy trap shut," Eugene shook his head as he looked down at Blackburn's rapidly cooling corpse. "What's the verdict, then?"

"Well," Hampton sniffed as he examined the wound to the back of the late doctor's head. "There are no ligature marks or signs of gunshot or stab wounds. The only wound I can see is this big dent in the back of his head. It's a savage blow. I'd say it killed him almost instantly."

"Any idea what the murder weapon could be?"

"Well, judging by the shape of the wound… a candlestick, maybe?"

"On a train? Don't be daft, Hampton."

Hampton frowned. "It could be any blunt object, a lead pipe or a wrench, perhaps. Look around, Sir." He gestured to the myriad shovels, picks, and other tools. "Take your pick… no pun intended."

"What the blazes are you two wittering on about like a pair of old washerwomen?" The military man, Colonel Tewksbury, grumbled as he climbed over the equipment to join Eugene and Hampton. Up until now, he had been at the far end of the carriage barking orders at his valet, Dwight LeBlanc. The Sikh, Arju, and Professor Mirabelle were in the opposite corner, looking on silently, leaving Sister Olive in the dining car to look after Ruby.

"The poor chap's had his head caved in," Eugene stated flatly. "From the looks of things, he was trying to pinch something from this crate, and got clobbered for his troubles."

"We'd better search the train then," Tewksbury puffed out his chest. "The murderer can't have gone far…"

Eugene looked pointedly at the other guests, then the Colonel. "No, he, *or she*, couldn't."

"What are you implying?" Tewksbury barked, his moustache bristling.

"Well, Hampton and I did a thorough search of the train when we left Edinburgh. Aside from a few staff, there is only us lot on board, so…" He shrugged and let his words hang heavy in the musty atmosphere.

"But, we were all in the dining car, surely."

Hampton looked up from his squatted position. "We don't know exactly when it happened, Colonel, it could have been any time between him *retiring* with Miss Radcliff and the alarm being raised."

"Hampton's right," Eugene added, producing his hip flask from his inside pocket. "We will have to appraise ourselves with everybody's movements, I suggest you all return to the dining car, and we will be along presently."

"Look here, Angove," Tewksbury growled. "I represent His Majesty's Army, I'm in charge here and I will not take orders from a drunken *adventurer.*" He let the final word ooze with disdain. Eugene had been a Captain during the Great War, but had left that chapter of his life close following the armistice. In short, he wasn't going to be taking orders either.

As a consequence, the two men had been butting heads ever since they had clapped eyes on each other. Hampton saw them as two over-the-hill stags locking horns.

"And, you look *here*," Eugene grinned, taking an official document signed by Edith Stephenson and Neville Chamberlain from his blazer, tapping it with his finger. "I think you'll find that both the Order of Tamesis *and* the Prime Minister have put *me* in charge... *Colonel*."

Hampton turned his attention back to Blackburn's corpse, desperately trying not to snigger. If it was a competition in condescension that Tewksbury wanted, he was fixing to be out-classed. Nobody could top Eugene when it came to being patronising and obnoxious.

Tewksbury was fuming. His cheeks flushed red as he turned sharply and made his way back towards the door. "Come along, LeBlanc," he barked at his faithful companion, as though the slight fellow was a green private, not an ageing valet. "I can tell when I'm not wanted."

"Very good, Colonel," LeBlanc simpered, holding the door.

Once they had left, slamming the door behind them, Eugene chuckled to himself. "That Tewksbury fellow really is a charmless blister, don't you agree, Hampton?"

Hampton raised a finger.

"I know, I know, the code forbids you speaking out of turn about your betters." Eugene smirked. "Fine... don't talk. Nod once for yes and twice for *no*."

Hampton nodded.

"Professor Mirabelle?" Eugene called out as she and Arju turned to leave.

"Yes, what is it, Angove?"

"Could you come over here and check that nothing is missing from this crate? You may as well go back to the dining car, Arju."

Arju nodded curtly before leaving.

"Um, why, yes... I suppose," Mirabelle arced an immaculately plucked eyebrow over her wire-rimmed spectacles, "what about... him?" She pointed at the corpse with a tremulous digit.

"He's not going to cause you any bother, Professor, surely, you're not squeamish?"

"Well," Mirabelle shrugged, her cut-glass voice wavering. "It's just that I've never seen a dead body before."

"Ha," Eugene erupted. "Did you hear that, Hampton? The woman that spends her life digging up skulls and cataloguing bones has never dealt with a dead body before."

"Yes, but they don't have *meat* on them."

Eugene chuckled, then had a gulp of brandy.

"It's alright, Professor, I've finished gathering his personal effects," Hampton added, helpfully. "If you could pass me that tarpaulin over yonder, I can cover him up for you."

"Thank you, Hampton," Mirabelle said as she passed over the bundle. "At least one of you is a gentleman."

Her cutting remark merely made Eugene chuckle even louder. "They don't have meat on them... priceless!"

"Oh, out of the way, you big oaf!" Once Blackburn had been covered, Mirabelle elbowed Eugene aside and picked up the crowbar. For one minute, Hampton thought she was going to brain Eugene with it. Thankfully, she didn't. Instead, she levered up the lid then started to rummage in the crate.

"What did you find on the late lamented, Hampton?" Eugene asked, finally pulling himself together.

"Not much, Sir. Just some travel papers, a cigarette case, a packet of matches, and a monogrammed handkerchief." Hampton passed the documents to Eugene. "Wait... that's odd."

"What is?" Eugene unfolded the documents and started to examine them.

"Well... this handkerchief, Sir. It's monogrammed, JS, not JB."

Eugene waved this off. "He probably bought the wrong ones, he didn't strike me as the sharpest knife in the draw, despite all of his fancy qualifications."

"True, Sir, but the cigarette case is also engraved, JS."

"Hmm," Eugene's brow creased. "These documents appear to have been faked, also. You see this squiggle down here?" He pointed to one of the signatures. "This is supposed to be our old chum Stephenson's mark... it's no such thing. It doesn't even look vaguely similar."

"Cripes, Sir, you are right. But... it managed to fool the bluebottles at St Pancras!"

"Yes, well... I have long since said that the British Transport Police haven't got a single brain cell amongst the lot of them," Eugene paused for a moment to put the pieces together in his alcoholically befuddled brain. "So, if our stiff here isn't the redoubtable Doctor Blackburn, then who the bally Hell is he?"

Hampton shrugged.

"Blast it!... There goes my thoughts of a nice relaxing journey. We need to get to the bottom of this or Edith will have me stuffed and mounted before you could say, *Sherlock Holmes!*"

"It gets worse." Professor Mirabelle added in dire tones.

"What is it, Professor?"

She turned to Eugene with wide eyes. "The amulet of Shub-Niggurath… it's gone!"

* * *

"What's so important about this trinket then, Professor?" Eugene asked as they made their way through the vacant sleeper car. All the compartment doors were now open, and the rooms appeared to have been ransacked.

"The amulet of Shub-Niggurath is said to be a powerful talisman… when used in conjunction with certain passages in *The Necronomicon*, it is said to…"

"Say no more," Eugene held his hand up, "anything even vaguely connected with *that* book can't be good."

"It's not. When a couple of hikers stumbled across what turned out to be the ruins of a shrine to the Black Goat of the Woods With a Thousand Young, the Order contacted me to search for anything *dangerous*."

"Why you?"

"Because, Mr Angove, I am one of Britain's leading experts on the Great Old Ones."

"Well, Hampton, that explains why we are here… Edith could have warned us."

"You mean, you didn't know *what* we were transporting?" Mirabelle was incredulous.

Hampton cut in before Eugene could answer." Mr Angove didn't attend the briefing at The Mitre, I'm afraid he was… *indisposed*."

Now it was Professor Mirabelle's time to roar with laughter. "Oh, bravo, Hampton! Delicately put. I'm assuming by, *indisposed* you mean, drunk as a newt?"

Both men flushed, one with embarrassment, the other with mirth.

"Well, to sum up, Mr Angove, the Amulet of Shub-Niggurath mustn't fall into the wrong hands… least of all those brown-shirted swines from Deutschland. You do know that Herr Himmler is trying to get his grubby mitts on as many occult items as he possibly can?"

"The Spook Brigade, you mean?"

"Yes, Der Ahnenerbe, The SS Occult Division. Well, our spies told us that they had gotten wind of the amulet and that Himmler prized it dearly…

hence the motley crew we have here today."

Eugene nodded. "I understand, it all makes a bit more sense now. I was wondering why we had a Colonel on board. I'm assuming that the nun is here for a bit of divine intervention should things go wrong?"

"I suppose so. I confess to not knowing much about our companions. Aside from Arju, that is."

"Ah, yes, the big chap. Who is he anyway?"

"He's my assistant, on loan from Oxford. We met on a dig in New Delhi. We were out there looking for the Temple of Yig. He proved to be a useful asset when things got a little *rough.* So, when this came up, I headhunted him, he's terribly knowledgeable about the Old Ones..."

"And built like a brick outhouse to boot."

"Quite."

Hampton nipped ahead and opened the doors to the next carriage for them. It seemed that there was some kind of ruckus going on down the far end. "Sir, I think we may have trouble brewing."

After letting Professor Mirabelle go first, he stepped into the carriage and surveyed the scene. Arju and Colonel Tewksbury were standing chest to chest, hurling abuse at each other. "What the bloody hell is going on now?" Eugene bellowed.

"This *kuta* wants to ransack my room," Arju answered, not taking his eyes off Tewksbury for a second.

Mirabelle looked in her own compartment and found that it looked like a bomb had hit it. The bedding had been tossed, and all the storage spaces emptied. "What the devil do you think you are doing, man?" Her notes and stationary were strewn across the floor.

Tewksbury puffed out his chest. "I'm searching for the intruder!"

"He's been in our room too, Mr Angove," Hampton muttered. Annoyingly, Tewksbury had rumpled the day's shirts that he had laid out flat on the beds. "He's made a right old mess."

"What the buggery are you playing at, Tewksbury?" Eugene exploded. "If you've smashed my bottles of single malt, I will not be held responsible for my actions."

"Somebody had to do something aside from stand around yapping... and I would remind you that I am a colonel," whether it was a conscious thing for effect or not, the man snapped to attention. "I was conducting a room by room search. Look..." He moved away from Arju and opened the adjacent room. "I've even searched my own quarters."

Eugene peered around the door and saw that it was in the same state as the others. "That's all well and good, but why the Dickens have you pulled all of the luggage out? Surely you don't think someone could be hiding in the overhead compartment? Who are you looking for... a blasted pixie?"

"My point exactly, Mr Angove," Arju nodded. "He can see that there is nobody in there. I just don't want him going through my things. He's tipped out the contents of my suitcase... look!"

"That was an accident."

"Accident or not. I don't want your grubby paws all over my clothes," Arju folded his arms over his muscular chest.

Tewksbury went to argue but was silenced by a sibilant, "hush" from Professor Mirabelle. "Let us all just calm down, shall we? Are you satisfied that nobody is hiding in any of the compartments?"

Tewksbury sniffed. "I suppose."

"Right. Shall we all go through to the dining car, then? I'm sure you could do with a brandy, Colonel?"

"Well... erm... A wee snifter wouldn't go amiss."

"Come along then," Mirabelle threaded her arm through his and steered him out of the carriage. Arju followed along after them, his eyes burning holes in Tewksbury's back.

Eugene was impressed. Professor Mirabelle had handled the situation deftly. Part mother, part headmistress, whatever she did, it worked. He made a mental note to try her approach in the future. Though, what the Colonel would think about linking arms with him was anybody's guess. Deciding that brandy was a fine idea, he took a nip from his flask before looking around in confusion. "Hampton, where the devil have you got to?"

"In here, Sir," Hampton called from the compartment adjacent to their own.

Eugene wandered over and peered through the door. Hampton was on his knees riffling through Doctor Blackburn's valise. "Find anything?"

"Not as yet... wait." Hampton upended the bag and tipped the contents onto the floor. Next, he produced his trusty butterfly knife and swung it open. It was an incongruous item for one so refined-looking. The valet carried it for self-defence.

"What is it?"

"There appears to be something sewn into the lining, Sir," With a *rip*, Hampton slit the fabric and reached inside. "Well, I'll be blown. Look... a German passport!"

"Ruddy hell," Eugene whistled as he snatched the passport from Hampton's hands. "Say hello to Doctor Jayson Schwarz!"

"It gets worse, Sir, It appears that our imposter was a member of the Schutzstaffel!" Hampton held up an SS ID card.

"Bugger me. Well, Mirabelle did say that Herr Himmler was interested in the amulet. He was obviously sent to pinch it... the sneaky bounder."

"Indeed, Sir. But, if he was the thief, where is it now?"

"I don't know yet, Hampton, but I intend to find out. Come on, let's speak to our suspects..."

* * *

"How dare you suspect me of murder," Sister Olive fumed, her thick Scottish accent rumbling from her larynx, making her sound like she was gargling jelly. "It's one of the Ten Commandments... Thou shalt not kill!" She stared unblinking at Eugene with her bulbous eyes. Her cold gaze made him shiver. She licked her wide fleshy lips before taking a deep breath.

Eugene quickly held his hand up, halting the incoming sermon. "I'm sorry, Sister, but I have to ask everybody. You've just watched me ask everyone else the exact same question... what were your movements before you came for supper."

"Of all the nerve... *Movements* indeed."

"Sister, please," Eugene held his hands up in supplication.

"Fine... if you must know. I was in the water closet... Travel makes me... *irregular.*" The corpulent nun blushed. "Happy?" And, with that, she stood up and stormed out of the dining car in the direction of the kitchen and standard carriages.

Eugene looked at Hampton. "Well, as alibi's go, it's hardly cast-iron. When I asked about *movements,* I didn't mean..."

Hampton sniggered, despite himself. "Her reaction was a bit fishy, sir."

"Hmm," Eugene stroked his chin. "*Fishy* is one word for her..."

"Good lord," Hampton whispered, leaning in so that nobody could overhear. "You don't think she's an Innsmouther, do you?"

"I'm afraid I do, Hampton. She definitely has *the look.* In any case, we need to find out one way or another."

"How do we do that, Sir?"

"You need to get a look under her habit... see if she has gills."

"What?"

"Keep your bloody voice down, Hampton."

"How the hell am I supposed to to get her to remove her habit?"

"I don't know, but you're a resourceful chap, you'll think of something... I have full faith in your abilities. Go on, off you toddle. I'm going to speak to Miss Radcliff. She has gone for a lie-down. So far, she's the most likely suspect. It was her that found the body, after all, and she has yet to explain what *she* was doing in the baggage car. Surely, she would have come here first if she was looking for Schwarz? I'm not buying her '*I went the wrong way*' explanation for a second."

"Fine," Hampton sighed. "Meet back here, Sir?"

"Indeed, Hampton. Now, you have *duties* to attend to." Eugene patted his valet on the shoulder and grinned widely. "Good luck, old chap."

Hampton watched his employer depart. "And you, Sir... with knobs on."

* * *

Eugene steadied himself with a hand on the cold metal safety rail as the train rocked as it banked sharply to the left. Pulling the door to the sleeper car open, he hurried inside. Passing the WC, the portly adventurer nearly jumped out of his tweeds as the door flew open, revealing the ashen face of Dwight LeBlanc.

"Blimey, LeBlanc, you nearly gave me a sodding heart attack."

"Apologies, Mr Angove," LeBlanc answered as he dabbed his lips with a crumpled handkerchief. The man was looking decidedly green around the gills and there was a distinct puffiness to his pinched features.

Eugene's nose wrinkled as the pungent aroma of regurgitated sausage and mash drifted from the valet's gullet. "Everything alright?"

"Pardon? Er, yes, quite alright, Sir," LeBlanc stammered, his eyes darting from left to right. "I'm afraid that I don't travel well. Now, if you will excuse me..."

"Yes, run along," Eugene said quietly as the furtive manservant scuttled out of the car like a whippet with a bee up its backside. "I wonder what the devil has put the wind up him?" With a shrug of his broad shoulders, Eugene turned and walked towards Miss Radcliff's compartment. She and the duplicitous Doctor Schwarz had the compartment to the far side of his own. Eugene had to fight the urge to pop into his own room and have a nip of his treasured whiskey.

Reaching Ruby's door, he wrapped on it with his knuckle. "Miss Radcliff, may I come in? I have a few more questions I'd like to ask, if I may?"

No answer.

Assuming that the distraught personal assistant was either sleeping or ignoring him, he knocked again, louder this time. "Miss Radcliff... It really is a matter of the utmost importance."

Again, there was no answer.

"Oh, bugger this for a game of soldiers... Right, I'm coming in. If you are undressed, you might want to cover your bits and bobs!" With a *click*, he opened the door and instantly recoiled.

Ruby Radcliff was lying half on her bed, half off, as though she had been dragged off by her hair. A dagger had been plunged into her chest. From the positioning of the incision, and the amount of crimson soaking into the sheets, it was pointless to check for a pulse. Eugene stepped into the room and surveyed the scene. Nothing else appeared to have changed since he and Hampton had been in there earlier.

"Poor woman," Eugene sighed as he leaned over her corpse to examine the dagger. "Hold on, this is Professor Mirabelle's." Mopping his brow with his sleeve, he turned and exited the compartment. "She has some explaining to do."

Hurrying through the carriage, Eugene made his way back to the dining car. Professor Mirabelle was still sitting where he had last seen her. Over by the window, scribbling in a notebook. She looked up as Eugene entered and one look at his expression told her that something was amiss.

"Is everything alright, Mr Angove, how's Ruby?"

"Dead as a bloody stone," Eugene didn't bother softening the blow, he wanted to gauge her reaction.

"What?" Shocked, Mirabelle rose from her seat, clutching her chest. "What do you mean?"

"I mean, *dead*, Professor. As in, not breathing, expired, passed on, pushing up the blasted daisies! What the Dickens do you think I mean?"

"But... how?"

"She's been stabbed," Eugene paused for effect. "With *your* dagger. That Indian one that you keep for *protection*."

"My dagger?" Mirabelle was aghast, if she did have something to do with it, she was a damn fine actor. "How did someone get their hands on *my* dagger?" Suddenly, Eugene's implication became clear. "Wait... you can't possibly think?"

Eugene shrugged. "Did you?"

"Now look here, you blustering buffoon, how could I possibly have killed her? When she left, I was sitting here. You and Hampton were between me and the door. You would have seen me leave. Or are you so drunk that you forgot that small detail?"

"Well... erm..."

"*Hercule Poirot*, you most certainly are not. Pull yourself together, man, the real killer is still on the loose!"

"LeBlanc!" Eugene exclaimed, startling the Professor.

"I beg your pardon?"

"Where's LeBlanc... the Colonel's valet?"

"He went that way," Mirabelle pointed to the opposite end of the carriage. "He didn't look at all well... you don't think?"

Eugene turned sharply while simultaneously patting his jacket for the comforting weight of his service revolver. Leaving Mirabelle to fuss with her papers, he strode off confidently. After all, Dwight LeBlanc was in his sixties and eight-stone when soaking wet. What possible trouble could he be if he turned nasty? Reaching out for the handle, he was nearly hit in the face by the door.

"There you are, Sir," Hampton grumbled. He was rubbing his jaw, and his cheek was visibly red.

"What the hell happened to you?"

"Well, Sir. Let's just say that Sister Olive didn't appreciate me tipping a jug of water over her, then trying to remove her habit so I could dry it... not one little bit." He worked his jaw up and down to check that it wasn't dislocated.

Eugene couldn't help chuckling. "Did you find anything out?"

"Indeed, Sir. She is *not* an Innsmouther... no gills. She does, however, have one hell of a right hook on her. If it came down to a championship bout with Len Harvey... my money would be on Sister Olive, the blasted woman's vicious!"

"Well done, anyway, dear fellow. You have helped narrow it down even further... For now, though, we need to have a little chat with Mr LeBlanc."

"Oh?"

Eugene proceeded to explain the recent developments to his personal gentleman. Hampton was particularly upset about Miss Radcliff's untimely demise. Judging her to be a true innocent in the whole affair, and a dashed nice girl to boot. First, she had been seduced by a German spy then slaughtered in cold blood by a Canadian valet. It was simply wasn't cricket.

"I'll give him a damn good thrashing, you see, if I don't," Hampton raged as they crossed into the carriage containing the kitchen and stores.

The galley was empty and in disarray, Eugene had told all of the staff to remain in the guard carriage until the amulet had been recovered. Dirty crockery was piled in metal baskets awaiting the touch of soapy water. "Well, where the ruddy hell is he then?" Eugene bellowed, placing his hands on his hips.

"Standard class, perhaps... I didn't see him on the way through."

"Maybe he passed you when you were, ahem, *otherwise engaged* with Sister Olive."

"Perhaps," Hampton rubbed his jaw, it still stung like hell.

Passing the range and food preparation areas, Eugene and Hampton hurried towards the next door. As they reached the storage area, the train rocked and there was a heavy *thump* against the door of the storage locker. Both men paused. Eugene drew his revolver instinctively, putting his finger to his lips, he backed away and took aim. Giving Hampton the nod, he prepared to fire.

Hampton reached out and pulled the lever to open the door. It creaked and swung ajar as the dead weight of Dwight LeBlanc slipped onto the floor at their feet. "Blimey, Sir, he's been garrotted!"

"Good Lord," Eugene pocketed his firearm and knelt down. The murderer had used so much force that the ligature had bitten into the skin, drawing rivulets of crimson that had stained the starched white collar of his shirt. "So much for him being our killer, we are right back at square one."

"Indeed, sir." Hampton turned the man's head to get a look at the garotte. "Hold on. This is unusual."

"What... the rope? How interesting can a bally rope be, Hampton?"

"Very, if you know what you are looking for."

"Smugness doesn't suit you, Hampton."

"Apologies, Sir... It's just that this isn't ordinary rope. it's not made from hemp or cotton, and appears to be braided Indian silk."

"Indian silk... Arju!" Eugene yelped in triumph. "Come along, Hampton, and bring that wrench with you. he's a big lad."

Hampton looked around and saw what Eugene had indicated. He picked up the large adjustable spanner and followed on behind. "I don't understand it, Sir, the Sikhs are an honourable bunch, this kind of cloak and dagger business is anathema to them."

"That's if he is a Sikh, Hampton, we only have his word for that. Need I remind you that the garotte is the favoured weapon of the Thuggee?"

"Point taken, Sir," Hampton shuddered, he and Eugene had spent some time in India after the war, and he had seen up-close the handiwork of those notorious bandits.

Hampton led the way as they crashed into the first standard class carriage. Sister Olive was presently perched in a seat to the centre, knitting furiously. Hampton's pace quickened ever so slightly as he passed. The former regimental boxing champion knew when he was outmatched.

"Stay in your seat, Sister." Eugene bellowed, nearly making the nun drop what looked like a woollen nightmare into her lap. "There's a maniac on board."

She tutted then glared after Hampton. "How right you are!"

The two men crossed to the next carriage, with Hampton opening the door for Eugene. He stepped inside and drew his revolver. "Arju, halt!"

Arju was standing over Colonel Tewksbury brandishing a length of lead piping. The military man was on his knees, clutching his shoulder in pain. Arju turned, startled. "Mr Angove, you're just in time."

Bang!

Before Arju could say anything else, Tewksbury drew his own pistol and fired, hitting him in the right shoulder. The big man spun and collapsed in a heap.

"Tewksbury, what the hell happened?"

The Colonel ignored Eugene and started to riffle Arju's clothes. The archaeologist was bleeding profusely and groaning in pain. "Where is it?" Tewksbury was like a man possessed. "Where is it, you bastard?" He took his pistol and whipped Arju with it.

"Tewksbury, stop. For the love of God, what's wrong with you, man?"

"There you are... I've got it." Tewksbury stood, holding the Amulet of Shub-Niggurath like a prize.

Arju backed against a seat, clutching the exit wound just below his collar bone. Eugene and Hampton rushed over. Hampton bunched his hankie and pressed it to the wound.

"Why?" Eugene demanded. "Who do you work for?"

"To keep it out of enemy hands..." Arju produced a flat stone from his pocket. It was emblazoned with a star design. It was a river stone from the Thames, the seal of the Order of Tamesis.

"What? Explain yourself."

Click

The unmistakable sound of a revolver's hammer being cocked stopped Eugene's interrogation. He rose slowly, turning to face Colonel Tewksbury. "Stay where you are. Don't move a blasted muscle." Tewksbury grinned as he stuffed the amulet into his pocket.

"What's the meaning of this, Colonel?"

"Power, that's what. This amulet will give the British Army the power to wipe its enemies off the map! When I call Shub-Niggurath and bring her Thousand Young to our reality, nobody will stand in our way... The Empire will rise again!"

"You're as mad as a blasted March hare," Eugene spat. "You're no better than that SS bounder!"

"How dare you," Tewksbury levelled the gun at Eugene's head. "I'm doing this for King and country."

"And what if the King doesn't want a bunch of eldritch monstrosities trotting about England's green and pleasant land, hmm?"

Tewksbury chuckled. "Oh, he will… when he sees the power of Shub-Niggurath, he will welcome me into the fold with open arms. Hell, he might even let me marry that pretty daughter of his, Elizabeth."

"Ha," Eugene guffawed. "I've never heard such balderdash in all my life!"

"Careful, Sir," Hampton whispered. "This man's not the full shilling."

"You really think that the King wants the minions of Shub-Niggurath at Buckingham Palace. I don't know what the Thousand Young are, but I'd wager they will make a right mess of the soft furnishings."

"Silence, oaf," Tewksbury again pointed the gun at Eugene's head before relaxing a little. "No, I won't shoot you. This seems like a perfect opportunity to see if this fabled bauble actually works." Tewksbury grinned maniacally as he reached into his inside pocket and took out a notebook. "I had a chap at the MOD copy me the relevant passages from the copy of *The Necronomicon* that they have in Cambridge. Now, let's see…" Tewksbury cleared his throat and raised the amulet in his left hand. "*Iä Shub-Niggurath, mglw'nafh hh'ahor syha'h ah'legeth fhtagn!*"

Instantly, the carriage shook, and the panelled wall at Eugene's elbow started to darken and grow indistinct. The shimmer in reality was accompanied by a mephitic odour and a hellish din akin to someone raking a scythe down a blackboard.

"Look out, Sir!" Hampton cried as a thick rope-like tentacle whipped through the widening gap in reality. It thrashed to the left, splintering a crate and scattering its contents, a dozen or so large potatoes, across the galley floor. Ducking and weaving the valet dodged the appendage while Tewksbury laughed like a drain.

"Marvellous! It works, it dashed well works. Now, if I can find the correct words, I can get the creature to fully emerge and pull your wretched arms off!" Raising the amulet once more, the Colonel resumed his chant. "*N'ghftephai n'gha ahornah ah'mglw'nafh!*"

This time, the tentacle of the Dark Young thrashed in Tewksbury's direction, almost catching him a wallop in his belly. "Blast it. That's not it. To the left, you stupid creature!"

Eugene erupted with laughter. "You big nelly, you've got no more control over that thing than I have over a cricket bat after ten pints!"

"Silence!"

Eugene chuckled as Tewksbury threw the notebook to the floor and levelled the gun at his head.

"I guess a bullet will have to do after all."

"Go ahead, if your marksmanship is on a par with your reading skills, you wouldn't be able to hit a barn door!"

Tewksbury snarled and cocked the hammer, all the while, the rift widened and the tentacle continued to quest for a tasty morsel.

Eugene raised his hands and grinned, his taunting hadn't merely been for his own amusement. It was also a careful ruse to stop Tewksbury from looking behind him. Eugene's laughter, and the din of the portal, had covered the sound of the door opening. The bluff chap was perfectly unaware that Sister Olive had crept up behind him with her knitting needles clasped in her right hand...

Tewksbury screamed as Sister Olive rammed her needles into his right buttock. He jerked forwards, losing his footing. The amulet dropped from his hand and clattered to the floor, the incantation incomplete, the tentacle withdrew and the rift winked out of existence. As Tewksbury grabbed his posterior with both hands and turned unsteadily, the violent nun swung with all her weight and walloped him in the left temple with a hardback edition of the Catholic Bible.

Colonel Tewksbury hit the floor with a dull *thud.* Seconds later, Professor Mirabelle entered the carriage. "What in God's name is going on here?"

Eugene smiled as he pocketed the Colonel's revolver and the amulet. "Just a bit of divine intervention, Professor... that's all."

* * *

"Here, a nice cup of tea," Hampton placed the cup down on the table in front of Arju, then turned to Eugene. "Do you want one, sir?"

"No, Hampton. I need something a little stronger." Eugene unscrewed the cap on his bottle of single malt and glugged a hefty measure into a teacup. "So, Arju, are you going to enlighten us as to what the hell happened?"

"Indeed... I have been in the employ of the Order for several years now. I was given instructions to accompany and protect Professor Mirabelle, and the amulet, at any cost. Mr Stephenson told me not to trust anyone."

"Funny, that's what Edith said to me. Bloody Stephensons. This would have been a hell of a lot easier had we known we were on the same team."

Eugene shook his head.

Arju nodded in agreement. "Anyway, when we met Doctor Blackburn, I instantly knew he was an imposter. You see, the real Professor Blackburn made a speech at Oxford last year. I didn't want to blow my cover, so I decided to keep an eye on him.

"Just before I joined you for supper, I heard his door open. He didn't pass mine, so I knew he was up to something. To cut a long story short, I followed him, and when I saw him take the amulet, I clobbered him with a length of lead piping. I'm afraid that I hit him a little too hard. I only meant to incapacitate him."

"But, why did you take the amulet?" Hampton asked as he sat down next to Eugene.

"I didn't know who else was in on it. I thought for certain that Miss Radcliff was... poor woman. I assume that Tewksbury thought the same?"

"Indeed," Eugene nodded. "he has told me everything. The damn fellow won't shut up... He's locked up in the guard's cage, by the way... Well, when Schwarz was found dead, he hid in an empty compartment until you had gone then lurked outside while Mirabelle looked for the amulet. When he heard that it was gone, he searched the rooms. That's when he had a set-to with you, Arju. Later, when we were talking to you and Mirabelle, he snuck out after Ruby, believing her to have the amulet."

"That's why he killed her?" Hampton asked.

"I'm afraid so. Tewksbury didn't want Ruby making a fuss while he riffled her effects. Unfortunately for him, LeBlanc saw him come out of the compartment while he was throwing up. Tewksbury knew that when Ruby was found, his valet would put two and two together. He had to be silenced. I can only imagine he took Mirabelle's dagger and Arju's braided silk to throw us off the scent... sneaky blighter."

"So, what happens now?" Arju asked.

"Well, we will be arriving in London shortly where I will hand over the amulet and Tewksbury to Edith Stephenson and her pet constables... then go and get blind drunk."

Arju laughed. "Sounds like you have it all planned out. I should go and see Mr Stephenson."

"If you do," Eugene smiled. "Give him a kick in the plums from me, there's a good chap."

THE SQUIRMING SCRIPT

I.A. WATSON

"The man has the most abysmal handwriting I have ever seen," I suggested to A.H. Whitstable. "Surely he has abandoned all attempt at the alphabet and has simply filled page after page with random scrawls and doodles?"

My academic friend shook his head in mild reproof. "Push past your preparatory-school lessons, Captain Ashworth. Suppress your inner English-teacher's tutorship in copperplate. There is writing here, just not in the characters and language to which you are accustomed."

"You think so?" our visitor at Whitstable's London lodgings asked eagerly. "I had hoped..."

Whitstable held up one long, spindly finger for silence. He was still examining the journal before him and preferred to draw his conclusions uninterrupted.

The document in question was a commonplace work-journal of the late Professor Aldwyn Enderlidge, an anthropologist of some repute who had passed away two days previously, during his visit to our capital. The anxious querent was his fellow scholar Dr Simon Appleby, the librarian from the New England academic institution at which Enderlidge had been tenured. Appleby had been diverted from his sabbatical at the Bibliotheque Nationale to supervise the recovery and return of the deceased researcher's notes and artefacts.

I examined the yellow-leafed writing volume more closely, trying to see it as my comrade Atherton Whitstable must perceive it. To me it appeared to be a standard leather-bound journal such as any man might keep as a diary or notebook. It was somewhat travel-battered and stained from its journey to the South Pacific, where Enderlidge had recently completed a two-year expedition amongst the indigenous tribes of Polynesia.

Whitstable, that eccentric doyen of K___'s College, seemed fascinated by the test. He ran his fingertips over wrinkled paper whose edges betrayed the moist conditions to which the book must have been exposed. The writing-ink was plain black and smeared only a little. Certain diagrams had been rendered in charcoal pencil. I estimated there must be a hundred pages in the journal, of which two-thirds were filled with Enderlidge's notes. Some quarter of the content was enciphered in the strange scrawling script that looked to me as if a fly had fallen into the inkpot then rolled in its death-throes over the page. I said as much.

"You would be doing a disservice to the writer, Ashworth," Whitstable corrected me. "A careful examination would reveal the delicacy of the author, a precision of penmanship that betrays a deep understanding of the language being written. I hesitate to use the term alphabet for this manuscript, since I see that no two characters recur on a single page."

"But it is a message?" Appleby ventured. "I was certain that – I hoped that – Aldwyn had kept some record of his findings other than the pottery shards and masonry that he shipped to London."

"Why London?" I wondered. "If your anthropologist was in the South Pacific, on an expedition funded by the Miskatonic Institute, Massachusetts where you both work, would it not be a significant detour to head to England on your way home?"

"The British Museum," the librarian explained. "Enderlidge uncovered a series of ancient ruins on Tuamotu and Mangareva, with some carved basalt blocks of vast antiquity. He retrieved a few of the smaller examples with carvings in this language and some fragments of pots or plates with much the same script imprinted on them. He felt he must divert here to compare them with certain artefacts held in the British Museum's archive, relics of a Royal Navy expedition to the Marquesas Islands in the middle of the last century; that unfortunate expedition where the crew ran mad with ergot poisoning. There was a significant similarity in the artefacts' provenance, possible evidence of a proto-culture predating the current indigenous occupation of those islands."

Whitstable flicked back and forward through the pages of the journal, comparing the writings. In between the slabs of incomprehensible rubbish were more mundane descriptions of Enderlidge's voyage and explorations, rendered in proper form except for some abominable American shorthand

and misspellings.

"Professor and Mrs Enderlidge and two assistants set out some twenty-three months ago," Whitstable surmised from the account, though this was only the most recent of the anthropologist's logbooks. "They progressed through the Eastern part of the French Polynesian chain, beginning at Cook Island. It was on some of the most obscure of the eighty-odd tiny islands and atolls that Enderlidge made his discoveries. This particular volume begins with their arrival on Anaa in the Tuamotu Archipelago."

The early pages of the diary included sketch-maps and some few drawings of crude stone implements and one fierce-looking blade, but more and more of the pages were copies of the unintelligible scrawl that had intrigued the anthropologist, and about which Dr Appleby was now consulting Dr Atherton Whitstable.

"It may be a significant breakthrough," the Miskatonic librarian asserted. "Enderlidge seemed very excited. We all were, eagerly awaiting his correspondence packets. The photographs he forwarded, of the stones and fragments, caused much excited debate in the common room. His death came as a terrible shock."

"So great that you were hauled away from your own research to catch the overnight boat-train from Paris and hasten here within thirty-six hours of his demise," Whitstable observed.

Appleby looked a little evasive. "Well, there was some concern about the academics of the British Museum… about whether they might try to hold on to the items that Enderlidge and his team had retrieved, to try and study them here. To be honest, the Miskatonic wired me to hasten over and maintain a firm claim on Enderlidge's finds and the academic credit for them. Not that we have not the greatest regard and respect for…"

"Enderlidge's team is still here?"

"Yes. Mrs Enderlidge and two post-graduate students, Clegg and Visitor. But it was felt that… you will understand that Mrs Enderlidge is rather devastated by her husband's sudden and untimely passing. The students lack the seniority required to… assert a proper claim." The uncomfortable librarian clumsily shifted the topic. "It will take two or three days to clear up the customs, legal, and academic issues, but since there will be a necessary delay… that is, I had the inspiration to think of you. This mystery script, and the chance for me to consult the author of such a monograph as *Notes Upon the Cargo Cults of the South Pacific, with Reference to the Protomyths of Ktul and Dag*, it seemed too good a chance to let pass."

"You expect Whitstable to make sense of this gibberish?" I challenged.

"My dear Ashworth!" Whitstable chided me, "Surely you are aware that the 8th century polymath Abu Mūsā Jābir ibn Hayyān, known now as the father of chemistry and by his Latinised name Geber,[1] recorded his research in a coded language of his own devising, which many ignorant fools took to be meaningless – the origin of the term gibberish? Modern language defines gibberish as without meaning, whereas its first usage comes from coded wisdom which appears nonsense to the uninitiated but is valuable, vital knowledge to those possessing the key."

"Surely," I replied vaguely. It is best to allow Whitstable his didactic moments and pass on.

"As for this remarkable document, Dr Appleby, I would appreciate an opportunity to study it further, or to take photographic plates if you would prefer to retain the original. I can already tell you that there is certainly a code here. Look at the characters of the untranslated messages. You see there are upper and lower flourishes quite independent of the central glyph? I posit that these peripheral flourishes differentiate the meaning of the text by their association with the characters before and after, and possibly above and below. The writing is therefore not linear but almost three-dimensional. Fascinating."

Whitstable reached for his sherbet box; it is his habit when he wishes to retreat into that inner cerebral world wherein he can think most deeply to resort to that disgusting Turkish soda powder as if he were an infant at some foreign bazaar. It was left to me to negotiate the temporary loan of Professor Enderlidge's final journal and to make proper farewell to Appleby, with an invitation for him to call tomorrow at the same time and discover what progress had been made.

"What do you make of it, Whitstable?" I asked once the librarian was dispatched.

I doubt that Atherton Whitstable even heard me speak.

After a time, one grows accustomed to my companion's odd moods and introverted ruminations. It is pointless to be offended, or to try and disturb him. Indeed, it would be both cruel and unproductive to divert the chain of thought of such a magnificent mind when it is working to capacity. Therefore I ignored him, made myself some buttered toast, and settled down to read the newspaper.

It was two hours later and I had just lit the lamps when Whitstable

---

[1] Abu Mūsā Jābir ibn Hayyān (fl. c. 721 – c. 815) is accounted the author of over 3,000 treatises on chemistry, alchemy, astronomy, astrology, engineering, geography, philosophy, physics, pharmacy, and medicine.

looked up at me with wide, urgent eyes and said, "Professor Enderlidge was murdered."

* * *

The St James' Hospital morgue attendant was fortunately familiar with Whitstable and I, which helped convince him to allow us access to the sealed metal drawer that held the mortal remains of Professor Aldwyn Enderlidge. It was not the only time we had disturbed Orderly Harris with an urgent request.

"Was there an autopsy, Harris?" I asked the man.

"Of course," the attendant assured me. "A forty-five year old man in apparent good health who drops dead of a heart-attack in the British Museum will require attention from the coroner. Dr Finch examined the corpse yesterday, not less than six hours after it came in."

"His verdict?"

"Previously undiagnosed heart-disease, exacerbated by recent strenuous foreign travel. Lungs, liver, and kidneys were in good order. The stomach contents were tested for the usual toxins, of course."

"He was murdered all the same," Whitstable insisted.

"Perhaps you might explain why you have drawn that conclusion, Whitstable?" I asked somewhat testily. "Whilst I am willing to be dragged down to the morgue at a time when I would usually be enjoying a pleasant supper, I would prefer some context. Have pity and explain!"

Whitstable snatched the paperwork from Harris and expounded as he flicked through it. "I have begun to decode the encrypted parts of the good professor's journal. It seemed logical to begin with his final entry, so as to understand where his thoughts were at his last writing. Also of interest was that this entry was made during the steamer voyage to London, over a week after he had departed from the sites he had been exploring. And yet there was new coded text. This suggested not a blind-copying of some ancient source, but rather new-originated material rendered into the unknown language."

"You have cracked it? You can read the journal now."

"The genius of that script is that the upper and lower modifiers render every single page different. I know the method of it, but each paragraph, each sentence, is unique. This is no simple substitution cypher, nor a pictographic language, but rather one of mathematical genius. As you saw, three hours cerebral labour won me the very final paragraph as best I could render it."

"And that informed your urgency to view Enderlidge's corpse?"

"Indeed. And informed me that Enderlidge was actually writing in English."

"English? But the scribbles..."

"Properly decoded, they translate as glottal codes, of throat and tongue sounds and movements. They are, in fact, pronunciation guides, forming comprehensible words in our own language. One need only shape the right vocalisms and the message is literally spoken."

"And the murder part?"

"As best I can interpret, the final paragraph of Enderlidge's journal reads: *I doubt now that I will live to prove my theories. I am marked for death. It grows within me. The curse proved true. The monsters will kill me. Now only horror remains.*"

I frowned. "Perhaps he was aware of his illness? He is speaking metaphorically."

"Or perhaps he knew that his end had been devised." He turned to Harris. "Please be so good as to allow us to view the corpse. I expect it to be quite instructive."

Harris reached down and heaved back the mortuary drawer. We all recoiled as a cloud of flies burst out of the confined space. The morgue attendant swore.

There must have been a hundred of the things, black bodied and dark red-eyed, about the size of my smallest fingernail. They swarmed from the metal container and dispersed lazily around the examination room.

I stared at the dead man and caught my breath. One of Enderlidge's eyes was gone, eaten away. The socket was now a crawling mess of fat yellow maggots, welling out to explore over the corpse's face.

Whitstable bent closer in fascination. "Tweezers, Ashworth," he prompted me.

I forced my attention away from writhing mass and buzzing cloud and found the instrument he requested. Whitstable picked up one of the wriggling larva and examined it under his magnifier. "Might I trouble you to apprehend one or more of those flies, Ashworth?" he asked, as equitably as if he had been requesting I pass the salt.

"This is wrong!" Harris stammered, backing away from the drawer. "Very wrong! Those things... they were not in there before. The drawer was sealed."

"Of course they were in there before," Whitstable told him scornfully. "Look at the dead man. Can you not see that the infestation occurred internally; almost certainly the *actual* cause of Professor Enderlidge's collapse and demise. Ah, you have acquired a sample for me, Ashworth – excellent. Now look!"

I was less filled with detective vigour for examining the specimen I had caught under a Petri dish than was Whitstable. I was all too aware that the hospital morgue was now swarming with the very creatures that had apparently gnawed their way out of their victim's skull.

But Whitstable was emphatic. "You recognise the species, Ashworth? *Cochliomyia hominivorax*, I'll warrant, though at first I had thought *Chrysomya bezziana*, the European counterpart. But of course, Enderlidge was in the Pacific. This specimen of *Calliphoridae* is undoubtedly from the New World."

"You have caught the, um, the murderer then?" I ventured.

"Hardly, Ashworth. But I have discovered the murder weapon. This little insect is colloquially known as the New World Screw-Worm Fly. And of course, the *hominivorax* part of its name means 'man-eating'. It is a known pest in South America, the South Seas, and the lower latitudes of the United States – known and feared."

"You know of it, then?"

"The female enters the body through an open wound or sore, or less often through soft membrane like the eyes, ears, nostrils, rectum, or generative organs, or a newborn's umbilical. She lays her eggs, perhaps two hundred and fifty to five hundred of them, which develop into larvae that burrow or 'screw' deeper into the flesh around them to feed. Three to seven days after hatching, they eat their way out to pupate. Four or five days after hatching, the adult fly, of which you have a new-born specimen under glass there, then mates and the 20-day cycle begins anew. A female can lay 3,000 eggs and fly a hundred and twenty miles in her lifetime."[2]

I failed to suppress a shudder. "Enderlidge had these things growing inside him?"

"A proper, competent autopsy will now be required," Whitstable declared in censorious tones, "but a preliminary view suggests that these larva hatched in the late doctor's brain and devoured it. They made their exit through his eye socket."

[2] Those wishing further authoritative data on the New World Screw-Worm Fly may refer to the California Department of Food and Agriculture's publication at
https://www.cdfa.ca.gov/ahfss/Animal_Health/pdfs/Screwworm_Fact_Sheet.pdf

Contemporary citizens of the United States can be assured at the species' eradication in North America since 1982, with the exception of isolated outbreaks from imported animals.

"*The monsters will kill me indeed*. Did he know?"

Whitstable would not theorise without more data. "There is another question, Ashworth. Some of the maggots are still in pupal form, but others are fully developed flies. This suggests not one but two infestations, some days apart. The most recent myiasis cannot have taken place more than a week before Enderlidge's death."

"While he was on the boat to England!"

"Indeed. And while one fatal exposure to *Cochliomyia hominivorax* in the South Pacific might just feasibly have occurred – though it would be notable in the medical literature – two such incidents suggests an artificial intervention."

"Or a curse."

"If there is a curse, it has a human agent," A.H. Whitstable growled.

* * *

The remainder of the Miskatonic expedition was lodged at the Bridge House Hotel, just south of the river across Tower Bridge. Dr Appleby effected introductions to the Widow Enderlidge and to the post-graduates Thomas Clegg and Harvey Visitor.

"You have heard from the Coroner's Office?" Whitstable checked with them by way of an opening remark. He has little patience for the common decencies. "You are aware that the matter of Aldwyn Enderlidge's death is now being reopened as a murder enquiry?"

"We have all received summonses," Appleby answered stiffly. "What we were told was gruesome and... surely not conceivably true?"

"We were the first witnesses," I assured the librarian. "Mrs Enderlidge, we are very sorry for your loss. The recent revelation can only add to your heartache."

"I am so amazed I do not know what to think," the bereaved woman answered. Her grief was evident to me, but she bore it gracefully. Anne Enderlidge was a comely woman, perhaps ten or fifteen years her husband's junior, and had formerly been his secretary before they wed. "So much has happened so quickly. Two weeks ago we were on Nukutepipi, one of the smallest of the Duke of Gloucester Islands, trawling the lagoon for more of the ancient soapstones with that extraordinary script on them. Three days ago we were still aboard the SS *Hosmer Small*, making for London – and Aldwyn was alive. Just the day before yesterday we were meeting Dr Murdoch at the British Museum, with Dr Smallhorn of the Royal Society, when... well, you know what happened."

"I would prefer a first-hand account," Whitstable replied, with little regard for the lady's feelings.

"I can tell you," Visitor chipped in valiantly. "We were all there. Professor Enderlidge was showing some of the carved artefacts we had dredged from the reefs and lagoons – all our discoveries were made in shallow water, similar to the pre-Roman sacrificial cult objects recovered from rivers and lakes in the United Kingdom. There was considerable excitement. It looked like the Brits were going to co-operate and grant us access to compare our finds with the sealed material in their 'black archive', the British Museum's closed storage for controversial and difficult items. We wanted to see the HMS *Doubtless'* finds from Fatu Heva in the Marquesas Islands, you see. And then the professor just stopped speaking, mid sentence. His eyes widened as if he saw something we did not. He tried to reach out. He tried to speak again. And then he fell down – dead!"

"Yes," agreed Clegg. "It rather spoiled the meeting."

Visitor and Appleby gave him annoyed glares at his inappropriate irreverence, but the student researcher didn't seem to care. Clegg was a small, somewhat dishevelled fellow in his late twenties. He looked as though he should have body odour, though he did not. I found myself disliking him, though I had little rational reason. Visitor was more presentable, an eloquent and well-mannered fellow who would at least meet my gaze.

"Aldwyn simply died, instantly, right there in front of us," Mrs Enderlidge whispered. "Cursed."

Whitstable jumped upon the word. "Why say that?" After all, the widow could not know of his translation of her husband's last journal log.

"Oh, it's what we were told all the time on the islands. Our excavations were not popular. We had great difficulties with our interviews."

Visitor explained more. "There are a good many superstitions amongst the indigenous races of the South Pacific. The Polynesians are generally thought to have slowly migrated west across the ocean from around two or three thousand years before Christ, arriving in the Cook Islands and Tahiti around the second century A.D. and arriving at Hawai'i and Easter Island towards the end of the first millennium. They have all sorts of stories about guidance from the gods and suchlike. But the tales that interested us the most were about the ruins and structures they found *already there* on the islands when they arrived."

"Nobody wanted to talk about that," Clegg grumbled. "Half of what they did say was made-up to get rid of us, or to milk the rich Americans out of their grant money."

"The carved soapstones and a few old blocks we unearthed – unsea'd actually – were the first solid evidence of a previous civilisation in the Pacific triangle," Visitor went on. "The locals knew about the sunken artefacts but they didn't like them."

"There was some reference to this in Enderlidge's English journal entries," Appleby recalled. "All sorts of wild legends about orgies with sea monsters – or sea gods, possibly – and sunken temples and so on."

"We found clear signs of cult activity," Visitor insisted. "There were certain sites, at sea promontories and lagoon spurs, where votive items had been dropped into the water. Ritual deposits, quite deliberately placed near the old carved blocks. Some of the offerings had been shattered first, like those stones with the five-pointed diagrams on them. That's where we recovered most of the materials with carvings and etchings on them, brought up by locals we paid to dive for us."

"Assuming those carvings *are* ancient," objected Clegg. "Once the natives knew we would pay for them, we probably spawned a cottage industry."

"The local people were superstitious and claimed there was a curse," Whitstable summarised impatiently.

"We laughed at them," Mrs Enderlidge confessed. Her sentence ended in a choked sob.

"Maggots in his eye? Really?" Clegg asked us.

"Perhaps we don't talk about this here?" Visitor challenged his fellow student viciously, with a significant glance at the distressed widow.

"It will need to be talked about sometime."

"Agreed. But not now."

Whitstable watched the rival interplay without comment. "What of the script in Professor Enderlidge's last journal?" he enquired.

"Copied from the stones we found," Visitor suggested. "Some of the blocks were too big to shift without heavy lifting gear. The largest were ten feet wide and twenty feet down."

"Rubbish!" Clegg snorted. "We never found any text as long as the passages in that journal. It doesn't match any of the photographs we took. Alright, the very first entry, the short one, that was copied from the Anuanurunga site. But the rest... no chance."

"Unless the professor found sources he didn't share with us? He wasn't above keeping a few secrets, you know."

Clegg glanced sideways at Mrs Enderlidge, then discarded discretion and delicacy anyway. "What, his 'special interviews' with young Polynesian girls? I doubt they were deciphering ancient translations."

"I know about his interviews," the widow snapped. "Aldwyn was a complicated man, a great man, and though he had... weaknesses, he was a brilliant scholar. I do not doubt that he was able to decipher the fragments we found and learn to write more."

Visitor glared at Clegg then deliberately turned from him to face us. "I asked the professor, on the voyage to England, how he was getting on translating the script. Knowing what the stones said – dedications, prayers, even curses, would have helped so much with insight into this lost culture we know virtually nothing about. He was more bothered by his imaginary stalker." The student looked to me. "Do you think the, um, the things worming into his brain might have made him see things? Or believe that someone was stalking him?"

Mrs Enderlidge frowned. "Stalking him? On the *Hosmer Small?* It was a small boat, with a compliment of no more than two dozen and eight passengers."

"Is *that* why he made the captain conduct a search for stowaways?" Clegg asked, in the tones of a man for whom a puzzle had been solved. "He was already going potty!"

"Mister Clegg!" Dr Appleby chided.

"A stalker?" Whitstable repeated. "Elucidate."

Visitor shrugged. "As the journey progressed, Professor Enderlidge seemed to become obsessed with the idea that he was being watched. Hunted. I told him he was imagining things. As Mrs Enderlidge said, it was a small vessel. But the professor claimed he had glimpsed a crooked grey-garbed figure – 'shambling' was how he described him – haunting the gangways and slipping between the crates in the cargo hold. He asked me to keep watch for him."

"You never mentioned this to me," Mrs Enderlidge objected.

"I didn't want to worry you. And the professor instructed me not to. He was... quite worked up about it. Perhaps he thought someone was planning to steal his discovery? Or... I don't know."

"Push brain-eating flies into his skull?" Clegg scorned. "The curse of the underwater orgy-monsters!"

I felt that the interview was slipping somewhat out of control. Though Whitstable seemed quite content to let the sniping continue, I felt for Enderlidge's poor relic. "There *is* the question of how the Screw-Worm Flies got into the dead man," I mentioned. "Can any of you offer any plausible suggestion?"

"Other than crooked shadows?" Clegg replied.

"Preferably."

"Suicide."

I raised my brows. "What?"

Clegg set his jaw. "I mean it. Old Enderlidge was getting pretty weird on the way back to civilisation. You both know it too, you're just too polite to say. I'm not surprised he started seeing shadowy shamblers. He locked himself in the hold with the assemblage we'd collected, all hours, poring over the site photos, scribbling in his damned journal, hardly eating, hardly sleeping. Not talking to anyone. God forbid he should share his academic insights with his students! I wouldn't put it past him to stick the damn grubs up his nose himself."

Appleby reacted. "Clegg! You go too far!"

He had. The widow's last courage deserted her and she dissolved into tears.

Whitstable was still watching carefully as Dr Appleby led her away and the interview ended in disarray.

* * *

"Cy-clop-ean," said Atherton Whitstable, without looking up from his studies.

"I beg your pardon?" I responded. I was on my way to bed, since I had no obsession with staying up all night staring at Professor Enderlidge's confounded notebook.

"Oh, just sounding aloud the syllables I'm decoding. I'm getting through it slowly, except for that first short piece. I can tell what that was supposed to sound like, I believe, but not what the words mean."

"So the rest is in English, just... written in sunken scrawl."

"Yes. A secret diary, if you like. Much like my brother Bancroft and I used, to write messages to one another as children. I suspect Enderlidge found a pleasant irony in encoding his thoughts in the very language he had striven so hard to decipher."

"You know what he wrote, then?"

"It will take days, if not weeks, to complete the calculations for all of it, Ashworth. Fortunately it will not require a full translation to get to the bottom of this affair."

"The vital clue is in the document?"

"The vital clue is the document." Whitstable shifted and turned to another bookmarked page. "To satisfy your curiosity, this is an early passage. I have not troubled with a full transcription, but here is as far as I got before I decided to turn my efforts elsewhere."

I looked over the notes he handed me. "'Silky nut-brown flesh…' 'half-formed bosom…' 'smooth naked…' Hmph. Is this a description of some amorous encounter that the professor enjoyed?"

"In some graphic detail, Ashworth. He evidently felt the need to diary his liaison but could not trust it to plain script. There are several similar passages in the first half of his… entries."

"Then Clegg's insinuation about Professor Enderlidge was accurate. The man was a philanderer."

"Other notation is of a more academic nature. It seems that the professor had doubts about his students. He felt he had made a significant discovery and was reluctant to share the credit."

I checked the next sheet of translation. "'I must find a way to keep Visitor and Clegg's ambitions under control and minimise their share. The discovery is mine, and I shall have it! It has been here for a thousand years or more and only I had the wit to find it, to reveal it. Visitor and Clegg contributed little, sacrificed nothing. It was meant for me, only me, and it shall be mine.' Well, that's an insight. Academic hubris and jealousy?"

"There is more like it, though I have not plumbed it all yet. The latter part of the texts is also illuminating."

I took the proffered work-sheet. " 'The crooked thing has followed me aboard,' " I read. " 'I have seen it twice now, once as I examined artefacts in the hold, and again as I passed down the companionway to my cabin. It chills me to the marrow. I feel that it is wholly malevolent. Yet Visitor claims it is only my imagination and the captain is sceptical of a stowaway. I begin to wonder about the natives' talk of curses, of sea-horrors. We cross a vast unknowable ocean of uncharted and alien deeps. What did those primal men who raised those ancient temples know of it that we do not? How much of what was born under different stars yet survives to haunt our sane rational world? I dread to know.' " I ignored a chill down my spine; it was not enough years since the *Titanic* was lost with so many hands – and my heart.[3] "How far into the voyage did Enderlidge write this? Would he have been infected with the larva yet?"

"Perhaps at that very time," Whitstable considered. "The first myiasis, that is. The other must have occurred perhaps two or three days later, about the time that the captain gave in to the doctor's portuning and conducted a search of his vessel."

---

[3] Ashworth's first wife Louisa died on 15th April 1912 when the Olympic-class ocean liner RMS *Titanic* on which she was travelling struck an iceberg and sank with immense loss of life.

"So the murderer was on the *Hosmer Small*. The mysterious crooked man?"

"Ah, he is a very helpful phenomenon. The first time that Enderlidge saw him shuffling in the cargo bay, Visitor was close by. The professor called him and pointed out the retreating figure, but Visitor could not perceive him – or was possibly just a second or two slow looking at the right shadow. The second time, Clegg was witness to Enderlidge rushing up to inform the captain of an intruder. You see the significance?"

"Not immediately. I'm sure you'll be happy to lecture me."

Whitstable chuckled. "You get testy when you are baffled, Ashworth. And you are testy so often. Well, I am afraid you will be testier yet before morning. We have a long night's vigil ahead of us."

"And the purpose of this vigil?" I demanded,

"My friend," Whitstable replied. "We are going to catch a monster."

* * *

The katuali[4] is a yard-long sea snake found exclusively in waters off the island of Niue in the South Pacific.[5] Its venom makes it one of the most dangerous creatures on the planet.

As midnight approached, an intruder forced the larder window at Whitstable's lodgings and stole upstairs in search of my academic friend. He bore with him a native blowpipe and darts soaked in katuali toxin.

The grey-swathed assassin's target was still hunched over a desk despite the lateness of the hour, his back to the door, his head resting in his palms, looking down at Enderlidge's journal. The killer did not need to shift into the room, only to intrude that long hollow reed. He puffed a feathered dart into his victim's neck, injecting a lethal dose of katuali poison.

He waited for it to take effect. The ormolu clock on the mantel ticked away the quarter-hour. At last the murderer ventured in, pausing to check that his quarry breathed no more. He passed over to the desk to retrieve the coded book from the unseeing eyes that stared upon it.

I drew the hood from the dark lantern by my chair, flooding the corner

[4] Also known as the flat-tail sea snake (*Laticauda schistorhyncha*), the katuali dwells in warm salt water but resorts to dry crevices in sea caves to lay and hatch its eggs. It is indolent and docile unless provoked or threatened, but has an extremely toxic bite.
[5] Niue, "the Rock of Polynesia", is a 100 square-mile former British protectorate west of the Cook Islands, and is now an independently-governed nation "in free association with New Zealand". Its head of state is Queen Elizabeth II in her role as Queen of New Zealand.

with light. The dart-stabbed figure at the desk was revealed as a wax mannequin, positioned as if reading, wrapped in Whitstable' quilted dressing-gown. The actual Dr Atherton Whitstable aimed his revolver at his would-be murderer.

"Be careful not to hiccup, Mr Visitor," my friend warned our intruder. "Swallowing a dart laced with toxin would not enhance your health."

The postgraduate swung round, his face pale and horrified at his discovery. Shock turned to anger and then, as he observed our firearms levelled at him, to despair. "You devil," he said to Whitstable.

"I am not the one sneaking in to commit murder, dressed in the grey boat-cloak that Professor Enderlidge saw upon the creeping, limping figure that so disturbed him."

Visitor managed a flash of defiance. "You think that was me? I was with him the first time he hallucinated that."

Whitstable smiled thinly. "It was Clegg that your professor encountered the first time, when Enderlidge took you unexpectedly to your steamer's hold to examine some find or other. You pretended not to see the figure, hoping your tutor would dismiss what he saw as his imagination. Instead, he decided it was some sinister stalker, possibly of supernatural origin, that only he could perceive. But explanations must wait for a short while. Kindly divest yourself of that blowpipe and those toxin darts – there, on the side table will be fine – and be so good as to sit without trouble in the wicker chair. Ashworth, would you be so good as to tell Inspector Keyogh that he can join us?"

I lifted the window sash and signalled to the carriage opposite. The Scotland Yard detective emerged from it, ushering the three people that Whitstable had instructed him to bring: Dr Appleby, Mrs Enderlidge, and Mr Clegg. Our housekeeper Mrs Johnson showed them up to our rooms, and to gave notice that she expected compensation for her broken larder glazing.

Our guests crowded into the lounge. I yielded my seat to Mrs Enderlidge, who was pale and unhappy. Clegg was so scarlet that I feared he might pop an artery. The Miskatonic librarian Appleby seemed only confused.

"Why have you dragged us all here at this hour?" he wanted to know. "And, good grief! Why are you levelling guns at Mr Visitor?"

"Mr Visitor just attempted murder on our shop dummy here," I answered. "He expected to be ridding the world of Atherton Whitstable, of course. Many have tried."

"We rather caught Visitor in the act," Whitstable explained. "The fingerprints on that cane blowpipe will be quite enough to verify our own testimony."

"He tried to murder you?" Clegg questioned. "But why?"

Whitstable looked at the other student pityingly. "You know exactly why. But I shall lay it all out simply for the benefit of Scotland Yard and for my friend and chronicler here, Captain Samuel Ashworth."

"I should certainly like to know why I had to grab all these people and drag them here at this hour," Inspector Keyogh grumbled.

"We are here to discover a murderer," Whitstable promised him.

"Very well," Visitor snarled. "I killed Professor Enderlidge. I tried to kill you. I confess it. Well done."

"You tried to kill me, yes," the academic agreed. "But that was to protect the murderer – or rather the murderess."

Mrs Enderlidge flinched and gasped. Her fingers gripped the arms of the chair but she did not speak.

"Here is my reasoning," Whitstable told us. "There is a passage in the journal which I translated: 'The discovery is mine, and I shall have it! It has been here for a thousand years or more and only I had the wit to find it, to reveal it.' At first reading I assumed that the professor was referring to the academic glory of his discovery of a possible ancient civilisation; my error of assumption. Then I began to think about the lurker in the SS *Hosmer Small*. Someone shrouded himself in a boat-cloak and went to examine the finds from your recent expedition – without Enderlidge's supervision."

"Someone wished to usurp his research?" I supposed.

"Someone wished to check what he was concealing. Not all the stones drawn up from the water were calcified carved rock, were they? Under the crust of a thousand years or more of sea-silt, some of them were, what, gold? Silver? Olivine? Peridot? Black coral? Something of significant market value, anyhow. Enough to smuggle back to the United States and sell off for a rich retirement; or, I suppose, to fund more research expeditions. There is no point denying it now. Your cargo can be searched."

"You found buried treasure?" Professor Appleby challenged the expedition.

"There were some items of precious metals," Clegg agreed sullenly. "Certain crusted objects turned out to be inlaid with pearls or semi-precious stones. Votive gifts, given into the sea by a forgotten people long ago. Professor Enderlidge deciphered enough of the writing for us to discover a cache below the waterline of the Nukutepipi lagoon. He claimed we had no share in it, underplayed what we had found. So on the journey home, I crept in to see for myself how badly he was cheating us."

"And Visitor guessed what you were up to, and denied seeing you,"

Whitstable accused. "Being with the ship's captain, you had an alibi for later appearances of the shambler. But Harvey Visitor donned a similar boat-cloak and adopted a similar gait to hide himself when he made his own midnight excursions."

Clegg's expression was sly, but for once he kept his mouth closed.

"I am referring to your visits to Mrs Enderlidge, Mr Visitor," Whitstable continued inexorably, "whilst her husband was sealed in the hold, working on his translations, preparing his report, beginning his thesis, perhaps even counting his spoils."

Anne Enderlidge flared up. "And why should we not be together, Harvey and I? Aldwyn had his Polynesian beauties, his pretty native girls who sold themselves for baubles! Why should I keep fast to stale wedding vows when he would not?"

"I cannot speak to your fidelity. Only to your culpability in the matter of the Screw-Worm Fly Larvae. The parasites could only have been introduced into your husband's brain through the ear, and then only as he slept. Beside you."

"I told you, *I* did it," Visitor insisted.

"This is why you tried to kill Whitstable!" I realised at last. "To protect your lover! You knew that only she could have inflicted that devilish fate upon Professor Enderlidge – twice! No-one else could get so close without him noticing, except when he was insensible in bed. And you feared he knew what had been done to him. *He* feared the monsters. And he wrote it in his journal."

"I needed to recover that book," Visitor admitted. "To destroy it."

"There was a fortune in our finds," declared Clegg, "Enough to make us all wealthy. Enderlidge tried to keep it from the rest of us. Visitor and I planned to steal it. Harvey and Anne could run far away with their share. I... well, my plans are irrelevant now. But I swear, neither of us considered *murder!*"

"Visitor seems to have stacked away some poison darts," I pointed out.

"Those were just part of our anthropological collection," Visitor responded. "When it became clear that I had to act quickly, desperately, to save Anne..."

"Then it was the lady who murdered her husband?" Keyogh understood.

"So the clever Atherton Whitstable asserts," the widow replied. "Proving it is a different matter."

"I suspect a search of your belongings will correct that lack," Whitstable mentioned. "A case of *Cochliomyia hominivorax* larvae, perhaps, retained in case the other applications of the maggots did not work? A jar of the adult flies? I read from your reaction that I have hit the mark."

"I tried to protect you," Visitor told his illicit lover sadly. "You need not have killed him."

"We would never have got away if Aldwyn was not dead," Mrs Enderlidge cut in, coldly, sternly. "It would never have been *allowed*."

"Whatever do you mean?" Dr Appleby puzzled.

A twitch rippled down the lady's cheek. "Fools. Do you think only Aldwyn learned to read those stones? Understand that script? Do you think his comprehension of their meaning was greater than mine, who worked ten years at his side, transcribing his notes, ordering and improving them? Do you think he read any inscription, saw any glyph, that I did not view also?"

"We all saw the writing," Clegg protested.

"Saw but not understood!" the woman spat. "I knew that Aldwyn suspected me. I read it in his journal, his vaunted coded notebook where he so-cleverly ciphered his confessions of infidelity and congratulated himself on his scholarship. But I knew more than that, more than him. I felt the words, in my heart, in my mind and loins and soul. In robbing the offerings from the Old Ones, Aldwyn provoked their curse. Without sacrifice, none of us would survive."

"What are you saying?" Appleby objected. "That you killed your husband to placate some pagan idol?"

"There are ancient things, Dr Appleby," Mrs Enderlidge rasped in a voice quite different to her normal tones, "Things ancient and vast beyond our comprehension, from a time when the stars were different and giants ruled our Earth under alien skies. They are dead now, mere echoes that rake at the edges of our consciousness, beckoning us to madness. But they will not be dead forever. *That is not dead which can eternal lie!* I have read it. I have felt it. And in sacrificing Aldwyn I have saved us all, all of humankind, from their premature awakening! I saved us, Harvey! I *saved* us!"

"You have your confessions, Inspector Keyogh," Atherton Whitstable said soberly.

Dr Appleby looked unhappily on the devastation of the Miskatonic expedition. "I had only hoped for a key to understanding the language of the stones," he told us in a small, stunned voice.

A.H. Whitstable shook his head at the librarian. "I think it best, sir, if I decline that commission."

MOURN NOT THE SLEEPLESS CHILDREN

BOB FREEMAN

Fog crept like a living thing across the graveyard, mindful and with purpose. It masked the cemetery's landscape with malicious intent, stealthily concealing whatever evil lurked within the ineffable mist. Watching from the balcony of Grandstaff Hall, Brianna Moore surrendered to the fear that grew inside her.

A pall hung over the inhabitants of Grandstaff. For a score of nights the fog had come, thick and oppressive, and with it the mournful repine of some godforsaken spirit. It was a maddening clamour, like a demonic din rising up from the very aperture of Abbadon itself.

The young governess' attention was drawn to the ruins of the old Kirk at the periphery of the cemetery grounds. Lantern light struggled to cut through the assaulting mist and the sound of human voices floated up to her from the sacellum. She was unsure of what troubled her more, the anticipation of the wail's return, or the presence of the man in the company of the Grandstaff Lord below.

"We'll not be waiting much longer, Old Crow," she heard Lord Grandstaff say. His was a commanding voice, used to issuing orders and seeing them carried out in due haste. The serpentine tongue that responded commanded equal attention, but for altogether different reasons.

"I need not hear the banshee, Sir Stuart, for already I sense a presence among us wholly unnatural. It feeds off the fear that emanates from

Grandstaff Hall. It is a type of psychic vampire, if you will."

"Aleister, I knew you were the man to call in. Your knowledge of the esoteric knows no peer. I trust within your magical arsenal you have the means to dispose of this beastie?"

"I would need to gather some things from Boleskine. I could return within a fortnight and see to the exorcism of your earthbound spirit. Of course, there would be the matter of compensation; travel, the expense of the material components, my time and, I should add that my considerable expertise does not come cheaply."

"Yes, yes, old friend," she heard her employer say, "coin is of no consequence, if I would be free of this damnable apparition once and for all."

Brianna returned to her room, distraught. *A fortnight?* she thought. She feared she'd not last another night, let alone two weeks. She crossed the cool marble floor and stoked the fire against the autumn chill. When the wailing began, she was quick to bed, burying herself beneath thick woolen blankets and praying that morning would come faster than was its natural course.

* * *

"Gone," the lady of the house moaned, "all gone."

"Pardon me, ma'am?" Brianna asked, surprised to find Lady Grandstaff toiling over a pot of tea in the Manor kitchen.

"The staff," she muttered, "all gone save for you and Ewan." Ewan Pitcairn was Lord Grandstaff's retainer.

"Gone," Brianna repeated in a low murmur. The thought had occurred to her; to flee into the night. But when all was said and done, she had nowhere to go.

Lady Grandstaff turned to face the governess and Brianna was struck by how much older the woman appeared. Her eyes were dark and puffy, her chestnut hair now touched here and there with gray. Three weeks of ghostly manifestations had taken their toll.

"What shall we do, ma'am?" Brianna asked, lowering her gaze to the tile floor.

"We shall persevere, dear child, for we are Grandstaffs and that is what Grandstaffs do," the proud woman proclaimed. "If you would see to the children, Brianna, I will see that my husband gets his morning tea."

"At once, ma'am," she responded, shuffling off toward the great stair and the children's wing.

The long hallway that led to the children's rooms was paneled in dark wood and ill-lit. At the far end of the passageway was a high window that would normally spill daylight down the hall, but the heavy drape was pulled tight. Brianna's footfalls fell silent, masked by the oriental runner that stretched the full length of the space. Nearing the twins' room she heard their animated speech. Taking pause, she listened.

"Walter, must this most unnatural conveyance return to bother us this night?" a thin voice asked. It belonged to Wallace, the fair-haired twin. Where Walter was energetic and robust, Wallace in turn was frail and weak. Wallace was the sharper of the two, blessed with an innate knowledge of the world around them. Walter, though no dullard, deferred to his twin in matters of intellectual dissection.

"Must you be such a frightened ninny, Wally?" Walter chided his brother.

"But they've not kept their promise," Wallace said.

Brianna could take no more. She burst into the room.

"What promise?" she demanded. "What do you hear at night?"

"Miss Moore," the boys said in unison, startled by her sudden arrival. She flew across the room and snatched Wallace up, holding the boy about the shoulders and drawing him in close.

"Speak up you little heathens," she raged, flashing a disapproving look towards Walter. "What do you know? What devilry have you been up to?"

Wallace was beside himself, tears streaming down his cheeks, while his twin backed away to the far wall.

When Wallace refused to answer, Brianna tossed him aside, then turned and stalked across the room to confront his brother. "What about you Walter? Have you something you'd like to share with me?"

"I'm not scared of you," the boy said, puffing his chest out.

"Tell me Walter," she fumed, "or so help me..."

"So help you?" the boy said with a wry smile. "There's no help for you. Not after what you did when you were dollymopping the dockers."

"When I..." the governess stammered, "I... how could you?"

"Know?" Walter said, finishing her bewildered statement. "I know because they speak to us on the wind. At night. When the banshee comes. Oh, we know all about you, Miss Moore. We know all about how you spread it for a tanner, or less when you were hungry. And we know what happened the night of the blood moon, of how you..."

The sound of shattering glass somewhere deep inside the manor silenced the young Grandstaff. But the reprieve did little to alleviate the governess of her ire and embarrassment. When a remote scream followed the crash, Brianna raced out of the room and down the hall, relieved to distance herself from the twisted smiles exchanged by her twin charges.

The governess followed the sound of muffled whimpers to the dining room. It was dark, curtains pulled tight against the beckoning day. Still, she could see the shards of fine porcelain that lay scattered across the mahogany floor, and in the midst of the destruction, the Lady of the House, kneeling, rag in hand, sopping up steaming tea from the floor and rug.

"Lady Grandstaff?" The woman looked up and Brianna gasped as she saw the hand-shaped red mark across her face. "Oh, ma'am, I'm so sorry. Here, let me get that for you."

What was going on around here, Brianna wondered? *Were they all going crazy? Had madness settled in and taken root in their minds? How long before something truly horrible took place? How long before... No*, she thought, *not that. Why even consider that?*

"I... he..." Lady Grandstaff stammered.

"It's all right, ma'am. I understand," the governess sobbed.

"Do not cry for me, Miss Moore," the Lady said.

"I do not cry for you, ma'am," Brianna replied, fearing to look up. "I cry for us all."

The rest of the day was filled with tension. The whole household seemed ready to explode. Nightfall came, and with it, the horrific wails of the demon spirit. Four days later, Lady Grandstaff would be gone. Two days after that, Ewan too was nowhere to be found. Soon the house was filled with naught but the brooding visage of the Lord of Grandstaff Hall, a morose and despondent governess... and the sound of laughing children.

* * *

Brianna Moore watched as the fog returned once more, rolling across the aphotic grounds. *How many nights had they been besieged*, she wondered. *Thirty-eight? Forty?* It wouldn't be long now. Soon the wail would begin and she would once more sink into madness.

She hadn't seen the twins in three or four days. Had they been spirited away? Or had they simply run off, no longer able to withstand the strain of the conditions they were living under? Or worse? She feared the boys now, perhaps even more than the wailing demon. How could they have known about...? No, she couldn't even bring herself to think upon those horrible days, nor could she face the twins. She had been shamed by mere children; children with a knowledge that burned her to her very soul. She had been unable go to them. She lacked the courage to look them in the eye. Had this decision doomed them? Was her own demise destined to follow?

A resounding knock upon the great Manor door roused her from her melancholy. She descended the stair and made her way through the maze of rooms, pausing when she heard voices coming from the parlor. The visitor had already been let in. She crept forward, opened the servant door but a crack, and peered inside the Stygian room.

Lord Grandstaff sat hunched in a high-backed chair, more throne than seat. Before him stood a pompous aristocrat, bedecked in full Scottish regalia, leaning regally on an elaborate cane.

"I wondered if you would return, Master Therion. Have you come to exorcise the demon that plagues this house at last?" the beaten patriarch bemoaned.

"First, Lord Grandstaff, is the matter of payment. The spells which I intend to unleash in your service come not cheaply."

"I assured you that cost would be no object, my old friend" the Lord responded.

"Old friend," the guest muttered. "Old friend – is that what we are then, Sir Stuart? Old friends? Tell me, how long have we known one another?"

"Well, I'd say, what?" the Lord mumbled. "Nearly thirteen years, I suspect? Since our Malvern days."

"Yes, quite right," the man responded, indignant. "Malvern, wretched place, what with all that buggery."

"Here now, Crowley," the Lord started, leaning forward in his withered throne. "What is this? Do you begrudge the trifling flirtations of schoolboys?"

"Trifling?" Crowley scoffed. "Then what, pray tell, Lord Grandstaff, of our later years then? Trinity... do you recall our camaraderie while installed upon those hallowed grounds of learning?"

"Damn you, Old Crow," Grandstaff huffed. "Damn you and your warped and twisted mind."

"Boys will be boys, won't they, my Lord?"

"You asked for everything that befell you, you damnable wizard," Grandstaff barked. "In this, my hour of need, you fall upon me like a sick and wounded pup? Did I not defend you, you awkward, socially inept wretch? When the fists flew, who came to your aid then?"

"You're a revisionist, old friend. It was by Will alone that I overcame my enemies, and by Will alone that I did master not only my fear, but by which I have begun to unlock the most esoteric of mysteries."

"Why did I send for you? I should have known," the lord grumbled, rising weakly to stand before the pompous magician. "You were a pathetic schoolboy, deluded and maladroit. I see that maturity has eluded you and you are little different. I had hoped for better, but it seems I am to fend against this fiend on my own terms."

"Your arrogance has remained unchanged as well, *Lord* Grandstaff," Crowley scoffed. "Do you think it an accident that you are beset by this malefic entity? You belittle me, the only man in Britain that might give you aid, just as you saw fit to see me debased when we were but aspirants. This shall be your undoing."

Brianna was drawn from the two men's dialogue by the sound of the twins' laughter. She looked back to the parlour and saw that Lord Grandstaff had brandished a weapon, an ancestral claymore from his private collection. She was torn between rushing in to her lord's aid and investigating the children's whereabouts. The prattle of a woman's soft murmurings led Brianna away from the parlour, entranced by the sounds down the hall, sounds soon drowned out by the mournful wails descending once more upon Grandstaff Hall.

The governess passed through the butlery and paused to listen in the kitchen. The youthful mirth, tempered with a palpable darkness rose from the winery door just off the dining hall. She crept forward uneasily, trepidation clinging to her heart. The banshee wail that laid siege to Grandstaff weakened her resolve, but when the mournful repose of a pained woman once more danced amid the sounds of youthful revelry, she steeled herself and slowly opened the door, descending the dark stair toward the lord's private stock.

Dark shadows performed a minuet with the candlelight that caressed the narrow climb. She traversed the stairs with care and set her feet firmly upon the doglegged landing. The boys' rapture had ceased, leaving naught but the whimpering of the shadowed figure before her. Drawn out on the service table she laid, arms outstretched in mock crucifixion. Her flesh glistened wetly in the half-light.

"Blessed Virgin," Brianna gasped.

Before her lay Lady Grandstaff, naked to the waist. Her chest, a gaping wound that hid not the organs within. Lungs rose and fell weakly, the heart pulsating in a dangerous rhythm. The governess felt her stomach's meager contents rebel and she spewed hot bile upon the cellar floor. She was frozen in place, feet unable to carry her away from this scene of utter horror.

"We feared the ribs would have been difficult to remove, you know," young Wallace said, stepping from the shadows with his brother in tow. "Strangely enough, it was the skin itself that proved more bothersome." His hands and face were covered in blood, his teeth and lips stained crimson from his inhuman activities.

"How… why…" Brianna stammered, what little sanity she had been able to cling to slowly slipping away. "You're monsters."

"No, silly cow," Walter scolded. "We are reborn. We have answered the call of our true mother. Her lullaby has raised us from the dead sleep that this house has fettered us with. Her song has called us home and we are reshaping this dwelling to meet her desire."

"You're mad," the governess spat. "The both of you. Driven mad by the very demon that haunts this place."

"A whore for sixpence with blood on her hands," Wallace spoke, "dares to call us mad."

"Shut up!" she screamed. "You don't know me!"

"Don't we, little dollymop?" Walter giggled, licking his fingers clean. "Were they someone else's hands clamped 'round the throat of the newborn babe that clawed from your putrid womb?"

"Shut up, damn you!" Brianna wailed. "You don't understand! How could you?"

"We understand plenty," Wallace said coldly. "We're all damned in this house."

Brianna froze as she heard a metallic click behind her.

"I couldn't agree more, foul spirit," sounded a serpentine voice from the stair. An explosion cut through the tension as a shadowed figure fired a revolver into the room. The slug caught young Wallace squarely between the eyes, showering his twin with blood and grey matter. The governess turned to face Mr Crowley, his eyes cold and piercing, their gaze the very essence of championing death. The Englishman let loose another round that sent the boy Walter scurrying for the cover of darkness.

"Hell is waiting for you, Old Crow," the boy called out. "Your wickedness is a one-way ticket into the arms of your true lover."

"In the name of all that's Holy and all that is Profane," Crowley called out, "you'll be sent back to the bowels from which you've sprung!"

"What are you doing?" Brianna mouthed, unsure if she even spoke the words aloud in the midst of the spectral cacophony and the reverberations of the weapon that the magician wielded.

"Saving your life, I think," Crowley answered. He reached out and pulled her to him. The governess was surprised by the strength of his grip. She clung to her benefactor even as thoughts of being trapped between two devils filled her head. "We should ascend with all due haste, my frazzled beauty," he said, urging her up the narrow stair. "I've but two shots left and I'm afraid these wee bairns have decided to raise the stakes in this gambit."

The governess' eyes were drawn toward Walter and she was stunned to see the boy rising up and scurrying over his mother's eviscerated corpse. He no longer looked human; scaled tentacles had sprouted from his ribcage and a mottled fin now bisected his skull, fanning out along his spine and forming a grotesque tail that whipped about like a thing independent of its host. Behind him, his brother writhed in pain, but she could already see the wound delivered by the mage's pistol knitting itself whole once more.

"Oh bloody hell, do something!" she exclaimed as she clamored up the stairs.

"I am open to suggestions," Crowley responded as he released one of his two remaining bullets.

"Your reputation..." she shouted, gasping for breath as she raced forward, crashing through the winery door into the dining hall, "... precedes you sir." She sprinted through the dark room with reckless abandon. "Can't you cast a spell or something?"

"Don't believe everything you read in the papers, Miss Moore," he chided. She was sure he would have been amused were they not running for their life.

The governess crossed the grand entry and slammed hard into the front door. She tried to open it, but it held fast. "Damn it!" she exclaimed, pulling with all her might.

"It's been nailed shut!" Crowley barked. Brianna cowered behind her Byronic savior as he turned to face the creatures that were slithering toward them.

"By who?" the governess asked.

"By me, Miss Moore."

Brianna and Crowley looked toward the parlor door and saw Lord Grandstaff standing there, seemingly oblivious to the seeping wound in his stomach put there by Crowley's revolver.

"Why?" she pleaded. The inhuman creatures that had once been her charges ceased their advance and now sat coiled, as if ready to pounce, at their father's feet.

"This has all been my doing, I'm afraid. My children needed to eat. You see, my wife and I had struggled to bring forth an heir to ensure the legacy of Grandstaff. Something had to be done. We had been to every physician, consulted every expert at our disposal. Still, nothing. My beautiful wife was barren. You can imagine our heartbreak. So, with nowhere else to turn, I called upon the Ancient Ones. I made a pact with them and they delivered not one but two children from my wife's barren womb. Their hunger was small at first. Slowly they went through their wet nurse, then a small parade of governesses. But their hunger was growing. Something more needed to be done."

"Why bring me into this, Stuart?" Crowley asked, keeping the gun leveled on the Lord of Grandstaff Hall.

"Because human flesh was no longer enough. They needed something more. They needed to feed on someone more satisfying, someone with power. So I devised a ruse and invited you here, appealing to your inflated ego and your appetite for the supernatural."

"The banshee, she is the Ancient One you bargained with," Crowley spat. "You offered her something she couldn't resist, a foothold in this plane of existence, a base from which she and her offspring could grow in power. You damnable fool, you've placed all of Britain in jeopardy, if not the entire world."

"You are without a doubt an adept of the first order," the lord choked, grimacing through the pain of his stomach wound. "I knew you would not be able to resist a challenge such as the one I had presented, nor the funds I waved under your nose. For all your knowledge and proficiency Aleister, you have always had a weakness for sycophancy."

"He's right, you know," Crowley quipped with a wink toward the governess.

"And me, Sir Stuart?" Brianna asked. "What part in your game did I play?"

"The children feed on fear, as well as flesh, but they are also nurtured by darkness, and we both know your sins, dear Brianna."

"Very well, Grandstaff," Crowley said, "you've played your game and lost. We're not cattle for your brood. Blood has been spilled enough this night. The girl and I shall take our leave and you shall darken our paths no more, or by all the gods of heaven and hell, I shall see you cursed in a manner that shall boil your very soul."

"False bravado, Mr Crowley. I still have the upper hand, and hungry mouths that need to be fed. Walter, Wallace," Lord Grandstaff said, addressing his children, "your feast is prepared. You may eat."

The beasts lurched forward, propelling themselves swiftly towards their prey with powerful tentacles. Their twin jaws dropped low and protruded unnaturally, the children's teeth now razor sharp and housed within demonic maws.

"I think not," Crowley said calmly. "Magick is an act of Will in concordance with action."

He stepped in front of the governess and steeled himself, staring down the grotesque younglings. He thought of his years of training at the feet of lesser men, men who had knowledge but not the Will to use it. He would show them what true Will could produce. He reached down into the depths of his being and ignited the spark of magickal energy that was alive within him. Crowley spread his hands wide, bending the ring finger of each and slowly bringing his thumbs forward to touch the fingertips, completing a magickal circuit.

Brianna stepped back, feeling the surge of preternatural energy emanating from within her benefactor. It frightened her in a way that even the beasts that charged toward them could not. Her mind told her that those ungodly creatures were an aberration, but the energies flowing outward from this man, this magician, resonated in her soul. Who knew that such power could lurk behind a human face?

The beasts were nigh upon them, their black tongues licking at the air, their tentacles slithering forth, their eyes ablaze with hatred and insatiable hunger – hunger for human flesh. Brianna Moore cowered behind Crowley, he being, she thought, the lesser evil, and as he spoke words that she could not comprehend, she felt the heat of the magickal flame as it sprang forth from the magician's hands and into the faces of the demonic twins. In that moment, she prayed not to God, but to an infernal spirit, and knew she was lost.

"I believe that is more to what you had in mind," Crowley said to the governess with a wink. He offered her his hand. He was shaking almost as badly as she was, but for an altogether different reason; her from mind-numbing fear, he from preternatural exertion. The stench of brimstone filled the acrid air, while the flames took root and slowly began to spread throughout the great Hall. The bodies of the twins were blackened and smoldering; their father hunched over their lifeless forms.

"What have you done?" Lord Grandstaff bellowed. "My boys! My beautiful boys!"

"Stuart," Crowley said.

Sir Stuart Grandstaff, Lord of Grandstaff Hall, looked up at his former schoolmate with a mixture of anguish and loathing. He clutched at his wounded stomach with a grim determination. Crowley hovered above him, revolver once more in hand. He steadied it, centering it on the Lord's forehead.

"She'll never let you leave here alive," Grandstaff moaned. "She was their mother. She will have her revenge."

"Do you think I fear her, you fool?" Crowley asked.

"What are you waiting for," the Lord growled. "Do it."

The revolver exploded, the bullet ripping through the Lord's head, tumbling through his brain, spraying bone and grey matter out the back of his skull.

"Black blood upon the altar!" Crowley said, "and the rustle of angel wings above! Black blood of the sweet fruit, the bruised, the violated bloom – *that* setteth the Wheel a-spinning in the spire. Death is the veil of Life, and Life of Death; for both are Gods."

Brianna came to stand beside Crowley and the magician slipped his arm around her waist.

"It is finished," he said.

"Aleister, listen," the governess said, "the banshee's wail. It's silenced."

"Grandstaff didn't realize that when he brought her forth, it was his life force that she fed off of. When I silenced him, I laid that hellspawn to rest as well, at least until the next blackheart comes along intent on making a pact with the devil."

EPILOGUE

Brianna watched as Grandstaff Hall burned. Crowley had scoured the dwelling for prizes that he could not give up to the pyre. Art, silver, jewels, cash, and rare books as well. All these he carted away with him. His offer to take the governess in as both pupil and concubine was rejected, though she had allowed the magician to seduce her into an act of Tantric coupling. She had been a prostitute in another life, after all, and before the heat of the conflagration and the fire that burned in her heart after nearly having her life stolen from her, she relished in the wantonness of it. A new lease on life had been offered.

She reflected, as she gazed into the fiery shell of what had been, and wondered about the new road that was now laid out before her. She had a bit of cash but no course. Perhaps America beckoned? Yes, that was it. America. Land of opportunity, they said. She could have a fresh start in a new country, with naught but fading memories of an ill-fated past and a devilish misadventure with the so-called Wickedest Man in the World. *Not so wicked*, she thought, as she turned away from the hellish ruin. *Not so wicked at all.*

DESCRIBIN' THE SCRIBES

PAULA D. ASHE (she/her) is an author of dark fiction. Her debut collection *We Are Here to Hurt Each Other* (Nictitating Books) was a Shirley Jackson Award Winner for Single Author Collection and a Bram Stoker Award Finalist for Superior Achievement in a Fiction Collection. She is also an associate editor for *Vastarien: A Literary Journal*. She lives in the Midwest USA with her family.
Newsletter: https://pauladashe.substack.com/
Amazon Author Page: http://t.co/y4nH39chRa
Facebook Author Page: http://www.facebook.com/pauladashe
Twitter: @pauladashe

JAMES BENNETT is a British writer raised in Sussex and South Africa. His short fiction has appeared internationally, and he's been twice shortlisted for a British Fantasy Award, first in 2017 for his acclaimed debut *Chasing Embers* and again in 2023 for his short story *'Morta'*, which appeared in the well-received *The Book of Queer Saints*. His latest fiction can be found in *The Dark* magazine, *BFS Horizons* and *Occult Detective Magazine*. A short story collection *Preaching to the Perverted* should see the light of day in 2024. James lives in the South of Spain where he's working on a new novel. Feel free to follow him on Instagram: @JamesBennettEsq
Blog: https://jamesbennettesq.blogspot.com

PAUL 'MUTARTIS' BOSWELL is a self trained artist, illustrator and screen printer creating weirdo drawings, freaked out creatures from other dimensions, sculptural mutations, and occasionally wall scrawlings. influenced by nature, the supernatural, weird and strange literature, primitive musics, obsolete technologies and the human psyche.

Emerging from Rural Somerset Mutartis Boswell presents us with a mixed up twisted world where the likes of freakish anthropomorphic creatures stalk apocalyptic landscapes co-existing with lost technologies, which have mutated and taken on a new life. Boswell's weird and wonderful visions are fueled by a powerful imagination, a soup of the mind whose ingredients range from a childhood brought up on comics, old horror movies, sci-fi, northern European folk tales, weird 1970s kids TV, and Punk Rock to name but a few of his influences.

More recently he has been screen printing in his home print studio using ethical materials, which has enabled him to put his work and ideas on garments and limited edition prints.

www.instagram.com/mutartis/
boswellart.blogspot.com
boswellart.bigcartel.com

SEBASTIÁN CABROL is an illustrator and comic artist based on Argentina. He's worked as a freelance inker and artist for Avatar Press, Dark Horse and Marvel among other publishers.

Website: https://www.artstation.com/cabrol
Blog: https://cabrol-art.blogspot.com/

PETE 'CARDINAL' COX has been having his various writings published in the small-press for approaching forty years. As well as his Lovecraftian *Codex* pamphlets he is a regular contributor to *Cyaegha* magazine. This led to the Swedish film maker The Lone Animator making a cartoon of his poem *The Night Land*. In the past he has been Poet-in-Residence for a Victorian cemetery (for three years) and *The Dracula Society*. The second of which led to his one-man show *High Stakes* (performed at Worldcons in Helsinki and Dublin) and his second collection *Grave Goods*, released by Demain Publishing.

DENISE DUMARS is a widely published author of poetry, short fiction, essays, articles, and criticism. She is best known for her short story collection *Lovecraft Slept Here*. Her current chapbook of poetry, *Cajuns in Space*, is nominated for the Elgin Award, and she has a poem nominated for the Dwarf Stars Award. In addition to writing, she helms Rev. Dee's Apothecary: a New Orleans-Style Botanica. She lives in L.A.'s beautiful South Bay area, but her heart is in New Orleans.

www.DeniseDDumars.com, www.DyanaAset.com

BOB FREEMAN is an Occult Detective, author, artist, and game designer. His lifelong passions for mythology, folklore, magick, and religion has led him to become a respected lecturer on the occult and paranormal phenomena. *Landon Connors*, an omnibus of his Occult Detective fiction, is available on

Amazon. Watch for *Vampirella: Dead Flowers*, written by Freeman with Sara Frazetta and artist Alberto Locatelli, and *Fire & Ice: Miniatures Adventure Game*, created by Bordermen Games, in association with Frazetta Girls, Bakshi Productions, and Dynamite Entertainment. Freeman lives in the haunted hinterlands of Indiana with his wife Kim and son, fantasy author Connor Landon Freeman.

Bob can be found online at occultdetective.com, bordermengames.com, and youtube.com/@occultdetective

MICHAEL KEYTON is Liverpool born and bred, and has worked in some of the dirtiest hotels in Wales, played in a semi-professional ceilidh band, and taught in a warm and challenging school in Newport before getting off for good behaviour. Now living in Monmouth.

His writing has been influenced by too many to mention, though he was once inspired by a young Ramsey Campbell, who not only gave a great talk in a Newport Library, but also conjured up a thunderstorm without moving his hands. His books include works on Anthony Trollope, the thriller writer Peter Cheyney, and occult thrillers like The Gift Trilogy. Mike Keyton is on Facebook and you can discover more books his author page
Amazon Author page: US amazon.com/author/michaelkeyton
Amazon Author page: UK amazon.co.uk/author/michaelkeyton
Blog: http://baffledspirit.blogspot.co.uk/

NICK MAMATAS is the author of several novels, including the Lovecraftian *Move Under Ground,* and *I Am Providence*, and the speculative thriller *The Second Shooter*. His short fiction has appeared in *Best American Mystery Stories, McSweeney's, Tor.com, Weird Tales*, and many other venues.

Nick is also an anthologist: his latest is *Wonder and Glory Forever: Awe-Inspiring Lovecraftian Fiction*. Visit him at www.nick-mamatas.com

TIM MENDEES is a rather odd chap. He's a horror writer from Macclesfield in the North-West of England who specialises in cosmic horror and weird fiction. A lifelong fan of classic weird tales, Tim set out to bring the pulp horror of yesteryear into the 21st Century and give it a distinctly British flavour. His work has been described as the love-child of H.P. Lovecraft and P.G. Wodehouse and is often peppered with a wry sense of humour that acts as a counterpoint to the unnerving, and often disturbing, narratives.

Tim is the author of over one hundred published short stories and novelettes, nine novellas, and two short story collections. He has also curated and edited several cosmic horror-themed anthologies.

When he is not arguing with the spellchecker, Tim is a goth DJ with a weekly radio show, one of the organisers of *The Innsmouth Literary Festival*, and the co-presenter of the *Innsmouth Book Club Podcast* & *Strange Shadows: The Clark Ashton Smith Podcast*. He currently lives in Brighton & Hove with his pet crab, Gerald, and an ever-increasing army of stuffed octopods.

Blog: timmendeeswriter.wordpress.com/

WILLIAM MEIKLE is a Scottish writer, now living in Canada, with over thirty novels published in the genre press and more than 300 short story credits in thirteen countries. He has books available from a variety of publishers including four collections of his *Carnacki: Ghostfinder* stories. His work has appeared in a large number of professional anthologies and magazines. He lives in Newfoundland with whales, bald eagles and icebergs for company. When he's not writing he drinks beer, plays guitar, and dreams of fortune and glory. Find him at williammeikle.com

WILL MURRAY is the author of more than 75 mostly pseudonymous novels and a lifelong Lovecraftian, Will Murray has been writing about HPL since the 1980s, chiefly in now-legendary journals such as *Crypt of Cthulhu, Lovecraft Studies, Studies in Weird Fiction, Dagon, Nyctalops, Books at Brown, Lovecraft Annual,* and *Fangoria*. He was one of the three founders of Friends of H. P. Lovecraft, which was organized to place the memorial plaque on the grounds of the John Hay Library on the 1990 centennial of Lovecraft's birth.

A contributor to numerous anthologies, Murray's Mythos stories have appeared in *The Cthulhu Cycle, Disciples of Cthulhu II, The Shub-Niggurath Cycle, Miskatonic University, Weird Trails, Reign of Cthulhu, Horror for the Holidays, Worlds of Cthulhu, Beyond The Mountains of Madness, That is Not Dead* and *Black Wings IV*. Many involve the semi-fictional Cryptic Events Evaluation Section of the National Reconnaissance Office. Several of his Mythos stories have been collected in *The Wild Adventures of Cthulhu.* Volumes 1 and 2.

Murray lives in Massachusetts, has explored Arkham Country extensively, and is a professional medium and a trained remote viewer, among other arcane accomplishments.

His website is: www.adventuresinbronze.com

PETE RAWLIK is a writer living in Florida where he collects Lovecraftian fiction and works on environmental issues surrounding the Everglades and related ecosystems. His research for a pseudo-history of the Miskatonic River Valley laid the groundwork for what would eventually become *Reanimators* (2013), *The Weird Company* (2014), *Reanimatrix* (2016), *The Peaslee Papers* (2017), *The Miskatonic University Spiritualism Club* (2021) and *The Eldritch Equations* (2022). His short story collection, *The Strange Company and Others*, was released in 2019. He has edited two anthologies one with Brian Sammons, *Legacy of the Reanimator* (2015), and *The Chromatic Court* (2019) a collection of Lovecraftian stories inspired by the King in Yellow. He is a regular member of the Lovecraft Ezine Podcast and a frequent contributor to the New York Review of Science Fiction.

ADAM BENET SHAW is an illustrator and painter based in Springdale, Arkansas. His published graphic novel work includes the fully painted *Bloodstream* for Image Comics and *Harpe: America's First Serial Killers*. His paintings have also been featured in publications by Dark Horse Comics, Akashic Books, Moonstone, New American Painting and Southwest Art Magazine. You can view more of Adam's art at ABShaw.com and instagram.com/abshaw_figurativeart.

RUSSELL SMEATON was Born from an egg on a mountain top, and has spent the past 40 something years doing stuff and things. After spending a decade travelling around the world he has now settled down in a small town in England by the North Sea. He lives with his lovely family, some rats, some fish and a very wayward cat. The cat most definitely knows far more than he should. Luckily he's not telling.
Amazon Author page: UK https://www.amazon.co.uk/Russell-Smeaton
Amazon Author page: US https://www.amazon.com/Russell-Smeaton

DJ TYRER is the person behind *Atlantean Publishing* and has been widely published in anthologies and magazines around the world, such as *Chilling Horror Short Stories* (Flame Tree), *The Mad Visions of al-Hazred*, *The Idolators of Cthulhu* and *Miskatonic Dreams* (all Alban Lake), *What Dwells Below* (Sirens Call), *EOM:Equal Opportunity Madness* (Otter Libris), and *Steampunk Cthulhu* (Chaosium), and issues of *Cosmic Horror Magazine, Cyaegha, Hypnos, Lovecraftiana, Sirens Call,* and *Weirdbook*, as well as having a Yellow Mythos novella available in paperback and on the Kindle, *The Yellow House* (Dunhams Manor).

Website: https://djtyrer.blogspot.co.uk/
Facebook page: https://www.facebook.com/DJTyrerwriter/
Atlantean Publishing website: https://atlanteanpublishing.wordpress.com/

I.A. WATSON stopped actively occult detecting in '09 after the Lochmerle Orphanage tragedy where the black waters rose. Once released from psychiatric care he immediately began scribbling blasphemous truths in the form of novels and short stories and has so far not been restrained again. Amongst his ramblings are a dozen or so novels and collections including *Vinnie De Soth, Jobbing Occultist*, and more than fifty short stories, a lot of them Sherlock Holmes or occult mysteries for which people keep giving him awards – the unknowing fools!
A full list of his literary misdeeds is available at
http://www.chillwater.org.uk/writing/iawatsonhome.htm

Made in the USA
Las Vegas, NV
10 November 2024